Belatedly coming to l
her gaze and cι

Lord Westrop cough _____ ___ _____
She watched him place his drink on a small side-
table from beneath lowered lashes.

"You must be the new housemaid." He turned
and came towards her. "Lily, isn't it?"

"Yes, sir." Lifting her head, she met eyes as blue
as a crisp winter sky.

He continued to study her. His eyes brushed
over her hair, her neck, her breasts. Lily flicked a
glance left and right as her body traitorously heated
beneath his gaze. The other gentlemen watched,
amusement twitching their lips.

"Are you ready to be seated in the dining room,
my lord?" Lily said, standing a little straighter.

"I'm sorry?"

"Your meal, sir?"

Lord Westrop blinked and the tension broke.
Lily held his gaze. She noticed the curiosity when he
looked at her not a moment before had vanished,
only to be replaced with mischief—or was it guilt?

His smile turned wolverine. "Oh, I'm more than
ready to eat, Lily. I'm positively salivating."

Lily smarted as his friends burst into a flurry of
mocking laughter, but kept her eyes locked on his.
The tone of Lord Westrop's voice disguised neither
the implication nor his obvious enjoyment at her
expense. A flame of indignation ignited inside of her.

Her smile was slow and intentionally
provocative. "I am so pleased, sir. For I would hate
for you to have to endure cold soup." Her gaze
lingered down to his crotch. "After all, you are quite
obviously still chilled from an afternoon of riding."

The Arrival
of
Lily Curtis

by

Rachel Brimble

To/ Julia,

·Happy Christmas, 2010

Rachel
Brimble x .

The Arrival of Lily Curtis

COPYRIGHT © 2009 by Rachel Brimble

Cover Art by *Tina Lynn*

The Wild Rose Press
PO Box 708
Adams Basin, NY 14410-0706
Visit us at www.thewildrosepress.com

Publishing History
First English Tea Rose Edition, 2010
Print ISBN 1-60154-792-7

Published in the United States of America

Dedication

To all my girl friends...
and a little place known as The Old Lane!

Prologue

Bath, England — August 1890

The door flew open with violence. Elizabeth struggled into a sitting position with her heart beating an out-of-control concerto in her chest. Her smile dissolved when she saw the furious look on her mother's face.

"Mother, you frightened me." She laughed, pressing a shaking hand to her chest.

Her father hurried in behind his wife and vigorously shook his head, warning Elizabeth that laughter of any sort was highly inadvisable at that moment.

"Frightened you? Frightened you?" her mother cried. "I'll frighten you, young lady."

Mary Caughley came toward her with such ferocity Elizabeth tensed, assuming an open-handed blow across her face was imminent. Instead, her mother leaned close enough for Elizabeth to feel her breath upon her lashes.

"You have really done it this time, Elizabeth May Caughley. No more. I will not let you make fools of this family for one minute longer."

Elizabeth swallowed. "Fools? What is it I have done?"

"What is it you have done? How can you have the audacity to ask such a question?"

Her father stepped forward and took his wife's trembling shoulders in his hands.

"Wife, please calm yourself."

"How can I? Look at her. She sees no

wrongdoing, no wrongdoing at all."

Elizabeth stared at her parents. Surely this couldn't be about this evening? Maybe she didn't behave in the required manner at the ball. Yes, she'd danced with not one but two, no, three different men and flirted somewhat with each of them...but her mother's fury surpassed anything she'd seen in her before.

"Mama, whatever it is I have done, I didn't mean to cause you this distress."

Her mother grappled from her husband's embrace. "You know just what it is you have done. Cavorting around the Assembly Rooms like a grand dame with her pick of men as suitors. I refuse to allow you to subject us to any more of it, Elizabeth. It stops right this minute. No more."

"But, Mother, please. I was merely making the most of..."

But then she stopped. Her father's hand still lay protectively upon his wife's shoulder and their faces were drawn into identical expressions of disappointment. Elizabeth swallowed. It meant trouble with a capital T when they stood united. More often than not, their father could be swayed to both Elizabeth and her sister's wishes, but when their parents stood together as they did now...

"Your mother is right. We have discussed this matter in length over a number of months. The decision has been made."

A feeling of foreboding dropped low into Elizabeth's belly. "Decision?"

He tilted his chin. "It is time you were married," he said. "We have made a stand, Elizabeth. Your days of thinking our way of life does not apply to you are over."

Icy-cold dread tripped up the length of her spine. "But I am not yet ready."

"You are three and twenty."

"But that is no age. You speak of me as though I am an old maid. I will marry in time but—"

"You will marry this year!"

Elizabeth jumped. Her mother's cry was high-pitched enough for the street cats to start mewling outside the open window and sweat to break out on Elizabeth's forehead.

"You have no further choice in the matter, my daughter," she said, her voice quivering. "We are your parents and our minds are set."

The room descended into silence. Elizabeth looked from one to the other. They were serious. Her blood heated in her veins as anger gathered momentum deep inside her. Her pulse thumped with each tick of the grandfather clock standing in the far corner of the room. She met her mother's icy-blue stare as resentment slowly rolled into a burning inferno that lodged painfully in the center of Elizabeth's chest. They would not break her. She did what she did tonight to feel blissfully unshackled for just one liberating moment and by God, she'd do it again. She drew in a long breath through flared nostrils.

She turned to her father, afraid she would say something to regret if she spoke to her mother. Mary Caughley's entire existence was based upon the importance of appearances and what should or should not be done. At least her father held a modicum of free expression.

"Am I to presume you have found a man you wish me to marry, Papa?"

Two pink spots of color stained his cheeks and his Adam's apple shifted beneath the skin of his neck. "Yes. Yes, we have."

Elizabeth's blood roared in her ears and her hands shook as she grasped them together in her lap. "I see."

"Darling, you have left us with no choice."

"Who is he?"

She watched her parents exchange glances before they turned and faced her. The slumping of their shoulders and the undeniable softening in their eyes told Elizabeth the man in question was dubious at best.

Had she behaved so badly that they would expect her to marry a monster rather than spend another minute unbetrothed?

She waited. And she waited. But neither of them spoke or as much as opened their mouths. Another ten seconds ticked by until it became glaringly obvious that neither her mother nor her father relished the task of informing Elizabeth of their choice.

Finally, she blew out an impatient breath. "Well?"

Silence.

Throwing her hands in the air, she leapt up from the chaise and toward the fireplace. The mantel seemed as good a place as any to cling onto. She glared into the dying embers in the grate. "Is there a particular reason that neither of you appears eager to share the name of my supposed beau?" she asked, quietly. "Or is the suspense designed to entice me to want to know more about the mystery man you want me to spend the rest of my life with?"

There was an awkward shuffle of feet but still she could not bring herself to look at them. A final spark of orange fire dimmed to nothing before her eyes.

"Surely you feel I deserve a man of the highest caliber, do you not?"

Silence.

"I'm confused. You have deemed this man suitable, yet do not have the courage to even tell me his name?"

At last her father cleared his throat. "Of course

4

we have the courage."

"Then who is he?" Elizabeth snapped her head up, her unshed tears stinging behind her eyes. His face blurred.

Gerald Caughley pulled back his shoulders in an act of authority yet his color was deeper than a fresh tomato. "It's um…um…it's Candle—"

"Candleford?" *No! No! No!* Elizabeth felt her eyes widen to manic proportions. "Are you about to say Candleford?" She looked to her mother but she appeared totally absorbed in a particularly interesting spot on the carpet. Elizabeth turned back to her father.

"Candleford? Thomas Candleford?"

"He's a good man, Elizabeth."

She pushed away from the mantel and threw her hand in the air. "A good man? A good man?" She laughed wryly. "I really don't know what to say. Thomas Candleford?"

Her father puffed out his chest. "And what of it? He is successful and hard working. A gifted lawyer who will no doubt make a fine judge one day."

Elizabeth gave a rather inelegant snort. "Yes, one day *very* soon, no doubt."

He narrowed his gaze. "And what is that supposed to mean?"

"It means the man is older than you, Papa! I'm sure he will be given a judge's position sooner rather than later for fear he will soon be too decrepit to climb onto the bench."

"Elizabeth! Do not be rude."

She turned abruptly to face her mother, anger burning hot in her chest. "Rude? Why that was not rude. Candleford is fat and bald and has enough hair sprouting from his ears to knit a bed blanket." She paused. "That, Mama, is rude."

"Elizabeth!"

Ignoring her mother's protestations, Elizabeth

paced the room. "I won't do it. I will not marry him. I am of age and cannot be forced."

"Then who do you suggest?" her mother snapped. "Your father and I have waited long enough for you to show even the slightest interest in taking a husband. Yet, here we are again. Another season has passed and you have wasted it with your endless flirting and dancing and giggling. We have been generous to let it go on this long. No, this is it. I will not allow you to put us through another year of anguish."

"Anguish? You make me sound like a tyrant. So I haven't found a man I wish to marry…"

"And we fear you never will." Her father came forward and took her hands in his. "You are spirited, my dear, and we both love you for it. But don't you see that we worry for your future?"

Elizabeth tipped her head back and looked into her father's eyes. They shone beneath the flickering candles in the chandelier above them. He suddenly looked so tired and forlorn that Elizabeth's heart weakened just a little.

"I will marry one day, Papa." She sighed. "I promise I will. Just not yet. I want to enjoy life a little longer, that is all."

"And you think once you marry your life is over?" her mother asked, her blue eyes wide. "Whoever put such an idea into your head?"

"No one put it into my head. I see it. I see it every day. Look at Isabella."

"What of her? Your sister is happy, she is with child."

"Yes, and she's half the person she was twelve months ago. Each of my friends has ended up the same way and I refuse to let it happen to me."

Her mother's laugh was drier than day-old bread. "You refuse?"

Elizabeth felt the pinch of heat in her cheeks.

"Yes. I will not marry and then have my husband tell me when and where I will serve him, when and where I will lie with him while he goes out and does whatever he chooses. I will not be a kept wife who sits at home, pregnant and forgotten."

"Oh, Elizabeth, I despair of you and this nonsensical way you insist on talking," her mother said. "Marriage is marriage; it is a way of life that has survived and will continue to survive. Your head is full of ideas that just have no place in society."

"Then I will remove myself from society."

Elizabeth froze. That's what she would do, remove herself from society.

"I beg your pardon?"

"What on earth are you talking about?"

Her parents stared at her. Her father's hands slipped from hers and her mother's mouth dropped open wide enough to catch a swarm of passing flies. But Elizabeth's heart picked up speed and her skin tingled as a burst of the unknown coursed through her veins on a tidal wave.

She brushed past her father and twirled herself around in a circle, her arms wide. "I will leave Bath. I will find a job far away from here where I can earn my own money and decide what it is I wish to do with my life."

"That's it," her father said, throwing his hands up in mock surrender. "She has truly lost her mind this time."

Elizabeth grinned. "Let me leave home, Papa. You can tell people I have gone abroad visiting family, but really I will be in the country earning a living. I will save enough money to go to France."

"France?"

"Yes." Elizabeth's mind raced with the images and stories she'd heard of this faraway and exotic place. "I have heard stories women live a freer life there. The pressure to marry the first man you so

7

much as kiss is not the same as it is in England."

"Oh, spare me." Her mother pressed a hand theatrically to her forehead, her eyelids fluttering closed.

"Mama, please. Give me your blessing to do this." Elizabeth laughed. "Let me have a different life than the one you plan for me. Please. Let me find my own way. I will write. I will reassure you that I am safe and well."

"But this is absurd! You are a lady, Elizabeth. We have given you a loving home, an education. How on earth do you intend passing yourself off as anything less?"

"Let me worry about that." She turned to her father. "Papa? What do you say? Will you help find me a position somewhere?"

Her father met her eyes. He had taken out his pipe and was now rhythmically tapping it up and down against his open palm. "This is madness, Elizabeth."

"Please, Papa. If I am not here, I will save you from further embarrassment, will I not?"

He shook his head. "You have no idea what you are suggesting."

"Then let me learn. Let me find out what it means to be in the real world. Aren't you always chastising Isabella and I for not respecting everything you have worked so hard to give us? Aren't you always saying we don't know we are born fortunate, compared to what working class lives are like?" Elizabeth looked from her father to her mother and back again. "Please, let me grow, let me learn, let me breathe."

The room fell quiet.

Her father looked to his wife—she shook her head. Elizabeth's heart sank. "Please, Mama."

"It is too much, you cannot ask this of us, Elizabeth," she said, a soft sob breaking her voice.

"How are we supposed to lie to our friends? Our associates? You will be missed at the Assembly Rooms, the theatre..." She let the sentence drift off.

"But I'll be happy, Mama; I know I will." She walked across the room and sat down next to her mother. "I can't marry. Not yet. I know you only want the best for me and I love you for it, but I won't be happy until I find a husband who understands what I want. Please, set me free."

Chapter One

En route to Colerne — One month later

"Now is not the time for tears, my dear."

"Sorry?" Elizabeth turned from the carriage window and the passing townhouses to face her father.

"You are crying."

Elizabeth swept a gloved finger beneath her eye and watched the dove grey cotton turn charcoal. "I didn't realize..."

"The time for tears has passed. Now is the time for action and restoration." He let out a heavy breath as the carriage bumped and jerked over the cobbled streets of Bath.

"Restoration?"

Reaching across, he took her hand. "Of your soul, my dear. This past month has been the strangest I have ever encountered but there is nothing, nothing I won't do for my children. Your mother is still distraught at your decision to leave home, you do know that?"

Elizabeth nodded, once again pushing aside the doubts and fears that had surfaced and ebbed away countless times in the last four weeks. "I know. But I have to do this, Papa. I want my independence."

His fingers tightened on hers. "But what does independence look like to you? Do you even know?"

Their eyes locked for a long moment before Elizabeth found herself having to look away. She stared through the open window again. Dusk had started to fall, turning the sky salmon-pink as they passed by the Abbey and out toward Pulteney Bridge. Bath was her home and she would be lying if she claimed she'd been unhappy here; yet it was the space of the country she craved. The society balls and grandeur suited many of the women of her age and class, but for Elizabeth it was nothing but a falsehood. She drew in a gulp of air.

"All I know is I long to breathe," she said watching the last of the shops and townhouses disappear as they edged on toward Colerne. "I know going to work for Viscount Westrop as a housemaid hardly equates to an independent life but it is a step toward it, Papa. I am willing to work hard in order to be free from the shackles of expectancy and social decorum."

"Has it really been as bad as all that?"

She turned, felt the flush of excitement in her cheeks. "To me, yes. It has been that bad. Ever since I turned sixteen and my entire existence was laid out in front of me, I have longed for something else. I want to sit with someone and talk. Really talk. Not about what color dress is fashionable this time of year or who has become engaged to whom. These things bore me beyond measure."

He watched her for a moment before a smile curved his lips and a fond twinkle glistened in his eyes. "Despite the fortunate comfort you were born into, you are forever to be found with your hands in dirty dishwater or digging in the garden wearing a dress meant for walking. Maybe you are right. Maybe you will never be happy leading the same life as your sister."

"I wouldn't and I know it isn't what you or Mama wishes to hear, but it is the truth."

He dropped her hands. "Oh, if you had been there to hear your mother's angst when I told her of the position I had found you. I thought I was going to have to ask the maid to fetch the smelling salts."

Elizabeth grinned. "Everything will work out perfectly. I promise."

Gerald Caughley's face sobered, his dark brown eyes, so like Elizabeth's, darkened to almost black. "Time will tell."

A weight dropped low in her abdomen but she pushed it away. She would not falter. It would be too easy to give in to her parents' wishes and end up living a life she hated forever. This was her destiny. Eventually she would have the means to live in gay Paris, maybe work as a seamstress to a famous dancing lady or a companion to a grand actress who treaded the boards of the many theatres there, performing and dancing and singing...

"Elizabeth?"

She started as her father's voice interrupted her reverie. "Yes?"

"I was saying Lord Westrop is a kind and fair man. The house is vast and no doubt you will be subjected to hard work of which you have never experienced before."

"I know, Papa. But I will endure. I will work harder than I have in my entire life."

"But will you be able to withstand the pressure without buckling, my dear?" he asked, sighing. "I fear you, or maybe it is I who has lost all notion of common sense." He paused. "You have six months, Elizabeth, and then you must have the integrity to come forward and admit to your mother and me, the independence you so passionately strive for is not the pleasure you first imagined."

Irritation prickled along the surface of Elizabeth's skin. She kept her gaze steady with his and sat up straighter in her seat. "I have no problem with admitting my mistakes, Papa. But I do struggle with my parents' lack of belief in me."

Color leapt into his cheeks. "I believe in you, Elizabeth," he said. "I'll always believe in you. It is my fear for you that holds precedence, not disbelief. So do you concur? Six months and you will return if your life is not how you imagined it. You will come home where you are loved?"

"But is that enough time to earn the money I need, if I do decide to still travel to France?"

"I'm afraid you will discover that maids don't earn that much. But, if you find your independent life agreeable...I might offer you a little to help you on your way to France, *if* you think you can manage it. I will ask Westrop if your work was satisfactory at that time."

"Oh, Papa." After a moment, Elizabeth dipped her head. "Then I concur."

The rest of the journey from Bath to the country passed in relative silence with only the horses' hooves and the carriage's wheels making any sound. The stone buildings gave way to open roads and fields as they neared Colerne. It wasn't until they were surrounded by nothing but green pasture that her father spoke again.

"There was something else I had to tell you."

She turned. "Yes?" He looked at her with such appeal in his eyes, Elizabeth reached out to take his hand. "Papa? What is it?"

He looked away from her face to their joined hands. "I really hoped you would change your mind, my dear. All your mother and I want is for your future to be secured in the form of a suitable husband."

"Papa, please—"

He held up a hand to halt her. "I know, I know. This is what you want." He paused and then reached across and gently cupped her jaw. "But this liberty comes with a price, I'm afraid."

"A price?"

He drew in a shaky breath. "Your mother insisted that if you go through with this, you were to

13

change your name so no one will know your lineage."
He rushed out the words.

"A different name? But—"

"You will be known only as Lily Curtis to the
viscount and his staff. I have secured this position in
that name and that name only. You are to keep your
new life as far away from your mother as possible,
Elizabeth. Do you understand?"

"But—"

"Do you understand?"

Elizabeth stared at him before her burst of
hysterical laughter bounced around the interior of
the carriage. "Lily Curtis? Lily?" she cried. "As in the
flower of innocence? Oh, how wonderfully apt!"

Color stained her father's cheeks. "Elizabeth,
please."

She lifted her chin from his grasp and wiggled
her finger in the air. "Ah ah ah. My name's Lily from
now on, remember?" she said, falling back against
the seat and clutching a hand to her stomach. "Oh,
what a delight! Don't you see? Mama has cut the
final tie holding me to my old life, now I am truly
free."

And with that, Lily was born and Elizabeth sent
to the grave.

****

Lily stood in front of the huge iron gates of
Cotswold Manor, her slender hands gripping the
metal pattern of tangled vines and leaves like a
lifeline. Her father had dropped her a mile down the
road so as not to evoke any curious glances from the
house—and now she was alone.

This was what she wanted. Four weeks of
planning and plotting and now she was here. A new
life was about to begin so she couldn't even
contemplate turning back. Not for one single second.

Screwing up her eyes, she strained to see past
the mass of trees lining a seemingly endless

pathway toward the house. She could not even glimpse a chimney much less anything else. Knowing she merely procrastinated, Lily pulled back her shoulders and opened the gates. Her fingers gripped her trunk of basic clothing and personal belongings as she began her trek along the graveled pathway. Darkness fell like an eerie blanket around her, but she strode purposefully forward.

I can do this, I can do this.

She repeated the words over and over in her head like a mantra, forcing her new persona to bind its limbs around her. She breathed in the fresh country air, drawing in the strength she needed to take these first few steps and not turn around and run back to her old life. The huge beech trees canopied above her head eventually gave way to conifers and low-lying bushes that stood like sentries either side of the path leading the way to the house. She pushed onwards, feeling her confidence grow just a little bit more with each step.

Who knew what mysteries laid in wait for her? Who knew what people she'd meet? Independence. That's what she was living. Independence.

She walked on until the path spread out to an enormous open space and Lily found herself looking up at Cotswold Manor for the very first time. Her breath caught and her trunk slipped unnoticed to the ground beside her.

"Oh, my."

She pressed a trembling hand to her stomach where a mass of butterflies had burst into flight.

It was a mansion. No, a castle. No, a palace.

Candles shone and flickered from deep within a few of the downstairs rooms but the rest of the house was shrouded in darkness. Her gaze roamed over its huge façade in an awe-consumed dance of excitement. Her fascination went from counting the numerous leaded windows to admiring the huge stone pillars flanking the carved wooden doors.

"So this is what it means to be rich," she murmured. "God bless my mother and her ideas of grandeur. If she could see this house, she would soon realize we are positively insignificant as far as society is concerned."

The impertinent squawking of a crow overhead roused Lily from her reflection and made her realize the master of the house could quite easily be watching her from any of the many windows. Her heart hammered in her chest as she hurriedly smoothed out the folds of her dress and tidied her hair with expert fingers. It was imperative she carried off her entrance to perfection, or she might be banished from her new and blessed independence before it even began. Picking up her trunk, she sent up a silent prayer for God's leniency and marched to the door. Pausing, she gathered her composure and then lifted the heavy iron knocker.

Barely a second passed before the door flew back on its hinges and she was dragged inside by a firm yank to the wrist. Her head snapped back on her neck as though attached to nothing more than a length of rubber.

"Excuse me, sir!" she managed. "What on earth—?"

"You're the new housemaid, yes?"

She estimated the man holding her arm to be in his late twenties. Dressed in a smart black suit and impossibly shiny shoes, his sandy blond hair was swept across his forehead from a side parting and his cheeks shone with rosy color. Yet it was his eyes that struck Lily, they were so wide in their obvious state of panic, she feared they would roll right out of their sockets.

"I'm sorry?" she said.

"Are. You. The. New. Housemaid?"

The ironic tone of his voice jilted Lily into

16

remembering exactly why she was there. She stood a little straighter and smiled. "Why, yes. Yes I am. My name is—"

"You are? Good. We are so glad to welcome you to Cotswold Manor, though you should have come to the back door." His smile manic, he released her arm. "The master has just come back with a few unexpected guests so the evening has been thrown into chaos, I'm afraid."

"Well, you're lucky I arrived when I did then," she said, collecting herself. "My name is Lily Curtis. How do you do?"

"Oh, yes, I'm so sorry. I'm Nicholas...Nicholas Little. I'm the butler."

She grinned, taking an instant liking to the effeminate, yet charming man. "I'm very pleased to meet you, Mr. Little."

They shook hands. "Nicholas, please. You'll soon see that Lord Westrop runs a very informal house. Often frowned upon by his peers, I know, but the master is as different a viscount as any you'll ever meet." He paused and smiled. "And fifty times as honorable. Now come, I'll show you your room and then we must get down to the kitchen."

"Of course."

But as Lily turned around, the magnificence of her surroundings hit her full force in the face. Her feet stuck fast to the gray and cream tiles beneath her. The foyer alone was as big as the entire lower floor of her family home. Huge, three-foot portraits hung along every surrounding wall. Great marble plinths holding beautiful bouquets of white and blue Michaelmas daisies and bright pink clematis stood at the entryway of the two sets of double doors to either side of her. She looked ahead and was faced with the most spectacular staircase leading to the second floor.

"Surely this is the biggest house in the country,"

17

she said in awe.

Nicholas laughed as he picked up her forgotten trunk. "Not quite. But we haven't got time for sight-seeing and gawking eyes at the moment. The tour will have to wait until tomorrow," he said, as he placed his free hand firmly at her elbow and steered her toward the stairs.

Forcing herself forward, they mounted not one but two flights of stairs until they reached the servants living quarters. He opened one of the doors and gestured her inside. The room was an ample size with an iron bed in the center, upon which lay a black dress and a starched white apron and house cap. The rest of the furniture was sparse and consisted of a chair, a small table and a cupboard as well as a washstand, bowl and jug. It was far more comfortable than the dire images that had flitted through Lily's apprehensive mind countless times over the past week. A little of her anxiety slipped away as her confidence grew that she would manage to adapt to her new lifestyle with minimal discomfort. She turned to Nicholas and smiled.

"It will do quite well, I think."

"The view's rather good from up here too," he said, walking into the room and toward the window. "You are facing the entrance so you'll have the best advantage of warning us who is coming."

She raised her eyebrows. "Warning you?"

He smiled. "Oh, don't look so worried. You'll be quite safe here. To a point."

"What do you...?"

"I'm playing with you, Lily!" he cried. "You are the luckiest housemaid alive."

She forced a smile. "I am?"

"Oh, yes. My lord is the finest gentleman this side of the Atlantic. I've been in his service close on eight years, you know. You are looking at groom risen to personal butler," he boasted, giving a mock bow.

Lily laughed. "And proud of it, I see."

"Well, of course." Taking her hand, he led her to the bed. "Now, this is your uniform." He paused. "I must admit we were not expecting you to be so...what shall we say? Curvaceous. But with a little adjusting, it will do just fine."

"Curvaceous?"

Nicholas smiled mischievously and nodded toward her bosom.

Heat seared her cheeks as she quickly slapped her palm across the upper curve of her breasts. "I say!"

He grinned and gently nudged her. "Oh, come now, Lily. You'll need to have a sense of humor if you are going to survive in this place."

She scowled. "Didn't you just say I was lucky to be working here?"

"Yes. And you are. The master is a rare and vibrant gentleman, Lily. He cannot abide snobbery of any sort."

"I see. Well, whatever kind of man he is, I just want it noted for future reference, I prefer that *any* man, whether he be stable-boy or a viscount, only cast his eyes at my bosom with my specific say-so."

He tipped his head back and expelled a laugh so genuine, so infectious it took all of Lily's inner strength to maintain her somber expression. "You are going to fit in here just fine, Lily Curtis. Even if you do talk as though you're a cut above."

She fisted her hands on her hips. "I do not."

He tilted forward on the balls of his feet and tipped her a wink. "Oh, but you do and it's positively endearing."

Lily tried and dismally failed to hide her smile this time. "I can see I'm going to have my hands full with you, Nicholas Little. A true rascal if I ever met one."

With a wiggle of his eyebrows, he brushed past her and picked up her dress. "Ha, ha. Now come my dear, the master has returned with several friends who will no doubt stay the night and so we have plenty to get on with." He gave the dress a sharp snap. "You need to change into this as quickly as you can."

She took the dress from his hands. "And what of her ladyship? Is she as carefree as the lord appears to be?"

His shoulders slumped. "Ah, now therein lays our current problem."

"Oh?"

"There is no lady, Lily. But very soon there must be. My lord's father, the Earl of Marshfield, is seriously ill and he has asked for the master to marry and his lady expecting a son before he dies."

"The viscount has told you this?" Lily asked, surprise lifting her brows.

"Oh, yes. He knows he must seek a wife and has shown a little more interest of late in his best friend's cousin, Lady Tasmin. But still he seems to be digging his heels in and delaying any kind of betrothal."

"Doesn't he wish to marry?"

"Oh, he does but in his own time." Nicholas shook his head and fluttered a hand in front of his face. "Listen to me telling you all this! I have no right. Now, listen, we must hurry. Quickly, get changed."

He walked toward the door, but when he reached it, he paused and turned to face her once more. Lily noticed his eyes were shining with unshed tears. "He's a good man, Lily. A good man who deserves an even better woman. You'll see that for yourself soon enough."

Nicholas left the room. Smiling softly to herself, Lily quickly undressed. Using the jug of water and end bar of soap, she swilled her face, neck, armpits and breasts. The walk from the carriage to the house had left her feeling less than presentable. But then as she dried herself with a scrap of toweling, she stared into the cracked piece of mirror hanging above the wash stand.

Her time had arrived. She dropped the towel. She was no longer a lady but a servant. A servant with intelligence, drive and hard work inside of her. She might not be as beautiful as the ladies who will sit at the viscount's table but she was just as important in God's eyes.

"Lily! Come on now. Time is wasting!"

Nicholas' hiss from the other side of the door made her jump and Lily hurriedly shrugged into her chemise. Getting the black dress on was a harder feat than she'd anticipated but she eventually managed to push and pull it over her breasts. She glanced in the mirror.

"Oh, no," she murmured upon seeing the way her bosom bulged against the dress. "There's every chance the master is going to think I'm here for services other than housekeeping."

"Lily!"

"Coming." She plopped the cap on her head and snatched up her apron. Hurrying down a narrower, back set of stairs after Nicholas, Lily tied her apron and shoved her unruly curls beneath the cap. "How many other staff are here, Nicholas?" She panted.

"The master keeps his staff to a minimum. There are four of us, well, five including you. We have Mrs. Harris, the cook cum housekeeper, Jane, the maid-of-all-work, myself as Butler and then Robert the footman cum groom."

They hurried through the rear of the house and down another flight of steps. Nicholas pushed open the green baize door of the kitchen and nudged Lily inside ahead of him. The huge room was a buzz of

21

activity. The heat hit her as soon as she stepped inside causing perspiration to burst onto her brow and upper lip. She squinted through the steam and smoke and managed to make out a thick-set woman in her mid-forties hitching a huge vat of rich-smelling liquid onto a hook above the roaring fire. At the scrubbed pine table that dominated the room, a young girl stood mixing what look like custard at an impossible speed.

"Ladies, may I introduce our new housemaid?" Nicholas shouted above the sizzling pans and spitting fire. "Her name is Lily Curtis."

The young girl put down her spoon, wiped a hand on her spattered and spotted apron and held it out to Lily. Her smile looked as soft and quiet as a summer meadow. "Pleased to meet you, Lily. I'm Jane."

Lily stepped forward and took her hand. "Pleased to meet you, Jane."

With a hand at the small of her back, Nicholas then urged Lily toward the fire. "And this is Mrs. Harris."

The cook turned her bright-red face from the vat and Lily swallowed. She was as formidable as a raging bull. Her eyes were like great glass marbles and her bosom so big, it looked fit to strangle her despite being strapped into a high neck blouse.

"How do you do?" she growled.

Lily curtsied. "Very well, thank you, Ma'am."

The cook slowly ran her wary gaze over Lily's face, down over her bosom which caused an inelegant snort, and down to the tips of the simple shoes upon her feet. "Nicholas says your references were second to none."

Lily nodded and clasped her hands in front of her to hide the shaking. "I am a hardworking girl, Mrs. Harris. I will do my utmost, always. I hope you will be pleasantly surprised by the attention I give to every aspect of my work."

"Is that so?"

Lily nodded again and stood stock still throughout the cook's second perusal of her body and face. But then the tightness of Mrs. Harris' features crumpled and she erupted into the loudest ground-shaking laugh Lily had ever heard. She clapped Lily so hard on the shoulder, Lily reached out to steady herself before she fell face first into the vat of boiling soup.

"Pretty as a picture and polite as gentry," the cook cried. "The master's going to adore her."

Nicholas stepped forward. "That's quite enough of your teasing, Mrs. Harris. Lily will be running from here without a backward glance if she listens to any more from you."

"I'm only playing. You're a little gem, sweetheart." She smiled, clipping a finger to Lily's chin. "You're one hundred percent welcome."

Lily released her held breath in a rush and grinned. "Thank you."

Nicholas cleared his throat. "Right then. Back to business. What orders has the master sent down? Has Jane served the pre-dinner drinks?"

With a wink at Lily, Mrs. Harris wagged a finger at Nicholas. "Now don't you go questioning my abilities when you ain't around, young man. I can keep this place running with my eyes shut."

He blew out a heavy breath. "I know, I know. Now come on, what are the orders?"

"He wants the full works tonight," the cook said, turning back to the pot and giving it a stir with the biggest wooden spoon known to man. "He has Lord Winchester up there and another two gentlemen. Lord knows what sort of state they'll be in later on. They've been knocking back the wine for the last hour and a half."

Lily's gaze wandered over the phenomenal

amount of food laid out on the table waiting to be served. It looked enough to feed fifty people at least. Mrs. Harris caught her stare.

"Now don't look like that. It won't be wasted," she barked. "The less they eat, the more for us later."

"I'm sorry, I didn't mean—"

"Ah, no need to apologize, girl. I expect you're feeling as though your throat's been cut coming all that way from...where were you before?"

"Bath."

"That's it. Bath. Well, you'll eat soon enough. Once the master's been taken care of."

Lily nodded. She was hungry enough to eat her own leg much less the golden chicken sitting amongst an array of richly colored vegetables and golden roast potatoes. But when Nicholas clapped his hands together, Lily knew the rumbling in her stomach would have to fend for itself a while longer.

"Right, let's get on with it, shall we?" he said. "Mrs. Harris? If you would do the honors."

The soup was transferred from the vat over the fire to a gleaming silver tureen. Nicholas turned to Lily. "If you please, Lily."

Lily stepped forward and carefully picked it up. And with another succinct nod of his head, Nicholas opened the kitchen door and Lily followed on behind.

"Are both ladies and gents staying this evening?" she asked as they marched along the corridor. He came to such an abrupt halt, the soup slopped audibly inside the tureen.

"Oh!" She cried as it wobbled precariously in her hands.

"Listen to me, Lily," Nicholas whispered urgently. "About what I was saying earlier. Maybe I shouldn't have told you about the master needing a wife but because I did, you need to know that although he has yet to pursue this goal, his father has threatened to break up the estate and sell it to the highest bidder."

"But he can't do that, can he?"

Nicholas lifted his shoulders. "Who knows? But my lord is far too proud to let that happen anyway. He says he'll die before he is the one to break the Baxter two-hundred year lineage."

"Baxter is his lord's family name?"

"Yes." He gave a swift look over each shoulder. "The trouble is because of all the pressure, the mere mention of women can set the master off with little warning at the moment."

Lily swallowed. "Set him off?"

"He has a sharp tongue, Lily. He doesn't use it very often, but when he does..." He let the sentence drift off.

The tiny hairs at the nape of Lily's neck stood at attention. "But he is expecting me, isn't he?"

Nicholas frowned. "But of course. Why do you ask?"

"Well, if he detests women so—"

He laughed. "Oh, he doesn't detest women, quite the opposite. He just doesn't want to marry one yet. Besides...you will not be a woman in his eyes, you'll be a maid."

He turned and continued to walk along the corridor as Lily stared after him. Not a woman, indeed! Narrowing her gaze she hurried after him, the tureen now heavy in her hands and surely the cause of the trembling in her arms. She opened her mouth to verbalize her grievance.

"And if you're thinking of getting on your high horse about being a woman and all that nonsense," Nicholas spoke first, "save it for later when we're alone. Right now we have work to do."

Catching the smile in his voice, Lily shook her head and bit back her own smile.

Very soon, working under Nicholas' precision,

the food was laid out on the beautiful mahogany
dining table in all its multi-colored glory. Nicholas
stood back and studied their handiwork.

"Perfect," he announced. "Right, Lily, his
lordship wishes to meet you prior to dining. Come
along now."

She flinched. "Oh, but I wasn't expecting..."

But Nicholas had already brushed past her out
of the door and her heart picked up speed. She
desperately tried to fight her presence but Elizabeth
pushed herself forward. This was the son of an earl.
A viscount. What was she doing? She couldn't
possibly carry off this charade. What was she
thinking?

Vigorously shaking her head, Lily chased away
the fear and trepidation building inside her. She was
no longer Elizabeth Caughley. She was strong,
independent Lily with fire in her belly and
excitement in her veins. She lifted her chin and
marched from the room. She could and would do
this. When she caught up with Nicholas, he turned
and took her icy-cold hands in his.

"Here is the drawing room. When he is finished
with your interview, lead the master and his guests
directly through to the dining room. Any questions?"

She only managed to shake her head.

"Good." And then with a final wink, he turned
and headed back down the hallway leaving her quite
alone.

Despite her preparatory talk to herself, Lily's
insides were a mess of knots and tangles. Sweat
broke out beneath the neckline of her dress.

Could she really pass herself off as a maid? To
attempt to hoodwink Viscount Westrop's staff was
one thing, but to try to dupe the gentleman himself?

Her father had given her very little information
on which to judge the man she was about to meet.
She knew his elderly father had retired to Bath in

order to take advantage of the healing waters but she'd had no idea his condition was terminal. His mother had died when he was just a young boy.

She stared at the closed drawing room door. *Come on, Elizabeth...Lily. You can do this.* Squeezing her eyes shut for a second, Lily inhaled a deep breath before stepping forward and pushing open the door.

Chapter Two

"Dinner is served, my lord."

"Ah, thank you."

He had his back to her. But when he turned...

Lily swallowed her surprise. He stared directly at her—his blue eyes widening, clear and intense. The crystal tumbler in his hand hovered at his lips, mid-sip. The erratic beat of her heart resounded in her ears. She was aware of other people in the room but there was no movement, no sound. *Say something, anything.* She opened her mouth and closed it.

Belatedly coming to her senses, Lily finally dropped her gaze and curtsied.

"My lord," she croaked.

It felt like an age before she heard the masculine sound of his cough as he cleared his throat. She looked up through lowered lashes to watch him slowly place his drink on a small side table. Sweat broke out on her palms when he came towards her.

"You must be the new housemaid," he said. "Lily, isn't it?"

"Yes, sir."

"Lily. Please. Won't you at least do me the honor of seeing your face when I am speaking to you?"

Lily lifted her head and met eyes as blue as a crisp winter sky. He said nothing as he continued to study her. His gaze brushed over her hair, her neck, her breasts. Lily flicked a glance left and right as her body traitorously heated beneath his scrutiny. The other gentlemen were carefully watching the exchange. Their curious eyes darted back and forth between the two, undeniable amusement twitching their lips.

"Are you ready to be seated in the dining room, my lord?" Lily said, standing a little straighter.

"I'm sorry?"

"Your meal, sir?"

He blinked and the tension broke. He hastily threw a look at his friends before turning to meet her eyes once more. He straightened his spine and regally lifted his chin. Lily held his gaze, noticed that his eyes now burned with something she couldn't quite decipher but whatever it was triggered her natural defenses to high alert. The curiosity when he had looked at her not a moment before had vanished, only to be replaced with mischief—or was it guilt? Whatever it was had him puffing out his broad chest making it impossibly wider.

His smile turned wolverine. "Oh, I'm more than ready to eat, Lily. I'm positively salivating."

Lily smarted as his friends burst into a flurry of mocking laughter. She gritted her teeth but kept her gaze locked on his. The tone of his voice had disguised neither the implication nor his obvious enjoyment at her expense. A flame of indignation ignited inside of her. She had dealt with dandies and philanderers on more than one occasion without any slip to her composure.

She wanted to mock him back. Was he embarrassed at having been caught staring so openly at a mere maid? Did he find her interesting? Pretty maybe?

But then Lily remembered her dress—or rather her breasts. Heat flooded her face.

Her face would be the last thing to catch his attention! So he was a viscount. Did that make him any less of a hot-blooded male? She thought not. Well, Elizabeth wouldn't stand to be made a mockery of and neither would Lily.

Her smile was slow and intentionally provocative. "I am so pleased, sir. For I would hate for you to have to endure cold soup." Her gaze lingered down to his crotch. "After all, you and your guests are quite obviously still chilled from an afternoon of riding."

The gentlemen's sniggers instantly halted and the lord's smile dissolved. He looked from her face to his crotch and back again. His eyes widened.

"Why, you..."

She quickly turned and left the room with her heart beating wildly inside her chest and her hands shaking. She had not been at the manor for more than two hours. Surely she had just ruined whatever chance she had of staying here. Silently counting to ten, Lily waited for him to demand she come back, insist she apologize then pack her things and go. But it never came—only a subdued ripple of male laughter traveled along the corridor behind her.

Her mouth slowly stretched to a grin. He was nothing like she had expected and fifty times as handsome. Of course, that was not necessarily a good thing, but she was grateful he appeared to at least have as wicked a sense of humor as she. She pressed a hand to her stomach.

Was she really doing this? Was she finally building her own life at the ripe old age of three and twenty? Her grin widened. But she must not assume she could get away with such banter often.

Lily threw another glance down the hallway. The master and his guests had yet to leave the drawing room and follow her. With a shaky breath, Lily hurried toward the dining room. Admittedly, he was handsome in a rugged way—maybe a little too rugged for a viscount but handsome all the same. His looks had thrown her at first sight but not enough to sway her. She would remain focused. She would keep France in the forefront of her mind at all times come what may.

She reached the dining room and stood ram-rod straight outside its open door as she waited. As the master was still dressed in his riding clothes, Lily could only presume he had returned home and taken his guests directly to the drawing room for pre-dinner drinks. Swallowing hard in an effort to ease her dry mouth, Lily started when she heard the tip tap of the gentlemen's shoes as they approached.

Casting a quick glance in their direction, she sucked in a breath when she met the viscount's impossibly blue gaze over the head of another guest. Her gaze dropped to the floor, she prayed he would walk straight past her into the room without saying anything further.

He stopped right in front of her.

She tipped her head up to meet his eyes. "Dinner is served, my lord."

He smiled. "I have the distinct feeling you and I are going to get along just splendidly, don't you, Lily?"

Icy cold perspiration broke out on the palms of her hands. "I hope so, sir."

And then with a final lingering gaze, he turned and walked into the dining room, leaving his band of friends to follow on behind. Lily released her held breath and vowed to curb her temper whenever in Viscount Westrop's presence. She may have gotten away with her quip this time...but if she was going to fulfill her dream of living a carefree life in Paris, she had to play the role of a servant better than she had so far or goodness knows where she'd end up if he decided to send her away.

Going home was no longer an option—at her father's insistence, she had more than agreed to go home after six months if her attempt at independence failed. She had agreed to marry whomever they chose.

Which meant she'd do her utmost to ensure that never ever happened.

****

"Thank you, Lily." Andrew didn't look at her as she topped off his wineglass. He didn't trust himself to look at her. Instead he picked up his spoon and dipped it into the soup. "I hope Nicholas has shown you where you are to sleep and introduced you to Mrs. Harris and Jane?"

"Yes, sir. He has."

"Good, good. My associates will be staying the night so the fires in the guest rooms will need to be lit."

"Yes, sir."

She moved away to fill the other glasses around the table and Andrew pondered on the mystery that was his newest member of staff. She intrigued him. How had a maid gained such unabashed confidence? Such an acute use of language? He watched her serve his best friend, Charles Winchester, sitting opposite him. Her uniform was far too tight across the bust, yet the waist and hips fit like a second skin.

He turned his attention back to his soup. Such observations had no place at the dining table. He would mention the inappropriateness of her dress to Nicholas as soon as he was able. Shifting uncomfortably in his seat, Andrew forced himself to take another spoonful of soup. Lily. Lily Curtis. He shook his head to clear it. Why a mere maid bothered him so much he had no idea.

He looked up and she immediately met his eyes as though she'd sensed his gaze on her. An uncharacteristic heat warmed his face as a knowing smile curved her full pink lips and her eyes, as black as ink, turned liquid. He wanted to avert his gaze but was caught, ensnared by the sheer power of her stare. For a long moment neither of them looked away but then she broke the silent contact by turning to pour the wine.

Andrew watched her and his jaw tightened. Surely she knew the curve of her breasts were now clearly visible above the neckline of her dress? What if she was being consciously provocative? Well, if she was, she played with fire.

"For God's sake, girl!"

The pitch of Charles' voice jolted Andrew from his turbulent contemplations. He looked across at his friend and saw that Lily had missed Charles' glass and a deep red stain spread across the table cloth like blood upon snow.

"I am so very sorry, sir." She frantically blotted the stain with the hem of her apron just as Nicholas came into the room.

Andrew rolled his eyes as his butler rushed forward, huffing and puffing like a baboon, his face turning much the same color as the aforementioned animal's rear-end. Knowing what he was about to say would cause eyebrows to be raised, but continuing nonetheless, Andrew stood up and dropped his napkin onto the table.

"Just an accident, Nicholas," he said. "Nothing to make a fuss about."

Lily lifted her head. The confidence had vanished. Her big black eyes showed nothing less than undisguised upset. She blinked once, twice. The gesture innocent, yet incredibly and inexplicitly sensual.

"You are very gracious, sir," she said, quietly. "I am so sorry."

Andrew came around the table towards her and then stopped, suddenly aware that he meant to touch her. He slapped his hands to his thighs and gestured toward one of the chairs.

He didn't want her to leave the room worrying

33

about such an insignificant mistake. He needed her to know that such things never bothered him. Even if they bothered Nicholas.

He cleared his throat. "Your hands are shaking, Lily. Would you like to sit down?"

She stared at him, her eyes wide. "Sit down, sir?"

"Yes, come. Sit here."

"Andrew? Are you all right?"

He turned to Charles. "What? Of course I'm all right." He forced a laugh. "Why wouldn't I be? It was you who almost had your riding breeches stained red, not me."

His friend continued to look at him, a line of confusion running between his dark eyebrows. "Andrew, this is most unusual."

"And what of it?" He looked at Nicholas. The man's face was scarlet. "What is the matter with you all?" Andrew asked with a laugh. "I just thought Lily might be put at ease over her accident if she sat with us awhile. It is her first day and a little wine has been spilt; it is not a disaster of manic proportions by any stretch of the imagination."

Charles stood up. "Andrew—"

"Shut up, Charles," he snapped. "Well, will you take a seat, Lily?"

Her dark gaze flitted around each face staring at her. Andrew had no idea if he had made the entire ordeal twenty times worse or better for her. Her face was unreadable. She was a mystery. The first woman he had come in contact with for years that he couldn't immediately mark her card. Her gaze narrowed as she looked at him.

"I am here to work, sir, not to impose on your evening." Her speech was stilted and a flash of color appeared high on her cheeks.

Nicholas stepped forward. "There really is no need, my lord. Lily will be relieved of her duties for

34

the remainder of the evening."

"Absolutely not," Andrew said, keeping his gaze locked with hers. "It was an accident, nothing more. I will not have any of my staff reprimanded for such a minor slip. Now, I'll ask you again, Lily. Would you like to sit down?"

The clock ticked like a heartbeat behind him, the fire crackled and spat. Andrew unconsciously held his breath waiting to see what this unpredictable woman would do. One minute she seemed so full of grace and intellect, the next full of fire and resentment. The two distinctions in her personality shouldn't have fit but they did—inexplicitly so.

"Well, what do you say?" he pressed.

She dropped her gaze and curtsied, throwing him off-guard once again. He felt his jaw tighten as he looked at her bowed head.

"I thank you, sir," she said. "But I know my place and to sit with you and your guests would be most unacceptable."

He stared at her. "Unacceptable?"

"Yes, sir."

Andrew watched her for a moment longer before slowly crossing his arms. "You have a very genteel way about you," he said. "One would almost suspect you have been educated."

She snapped her head up, another flash of color darkening her cheeks. "Not at all, sir. I...I try to better myself and the way I speak, that is all."

He smiled. "Really?"

"Yes, sir." She paused, a sudden glint in her eyes. "Of course, if it is not to your liking, I can always revert to common speech and bad manners. It comes easily to me either way."

Andrew felt the burst of laughter bubbling beneath his diaphragm and could do nothing to stop it erupting. It burst from his mouth and reverberated around the room. Uneasy laughter rippled around the table, joining him in his amusement. He ignored them, not caring about anything else but this enigma in front of him. His friends clearly laughed because of who he was rather than their shared delight, Lily on the other hand didn't seem to care who he was and would say just what she pleased.

"You are quite agreeable just the way you are." He grinned. "If you wish to continue with your duties, then I will not stop you." He walked back to his chair and sat down. "Nicholas, another bottle of wine if you please. I have the distinct feeling a long night is ahead."

"Of course, sir."

Andrew tried and failed to wipe the smile from his face as Lily threw him a look of satisfaction before obediently following Nicholas from the room. He picked up his glass and took a long mouthful. Lily Curtis may be just what Cotswold Manor needed right now.

****

Lily's heart thumped hard against her chest as she followed Nicholas to the kitchen. His admonishments and reprimands fell on deaf ears as she had little hope of hearing anything above the crashing roar of her boiling blood. The audacity! The incorrigible leering! She marched after Nicholas, her hands curled into fists as they swung back and forth at her sides. The viscount had been laughing at her. Actually laughing at her! But then a thought rippled through her conscience—what if he'd guessed she was not all she seemed already? A lead weight dropped into her abdomen.

She had to get a hold of her temper. It was as though the freedom, the blessed liberty from society and her parents, had turned her mind completely. She was here in this strange place, far away from anyone who knew her and now it seemed Lily, this audacious foolhardy mischief maker, was pushing herself forward and was certain to land herself in a whole lot of trouble.

She gnawed at her bottom lip. To lean so boldly across the table had been foolish. She hadn't realized what she was doing until it was too late. She pressed a hand to her stomach as nausea rose bitter in her throat. A man like Viscount Westrop would undoubtedly be experienced and aware of such immodest behavior—yet his condescension had been intolerable. The spark of those eyes, the toe-curling flash of his wide smile, even the clench of his jaw...she had wanted to kiss him, hit him, kiss him.

Lily's eyes widened as the thought rushed into her head unbidden. *What on earth am I thinking?*

She shook her head in an attempt to clear it. She was on the very first step of a very long road and she must remain focused. Money was paramount. This job was all she had to rely on. Her parents had granted her freedom but on a condition that was insupportable. Though her father had offered assistance if she succeeded. But how would he measure her success? She could not fail. She would do what she came here to do and then leave.

They reached the kitchen and Nicholas opened the door before flinging his arm out to the side, gesturing for her to enter ahead of him. Lily grimaced—his anger was radiating from him in waves. The door slammed behind her.

"Lily! For the love of God!"

"Nicholas, I'm sorry—"

He held up a hand. "Not a word. You do not say another word until I have finished."

Lily dipped her head and clamped her now shaking hands in front of her.

"Of all the ways to behave," he cried. "Where on earth did you work before? I have seen your references, your last employer's regret at having to let you go. This behavior makes no sense!"

Lily kept her gaze to the floor. Her father had thought of everything. The letters had been sent to Cotswold Manor weeks ago and not a question had been raised about them in the interim. Together, she and her father had painted Lily Curtis as the perfect and capable housemaid—a must for any aristocratic household. And now she risked ruining all their work by defying with the master of the house. She sent up a silent prayer that Nicholas wouldn't show her the door.

She opened her mouth to apologize again when Mrs. Harris stepped forward, a steaming gravy jug in her hand. "What is going on here?" she demanded. "If the master hears you carrying on like that, you'll both be in trouble. You know he likes a happy household."

"Oh, he'll know why I'm shouting, Mrs. Harris," he retorted. "You should have seen her up there."

"Who? Lily?"

Lily looked up and met the cook's confused gaze. "I don't know what came over me. It won't happen again."

Nicholas pointed a finger at her. "No, no, it will not."

"Reel your neck in, Nicholas." Mrs. Harris sighed. "Now, calm down and tell me what happened. It can't be that bad else she'd be out the door by now."

Nicholas huffed, flung an arm into the air. "Or so we would have thought. But it seems Lily has enamored herself to the master without as much as thinking about it."

Lily struggled not to cringe under the suddenly watchful and suspicious gaze that came into Mrs. Harris' narrowed eyes. Jane and Robert stopped what they were doing and also stepped forward to listen to Nicholas' account of the goings-on in the dining room.

"What are you talking about? In what way?" Mrs. Harris asked slowly.

"She just had him laughing out loud like I haven't heard in a long time past," Nicholas said. "Positively beaming he was."

"Laughing?"

"Out loud?"

"The master?"

Lily looked from one face to the other. Robert's eyes were wide with surprise, Jane had paled to the point she looked as though she might swoon and Mrs. Harris looked fit to keel over. And Nicholas was staring straight at Lily as though she was a conspiring con artist.

"Why are you all looking at me like that?" she said, feeling as though she'd committed murder. "Yes, he was laughing. But he was laughing *at* me, not with me!"

But none of their dumbfounded expressions changed. Nicholas slumped his shoulders and dropped into a chair. "Never seen or heard such a reaction in my life," he said, shaking his head.

"What happened?" Mrs. Harris asked.

He jerked a thumb in Lily's direction. "She spilt some wine, narrowly missing Lord Winchester's lap in the process—"

"Oh, mercy me," the cook said, slowly putting the gravy jug down on the table. "Didn't he go mad?"

"No. In fact..." He paused.

For dramatic effect, no doubt, Lily thought as the last of her remorse vanished. Their beloved master had laughed at her, and if these three didn't believe that...

"...he invited her to sit down," Nicholas finished triumphantly.

The sudden silence was deafening. All four faces

turned to Lily, their eyes wide and their mouths open ready to catch the dust motes dancing around the kitchen. But despite her bravado, Lily's foot began to tap nervously up and down. She crossed her arms to hide the shaking in her hands.

"I don't know why you're all looking at me like that," she said. "Maybe I shouldn't have been so...so...brusque with him, but as far as I can see the master doesn't want a maid, he wants a court jester."

They continued to stare.

"He was making fun of me in front of his guests. He wanted to see what I would do. He is drunk and he is rude."

"The real question that needs answering," Nicholas finally said. "Is why he just changed his entire personality of the last, oh, I would say two years because of you."

Lily's stomach lurched. *Has he?* "How do I know? I don't know what he was like before I came here but I do know what I saw. There was nothing more to his attention than ridicule. It was entirely for the enjoyment of his guests."

Nicholas crossed his arms. "You think so, do you?"

Lily swallowed. "Yes, yes I do. He purposely singled me out because I am young and a woman and new to this household. It is not the proper way for a gentleman to behave."

Nicholas slammed his hand on the table making her heart leap up and lodge in the middle of her throat. Would she ever learn to keep quiet? Didn't Mama always say her mouth would be the death of her? Now she'd surely die from exposure when she had to sleep in a field of cows for the night.

"Enough!" he yelled. "You have no right to stand there judging the master. You have barely been here more than a couple of hours. Viscount Andrew

Westrop is a good man. A proud man." He stood up and took three quick steps toward her. "We are not finished here. Not by a long shot, but I have to bring my lord his wine before he comes down here looking for it. As for you? I will decide what is to be done once Jane and I have served the rest of the meal. I suggest you use the time constructively and start cleaning up in here."

Lily's held breath came out in thick, harsh rasps as the chance of not being asking to leave inched a little closer. Her bosom rose and fell with each ragged inhalation. Nicholas had every right to ask her to leave—but he hadn't. She closed her eyes against the sudden stinging there before opening them again. "I'm sorry, Nicholas. I really am."

He stared at her for a long moment before his shoulders relaxed just enough to give Lily hope all was not lost.

"Dishes," he said, quietly. "Now."

And then he and Jane left the room and Lily busied herself cleaning a tower of pots and pans. The next hour passed in a blur until the kitchen gleamed and the pots shone. All of them hurried about their duties until the clock struck the eleventh hour marking the day's end.

"Come now, Lily. Put that cloth down. Time to eat, child," Mrs. Harris said.

Lily turned to see Nicholas, Mrs. Harris, Jane and Robert sitting around the kitchen table helping themselves to supper. Lily's stomach rumbled its approval. She hadn't eaten since tea time. Her gaze drifted over the steaming bowls of soup and thick chunks of buttered bread. Her mouth filled with saliva and she swallowed.

"Well, are you going to stand there gawking all night or grab yourself a bowl?"

Lily hurried to the table and sat down, trying hard not to snatch the bowl and spoon from Robert when he passed them to her.

"You hungry by any chance?" he laughed.

She grinned. "A little."

Mrs. Harris ladled soup into Lily's bowl and passed her three mammoth chunks of bread. "Eat up then, it will only go to waste."

Lily didn't need asking twice. She plunged her spoon into the soup and when the first taste touched her tongue, she understood what Lord Westrop had meant when she heard him boasting to his friends that he had the best cook this side of the country. It was aromatic, spicy, sweet, just delicious, and mere seconds passed before she had emptied the bowl and was wiping the final piece of bread around its sides and popping it into her mouth. She leaned back in her chair and ran an appreciative hand over her full stomach.

"That was the best soup I have ever tasted, Mrs. Harris." She smiled.

"Good," said Nicholas, stiffly. "Would you like some chicken now?"

The tone of his voice caused Lily's smile to waver. She turned to face him. The way his eyes glinted dangerously in the candlelight told her their discussion from earlier was far from its conclusion.

"Um…no…I'm quite full now. Is everything all right, Nicholas?"

"Oh, yes." He smiled. "I'm just waiting for you to finish, that's all."

She shifted forward in her seat, casting a glance around the table but everyone else was staring at him, their foreheads etched with confusion. "Is this about earlier?" she asked. "I have said how sorry I am."

"Indeed you did. And because of that you'll be pleased to know I've decided to give you another chance—"

Lily clapped her hands together. "Oh, Nicholas."

"I haven't finished."

Lily clamped her hands tightly together in her lap and waited. "Sorry."

"So if you're staying, you'll need these."

He stood up and walked to the counter before coming back to the table. He placed what looked like three black dresses on the table in front of her, all neatly folded into a bundle, pressed and laundered.

"Your new uniform," he said. "And this…" He put his hands out to Mrs. Harris who then leaned down, picked up a wooden box from the floor and pushed it across the table toward Lily. "…is a sewing box."

She looked from Nicholas to Mrs. Harris and back again. "I don't understand."

"You do know how to sew, I presume? I have yet to come across a maid who didn't."

"Well, yes, of course, I—"

"Good, well, these dresses are Mrs. Harris' old ones," he continued. "You will spend tonight altering at least one to fit you." He paused. "I suggest you leave ample material around the chest area."

Heat rushed to her face and she glanced down at the exposed curve of her breasts. "Oh. Yes. I see."

"Good. Then the matter will be resolved and I'll assume the master will return to a more normal state of mind. Not that I'm against him laughing, you understand, I'm just a little concerned about the origins of tonight's outburst, that's all. The other two dresses can be altered in your own time."

And then conversation resumed and the banter increased.

Despite her public reprimand, when Lily looked around the table at the quartet of smiling faces, her heart swelled.

Everything would be all right. They must like her to let her stay.

A tap at her ankle made her look across the

table and her eyes met Nicholas'.

He gave an encouraging wink and Lily's smile stretched to a grin.

Yes, everything would be just fine.

Chapter Three

Andrew entered the dining room to find her placing a steaming platter of bacon onto the table. She was humming a tune as she worked, oblivious to his presence—or the way the early morning sunlight came through the window and fell across her face creating a perfect highlight. A strange sensation skittered across his chest as he watched her.

One would almost describe the color of the hair falling from her mob cap as copper...no, bronze, he mused. Yes, her hair was bronze and her skin a startling contrast of the palest cream.

He was startled from his study when Lily began to jerk her head left and right as the overture in her head gathered momentum. He bit down on his bottom lip as he watched her, delight rippling across his skin and warming his blood.

The moment was quashed, when, at a particularly frenzied point, she gave a semi-pirouette and promptly froze when she saw him standing there watching her.

"Oh!"

Her smile dissolved but her cheeks remained flushed and Andrew wanted nothing more than to retreat from the room and leave her alone again to enjoy her time in private. But to do that would paint him as nothing less than an ogling imbecile, so the best he could do was put her at ease as quickly as possible.

"Lily, good morning. One of the more upbeat works of Tchaikovsky, I believe. You do the work great justice."

Her color deepened. "Thank you, sir."

He brushed past her and sat down, snapping open his newspaper and hiding his face behind it in an attempt to save her blushes. When he heard her footsteps whisper over the carpet, he sneaked a peek over the top. What on earth was she wearing? Gone was the revealing, skin tight, utterly bewildering uniform of last night. Now she wore a dress big enough to fit her own body plus that of a small child inside. He quickly looked away when he saw her turning around.

"Will your guests be joining you shortly, sir?"

"I've no idea. You will need to get used to Lord Winchester walking around the place as he sees fit," Andrew said, blowing out a breath. "He's my best friend and tends to take full advantage of the fact by treating my home as his own."

"It's nice that you let him do so, sir. I have met people of your position who would never dream of extending such a courtesy."

"Well, I would not have it any other way. The man is the person I trust most in the world and he will always be welcome here."

"Bacon and eggs, sir?"

"That would be lovely, thank you. Oh, and some black coffee, please."

"Yes, sir."

He laid the paper on the table as she put his breakfast down in front of him and turned to the coffee pot. "So," he said, "Who did you work for before me?" She stopped pouring the steaming liquid, her eyes staring into the half-empty cup. "Lily?"

"I…" She resumed pouring. "I worked in a house the other side of Bath, sir."

"And were they good to you? Were you happy there?"

"Yes, sir."

"Do you mind me asking why is it that you left?"

Andrew watched her hesitate for an almost indiscernible second before she very carefully put the coffee pot down on its stand. Obviously last night's mishap was still very much at the forefront of her mind. She slowly lifted her inky-black eyes to his and there was yet another strange lurch high in his chest. He swiftly turned his gaze back to his breakfast and waited for her to answer.

She gave a delicate cough. "I...I...the family moved abroad and they wanted their household to be entirely foreign. I feel the mistress had fanciful ideas of the exotic."

There was the most interesting tone to her voice. He could detect an almost self-deprecating laugh behind it. He looked up. "And you find such fantasies amusing?"

A splash of color darkened her chest and rose to her neck. "No, sir. It's just..."

"Yes?"

"I've found that living abroad is a fantasy a lot of people harbor."

He watched her for a few seconds and then turned away when he realized he stared. "Do you really? And that would be amongst the household staff you have met on your travels, is it?"

She opened her mouth, closed it, opened it again. "Yes, sir. We all...want more out of life, do we not?"

Never a truer word said. Andrew swallowed. "Indeed." He turned back to his plate. "Well, I am pleased to find you still here this morning, Lily, at least."

"Sir?"

"I have known Nicholas a long time and he views his job and service to me as the most important role in the world. Your mishap with the wine last night would normally cause him to suffer a seizure but it appears he's seen sense enough to allow you a second chance."

"He has and I am extremely thankful."

"Good." He met her eyes once more. "Nicholas knows I like my staff to be happy and hope in return, I have their loyalty. Mrs. Harris and the others have stayed with me for many years, I hope you will soon understand why."

For a long moment she said nothing and then a small smile lifted the corners of her mouth. "Even in the short time I have been here, I can tell that your staff are very happy here, sir."

"Good, that's good." He speared some bacon onto his fork.

"Is there anything else, sir?"

"No, that is all. Thank you."

She dipped her head and hurried from the room. He barely had time to lift another forkful of his breakfast to his mouth when the double doors swung open. Charles came into the dining room, his hair disheveled and his eyes bloodshot from the previous night's over indulgence.

"What in God's name is the matter with that new maid, Westrop?" he demanded. "She just rushed past me, mumbling something about families moving abroad and stupid girls and goodness knows what. I don't think she even noticed me."

"She's quite a character, is she not?"

"A character? My God, she's utterly insane."

Andrew shook his head, knowing his smile was wider than the River Avon and the inexplicable excitement running through his veins a hundred times more volatile.

"You, my friend, would think that of any woman who had more to say than yes or no to you."

"Nonsense." Charles turned to the long side table where the food was laid out. "I also always allow a woman the privilege to ask me whether I want her on her knees or in the bed."

Andrew shook his head. "You should have been put down at birth."

"Put down? You talk about me as though I am an animal."

"Exactly."

Picking up a set of tongs, Charles loaded bacon and then eggs onto his plate before sitting down. "I don't know what reason you have for taking such a liking to the girl."

Andrew looked at him from the corner of his eyes. "Don't you?"

"Well, look here. It's her second day and yet I am serving my own breakfast."

"That's my fault, not Lily's. I sent her on her way. Why should she have to stand around doing nothing while waiting for you to drag your drunken backside out of bed, eh?"

"All right, all right, point taken."

The two friends ate in silence for the next few minutes before Andrew spoke again.

"I have the distinct feeling she's just what the manor needs right now."

"What on earth are you talking about? She's a maid."

"Yes, but she's young, and fresh and full of gumption. She intrigues me, Charles. Haven't you noticed the way she speaks, the way she moves?" His friend didn't immediately answer. "Charles?" Andrew looked up to find Charles watching him through narrowed eyes. "What is it? Why are you looking at me like that?"

Charles put down his knife and fork, leaned forward on his elbows, his breakfast seemingly forgotten. "What's going on, Andrew?"

"Nothing. I'm just saying I think there is more to her than meets the eye." Andrew had the sudden urge to sketch the young woman. He sketched to relax...but what an absurd idea.

"And why do you care? She's a servant. She displayed her assets like a common whore at your dining table last night..."

His words were like a spark to a flame. The instantaneous anger that filled Andrew's brain blocked out anything further Charles said.

"...what's more, she shouldn't be answering you back, refusing your requests to sit down. Who does she think—?"

"Stop talking, Charles. Now." Andrew's voice was dangerously low.

His friend blanched. "What?"

The heat spread from Andrew's gut to his chest. "I will not have you talking about her that way. She is new here; we do not know her story or the reason she behaves as she does."

Their eyes locked and Andrew recognized the fire in his friend's gaze. He tightened his fingers around his napkin. As much as he wanted to slam his fist into his friend's condescending mouth, Andrew knew it would do no good. Charles' habitual childish jealously whenever Andrew took an interest in another human being was becoming more and more tiresome and it would have to be dealt with. Just not now—not when Lily was clearly causing a reaction to Andrew's sensibilities.

"Tell me this. Why do you even care about her story?" Charles ignored Andrew's advice to keep his runaway mouth firmly shut. He shook out his napkin and slid it across his lap.

"I care about *all* my staff."

Charles sniffed, gave a dry laugh. "Really? And you deny that this interest in the maid has nothing to do with that wonderful figure of hers, my friend? I saw the way you looked at her." He picked up his fork, drew in a breath. "There is absolutely nothing wrong with slumming it every now and then. If you want her, try her, go ahead. I like a bit of that every now and then myself. I'm not one to pass judgment."

Andrew brought his fist down hard on the table. "Try her? Good God, man! What is the matter with you? Have you no respect?"

Charles looked up from his plate, arched an eyebrow. "Respect? She's a servant."

Andrew's hands shook as he took a long breath through flared nostrils in order to rein in any further outbursts. "That does not give you the right to talk about her in such a way," he said slowly. "Are you listening to me?"

Charles' gaze didn't waver. But then eventually the fire in them cooled. He blew out a breath. "Fine. Fine. I will cast no further aspersions. I have never understood your affability with your staff, but it's far from me to tell you how to run your household." He popped some bacon into his mouth. "But I tell you this," he said as he chewed. "Your focus should be on getting a wife, not toying with a bloody maid."

Andrew poured more coffee into his cup. "And I am."

"How? When was the last time you paid a visit to Lady Tasmin?"

Andrew's stomach gave its customary roll whenever anyone mentioned his inevitable betrothal to the pretty and perfect Lady Tasmin. "I suppose it has been a week or so, but—"

"Three. It's been three weeks. You have not seen her since we left Bath after the season. You have to get over to the Lincoln estate. My uncle will be lining up someone else for her if you're not careful."

Andrew met his eyes and gave a small smile as his anger at his friend weakened. "Have you ever considered my reluctance to court Lady Tasmin might be due to the fact she's your cousin? Why on earth would I want to strengthen our bond from friends to cousins-in-law? God, the idea of us being united through family is repulsive."

Charles gave a weary sigh. "I know, I know, but it's all in the name of propriety. What can we do?"

Their eyes met and laughter filled the room. But deep inside Andrew felt the cruel pull of his duty as it yanked on every fiber of his being. Why had he promised his father he would see his only son married before he died? Time was running out. The Earl of Marshfield became sicker with each passing day leaving Andrew no choice but to marry Lady Tasmin, or send his father to his Maker incomplete.

"What troubles you, my friend?"

Charles' voice interrupted Andrew's reverie. He cleared his throat and picked up his coffee cup. "I am thinking that maybe you're right."

"About my cousin?"

"Yes. What do you think about a ball?"

Charles' mouth stretched into a grin. "There is nothing I like more than a ball, you know that. Dancing, champagne. Nothing loosens a lady's faculties like a night full of laughter and fan fluttering."

Andrew forced an enthusiastic smile. "Good, then it's decided. I will hold one here, at the manor. When shall we say? Two weeks from tomorrow?"

"Two weeks? My God, Nicholas will keel over. Is that enough time to organize a ball?"

"Who knows?" Andrew lifted his coffee cup to his lips. "Why don't you pull the bell and let the fun begin. Nicholas is always such a joy to watch over breakfast."

But as Charles scrambled from his chair, his juvenile amusement once more in place, Andrew's coffee scorched his arid throat like liquid acid as he drank.

He'd have to marry a woman who bored him to tears; a woman chosen purely because of her suitability as a countess to a future earl. Why did his father mention the lineage? The need to do the right thing? Andrew fought the nausea rising in his throat. Because his father knew him and knew Andrew would never ever break a promise. Never again.

****

Lily continued to mutter to herself all the way back downstairs to the kitchen. She was relieved to find it empty although not surprised considering the busy hour of the day. She walked to the window and pushed it open allowing the bright August sunshine to spill into the stagnant room and warm her face. She took a deep breath. The pleasing smell of freshly cut grass mixed with the perfume of roses filled her nostrils. The panic that had swept over her since leaving the dining room slowly diminished.

Nothing but acres and acres of grassland and the dense trees of the master's forest broke the perfect vista ahead of her. Both the house and the surrounding estate were stunning and Lily knew she had barely seen more than a fifth of it as yet. Both excited and nervous that she was even here, she had woken at sunrise and quickly washed and dressed. The rest of the staff had yet to stir so she'd gone down into the kitchen and brewed a cup of tea to drink while sitting outside on the servant's doorstep.

Even though her family dwelled in the city, she was a country girl at heart, preferring days out riding or picnicking. The hustle and bustle of town life was a permanent fairground, a kaleidoscope of colored dresses and top hats. The country was where Lily could breathe—for now at least. Deep in her heart, Lily knew her own tenacity was unmatched and she would prove it in her endeavor. There was not even the slightest doubt in her mind that she would be victorious in her independence and her parents' partial surrender to her wishes would be repaid in full by her making the best possible life for herself.

Lily knew Gerald and Mary Caughley, successful lawyer and housewife, were risking complete social disgrace by allowing their daughter to masquerade as a maid and earn her own money, but Lily would succeed. Of that she was certain. And then the whole town would be forced to acknowledge her accomplishment and concede her right to do as she pleased. Lily swallowed, felt her inner strength twitch and grow.

Never one to shy away from hard work, Lily would not give Lord Westrop any reason to suspect she had not been in service her entire life. Yes, she may have been born into privilege but her hands were used to working. Her father had taught her and Isabella their lessons, their mother how to run a household of their own one day—little did they know how those skills would serve their daughters in such completely different ways.

Lily's thoughts turned to the man whose money would ensure her future ambitions as she tightened her grip on the kitchen counter. His questions had been natural for any new employer but they had chilled her to the bone. She would have to concoct a plausible background for herself and stick to it. When the master had questioned her, the story she and her father had devised drained completely from her mind leaving nothing behind. She could not make that mistake again. Any questions he came up with next time, she would be quick to answer without staring at him as though he'd grown an extra head.

The kitchen door abruptly swung open and Nicholas bounded in looking decidedly pale. Lily spun around. "Nicholas?"

"Lily, oh, Lily. What are you doing?"

"I was just about to start cutting the vegetables for dinner. Is everything all right?"

He waved a dismissive hand. "You will have to do that later. We have more pressing issues to deal with right now."

"We do?"

"Indeed." He extracted a handkerchief from his breast pocket and dabbed it all over his perspiring face. "All the plans I had for today have been well and truly trod upon. You would think I would be used to this by now, but every time Baron Winchester—"

"Nicholas, please." Lily put her hand to her forehead as Nicholas' panic rushed over her. "Slow down. I feel as though I am on a carousel."

"Sorry, sorry." He fluttered a hand in front of his face.

"Just take a deep breath and tell me what has happened to get you into such a state."

"A ball."

Lily tilted her head to the side. "A ball?"

He nodded. "A ball."

"As in music and dancing?"

"Well, of course. What other kind of balls would I speak of?" he snapped. "The master has decided, on the advice of the baron no doubt, to hold a ball here the weekend after next."

Lily felt her eyes widen. "Next weekend, but surely—"

"Sit down, sit down." He flapped his hand toward a chair at the table.

Lily sat and Nicholas dropped into a chair beside her. "From now on, the ball takes precedence," he said. "Although I suspect the master only agreed to such a thing in the first place to keep his friend quiet rather than for his own pleasure. I cannot remember the last time I saw his lordship listen to the pianoforte, let alone dance with a willing lady."

Lily said nothing as she watched him chew at

his lip, dart his gaze manically around the kitchen before inhaling a deep breath and continuing with his rant.

"Of course, this does encourage me somewhat with regards to him finding a wife." He panted. "This ignorance of such an important matter cannot possibly go on for another six months and into next year's season. My lord's single status was the talk of society this year. Every mother from here to London flaunted their daughters in from of him as though they were attractions at a street market."

A small smile tugged at Lily's lips as evidence of the green-eyed monster reared its ugly head in Nicholas' disapproving tone. His sexuality was becoming quite clear to her and the master appeared to be high on his list of secret desires.

"Really?" she said. "Why, I cannot remember hearing any reference to Lord Westrop's eligibility." Maybe even for *her* mother, securing a future earl for her daughter was too much of a pipedream.

He arched an eyebrow. "And why would you?"

"Sorry?"

"Well, unless you know something I don't, I was unaware they were now admitting servants into the Bath Assembly Rooms." He emitted a shriek of feminine laughter at his own wit.

Heat flared in Lily's cheeks. "Oh, yes. No, of course not. I do talk nonsense sometimes."

"Indeed you do." He paused, his smile dissolving. "Although you do occasionally speak with the eloquence of the upper middle class, I must say."

Lily laughed. "Oh, Nicholas, you are funny."

He studied her a moment longer before standing and walking to the dresser. He pulled open a drawer and extracted a pad of paper and a fountain pen. "Alas, I fear there will never be a time when either of us becomes part of the social set, my dear."

Lily pursed her lips tightly together, not

trusting herself to speak. She sent up a silent prayer that he would forget her *faux pas* and continue with his panicked arranging of the upcoming ball.

"Now then..." He turned. "My lord summoned me to the dining room and he and Baron Winchester produced a list of approximately eighty guests."

"Eighty?"

"Well, yes. Don't look so surprised," he snapped. "There are many, many people who will be honored to attend a ball hosted by my lord."

Lily clasped her hands in front of her as yet another realization flooded her mind. "And where will all these guests be traveling from?" she asked, trying to keep her voice light-hearted.

"Oh, Bristol, London, Bath..."

She squeezed her eyes tightly shut and drew in a breath. Her days were numbered. The rest of his words melted into the background as she fought her rising panic. What would she do? Surely she'd be recognized.

"Lily? Are you listening to me?"

She blinked. "Yes, yes. And I'm positive eighty is a manageable number, aren't you?"

"Music to my ears! It has been so long since the master hosted a ball. I really want it to be a roaring success and him enjoy every moment of it."

Forcing a smile, Lily stood and clapped her hands together. "Then we will ensure that is exactly what happens. Did he mention a budget of any sort or has he given you free reign?"

His forehead wrinkled with sudden concern. "He didn't say, but I have never known him to hold back license before."

"Good, then in order to find him a wife, we will make not only the ball, but the master also, absolutely irresistible to every lady who comes here. That way someone will be powerless to resist falling in love with him."

The butler gave another feminine squeal. "You are absolutely awful, Lily Curtis."

She grinned. "Why?"

"Because the master is practically engaged to Lady Tasmin already, how can we possibly interfere?" He paused, his smile slipping. "Although I truly wish he would look at least a little celebratory about the prospect of his future bride."

A slow loop-the-loop swept through Lily's stomach but she remained stock still.

Why did it please her to hear him talk of Viscount Westrop's disinterest in the lady? What did she care what he felt for anyone? It was not her concern. Then why did sleep elude her last night because her mind was filled with thoughts of the master?

Lily swallowed. It had been two days, two days! She was in a strange place where she knew nothing or no one. The Viscount had shown her kindness and humor. There was nothing more to their relationship than that.

Nicholas sighed. "Now come, the master wishes to discuss the arrangements with us in his study."

Lily blinked and stood a little straighter. "Now?"

"Yes, there is no time to waste." He moved toward the door and then stopped. Turning, he came back to where Lily stood and completely took her by surprise by pressing a kiss to her cheek. "I was only teasing you before, Lily. You will attend a ball one day, I am sure. So you can change that glum face. Some fine young gentleman will snap you up and dress you in the finest jewels and silks one day, just you wait and see."

"Oh, I wasn't thinking about that." She shook her head to clear it. "Why isn't Mrs. Harris involved in the preparations?"

"She'll be busy with the food. The master asked for you, instead." He walked through the door before she could say another word.

Lily would have felt more comfortable if she helped from the background, but she followed.

When they entered the study, Viscount Westrop was bent over some papers on his desk. His thick dark hair gleamed from the spear of light coming through the big sash window beside him. Lily clicked the door shut and when she swiveled back around, her heart lurched inside her chest. He no longer looked at the paper, but at her, his eyes alight with amusement and good spirits. Their gazes locked for a brief moment but even when she averted her eyes, Lily still felt the heat of his gaze upon her skin like a silken film.

Icy-cold fingers of the unknown tip-tapped up her spine making her wonder what was happening inside of her to cause such a feeling. She didn't like it one bit, whatever *it* was.

"Ah, Nicholas," the Viscount said at last. "I see you have your trusted pen and paper."

"Yes, sir. I have the list of names you gave me and would now like to make a note of any food preferences, wine, etcetera."

"Good, good. I suppose these things must be dealt with as soon as possible if the ball is to be a success. Please, both take a seat."

Lily sat down quickly, grateful for the barrier of the huge oak desk between them. She may be young but she was far from foolish. She didn't want to acknowledge what was taking seed in her mind by naming it—that would be the worst possible thing she could do. She would curb it by distance. Silence it with ignorance. If she ensured she was never too close to the master, the feeling nipping at her center would soon evaporate.

Things only grew if they were nourished. Do not feed them, they will never evolve.

Nicholas made an elaborate show of clearing his

throat, propelling Lily's thoughts back into the room. She pulled back her shoulders as he poised his pen above his pad.

"Are we ready, sir?" he asked.

"And waiting, Nicholas," the master said. "You know I love nothing more than a flamboyant get-together such as this will be."

And despite her little talk with herself, Lily fought a smile while Nicholas steadfastly ignored his lordship's obvious irony. Instead, he pulled his face into an expression of a father tolerating a child.

"First of all we need to be clear of just how many guests you envisage staying overnight, my lord," he said. "That way Lily will know the number of rooms to be prepared and so forth."

The viscount reached out and gestured for the guest list. Nicholas passed it over.

"Well, the majority are coming from Bath so there will not be many in need of a bed. Which is exactly how I wish it, of course," he mused as he perused the list. "Mmm, let's see here. I would say…yes, him, her, him and him. Oh, yes, and her. If you prepare six of the guest rooms, Lily, that will be more than sufficient."

He looked up and met Nicholas' eyes. "I really don't want countless people loitering around the house the following day. God forbid Winchester should get wind of this, but the only reason I am even entertaining the idea of this ball is to see if there is anyone remotely near wife material in the county—other than Lady Tasmin."

Lily flinched as though he'd slapped her. She clenched her hands tighter in her lap. *Remotely near wife material other than Lady Tasmin?* Didn't Nicholas say that Lady Tasmin was more or less guaranteed in the master's affections? Dear God, one minute Lily wrestled with absurd feelings of attraction to the man, the next she wanted to strike him! It was preposterous how men think it acceptable to seek out wives this way. Where was the romance? The united interests, dreams and hopes?

"Is something wrong, Lily?"

She snapped her head up and heat flooded her face. "I'm sorry? Sir."

His mouth lifted at one corner. "You were mumbling to yourself."

"Was I?"

"Yes."

She looked to Nicholas for salvation; but he merely glared at her for obviously distracting the master from Nicholas' very personal crusade of finding him a wife. She had no choice but to provide an answer. She turned back to the master and swallowed the retort lingering on her tongue.

"It was nothing," she said, with a tilt of her chin. "I was daydreaming."

His eyebrows shot toward his forehead. "Are we boring you?"

"No, not at all."

He leaned back in his chair, his sapphire gaze glinting with blatant and infuriating amusement. "Surely a woman daydreaming does not clutch her skirts so tightly in her hands that her knuckles show white?"

She immediately dropped the material she wasn't even aware she'd grasped. "I…um…it was…"

"I would hate to think you disapprove of this ball, Lily?"

Heat rose in her face and her hands turned clammy. Did the man have a direct link to her thoughts? "Disapprove, sir?"

"Of my reasons for hosting such an event."

"It is not for me to comment on your methods of courting a new wife, sir."

Delight lit like a lantern behind his eyes. "Then

why do I see condemnation so clearly written in your gaze?"

Nicholas cleared his throat. "Really, sir. I merely think Lily—"

He stopped when the master stabbed a hand into the air to silence him. "Lily?" the viscount pressed, the tone of his voice decidedly colder as his jaw tightened. "Do you disapprove?"

Lily stared at him and immediately sensed this was a test. A test of what, she had no idea, but a test all the same. And what if she failed? Would he ask her to leave? Her heart picked up speed. Damn him. Is that what it meant to be in service? To allow a master to play a person like a ringmaster would a clown?

She drew in a breath and leapt to her fate. "It's not that I disapprove of the ball."

"All right then," he said. "So if it's not the ball, it must be about my finding a wife. Is there a reason you do not celebrate my wish to find a wife as everyone else on the planet seems to?"

Their gazes locked. And a potent mix of attraction and scorn battled within her. Lily was powerless to deny it and hated him all the more for that exact reason. The man had the look of a Lothario one minute and a dangerous predator the next. She should be repulsed, or frightened; yet it seemed she found the combination wickedly tempting and unbearably animalistic. It was as though she craved this challenge her entire life—and it had come in the worst form possible.

"Come now, Lily," he urged. "Despite the short time we have been acquainted, I am already confident you are by no means incapable of voicing your opinion."

He was goading her with unashamed enjoyment. Fine. If he asked her the question, she had no option but to answer. Pulling back her shoulders, Lily drew in a long breath. "Maybe I am not entirely comfortable with the way of the aristocracy, sir."

"The way of the aristocracy?"

"Yes, sir." She paused, her eyes never wavering from his. "That is to say, the way the upper class appears to canvas potential mates like a farmer would cattle."

Nicholas' sharp intake of breath was excruciatingly loud in the stillness of the room. Lily's heart thundered against her chest and her leg tapped up and down unbidden beneath the concealment of her dress. She waited. And she waited. And then the viscount's smile widened slowly.

"Cattle?"

She nodded. "Yes, sir. I would like to think that a man who wanted me in his life or his bed—"

"Lily!" Nicholas gasped.

His lord lifted a hand once more to silence him. "Go on. I'm intrigued to hear your view on courting and etiquette, Lily. Maybe I've been conducting myself incorrectly for the entirety of my adult life."

She widened her gaze with false innocence— praying the man had the intelligence to sense her overt irony less her respect for him be completely quashed. "Oh, surely that would be an impossible scenario, sir. After all, a man of your stature and prowess surely knows just how to deal with us delicate women and our little nonsenses?"

His cheeks darkened, his blue eyes grew even brighter. "Indeed...in fact, I am confident I know a lot more about women than just that."

His eyes flashed their meaning quite clearly and the implication caused Lily's breath to catch in her throat. She cursed the spark of his victorious grin. From the corner of her eye, Lily saw Nicholas' head batting back and forth between them with the jerky movements of a distressed puppet. It was safe to say his sudden and brusque hoot of laughter was evidence of a man nearing hysteria.

"Lily, you really are lucky the master enjoys your little outbursts otherwise we'd all be in trouble," Nicholas said, his ensuing laugh matching the noise of a chicken being throttled. "My lord, shall we continue? Lily, I suggest you remain tight-lipped for the remainder of this session."

Lily turned to him. "I was just answering my lord's question, Nicholas. It was not my intention to cause offence."

"That may be so but you need to heed your place in this household," he said, flicking a hurried glance at the viscount. "It will not do to pass comment on what the master chooses to do."

Lord Westrop's boom of laughter and rather inelegant snort made them both turn to face him.

"There is no problem here, my man," he said, keeping his delighted eyes on Lily much to her severe annoyance. "Lily is a breath of fresh air sweeping through the stuffy corridors of this place."

Lily dipped her head as a burst of butterflies took flight in her stomach. "Thank you, sir."

And with that, the conversation moved on to the menu, the wine, which guests liked to take a turn at the pianoforte and which guests liked to sing. Throughout the ensuing hour that Lily had to endure sitting across from the viscount, her impatience to leave the room scratched at her nerves like the savage beak of a vulture picking at a carcass. At long last the meeting came to an end and when Nicholas rose to his feet, Lily leapt to hers and hurried from the room with unbridled enthusiasm.

"What on earth were you thinking?" Nicholas ranted when they were barely in the kitchen. "Have you learned nothing of etiquette at your previous posts of service? How could you even think of questioning the master like that? Making your opinion, no..." He paused, his hand flapping back and forth in mid-air as he searched for the right word. "...your derision known with such open hostility. Never in all my life have I seen such a display of palpable disrespect!"

Lily dropped her bottom onto a chair, and then her cheek onto the smooth, age-old wood of the kitchen table. "He just infuriates me so."

"Infuriates you? Infuriates you, Lily? He is the master of this house. Your previous employer gave me a long list of your successful service yet you behave as though you have never worked in a house in your life. I have already seen evidence of how hardworking you are. You were up before everyone else this morning despite staying up all night altering your uniform, not to mention the fires had been lit and the water boiled. I didn't order you to do any of that, yet you did anyway. But your attitude, Lily, does not fit with your experience at all."

She closed her eyes against the hot sting of tears. How was she supposed to keep up the pretence? She was barely into her second day and already Nicholas saw things weren't as they should be.

"How are we ever to organize this ball if you are always snapping at the one person you should be doing your utmost to keep happy? Now I demand to know what is wrong with you?"

Lily swallowed. "Nothing, honestly." She wiped a hand across her brow and sat up in her seat. "I'll change, I swear."

He stared at her for such a long time that Lily felt an impending doom weigh heavy on her shoulders. It was over. Her playacting was no better than a busker's and twice as worthless.

"Nicholas, please..."

"You have one more chance, Lily. One more chance to prove to me that not only do you need to work here but you also *like* working here. I swear if the master had not thrown this ball on me without prior warning, today would be your last. However, now it is so, I need you here." He sighed, his shoulders relaxing as his anger dissipated. "How could you not like it here, for goodness sake? I don't understand this need to find fault when the master is so obviously fond of you."

She laughed wryly. "Fond of me? The man does nothing but play with me like I'm a mouse and he a cat."

He waved a dismissive hand. "He is merely passing the time of day with you. Would you rather work for a master who curses and rants and raves or works you to the bone for minimal pay?"

"No, of course not. You're right and I'm sorry for my outburst. It was his blasé attitude about the expected lady guests that angered me. That is all. It won't happen again."

"But what of it? He needs a wife and I am relieved to seeing him actually doing something about obtaining one. This idiocy that more and more women are shouting about is getting out of hand."

"Idiocy?"

"Oh, women wanting to do this and that; try their hands at things women have never done before. It has to stop before anarchy rules supreme."

Lily squeezed her eyes shut and counted very slowly to five before opening them and blowing out a slow breath through pursed lips. "You're right," she said, the words nearly choking her. "I have a lot of difficulty accepting things in our society, that's all."

"Well, that may be but even though my lord's and Lady Tasmin's marriage will not be any great passion, God willing it will at least be harmonious. A match well suited."

"But don't you see?" Lily cried, her feeble resolve to conform once more shattering to the stone floor beneath her feet. "That's exactly what churns me up inside!"

"What? Marriage?"

"No, not marriage. Passion. Passion and integrity. Lovemaking and sensuality. Building a life together while listening to each other's opinions and finding a way to make things work so both of you are happy."

He laughed. "Lily, you are talking about something that will never happen. If you continue to hold on to such flights of fancy, you will die a lonely woman."

Heat flamed her cheeks. "Really? Well, so be it then. I will never marry a man who expects me to parade around in front of him, dressed up in every piece of finery my family has seen fit to bestow on me. While I wait for him to decide whether or not I have the face that fits his perfect life or worse, as he calculates the wealth I have that will become his once his ring is on my finger!"

"You are doing it again. I fear this is never going to work."

"You don't like my point of view, I understand that but—"

He cut a hand through the air, slicing their conversation in two. "No, it just won't do. I will make do without you. You are going to have to leave. I have no choice but to sack you."

Her blood roared in her ears. "Sack me? But you can't."

"Oh, but I can. You are in danger of turning this entire household inside out if you continue with this outrageous carrying on—"

"And that is exactly why she will be staying."

Lily span around so quickly Viscount Westrop reached out and held her waist to stop her falling. Her hand slammed to his chest and lingered there just a moment too long before she remembered to snatch it away again. His hand slid from her waist, but the warmth where it had lain remained.

"Sir, whatever are you doing below stairs?" Nicholas cried.

The master stared straight at his butler. "Lily will be staying, Nicholas. Is that clear?"

Nicholas hesitated for a second before he straightened his spine. "Sir, I really feel Lily does not suit the house. She is far too volatile and opinionated."

"And your professional assessment has been noted. But I think Lily came here for a reason and until she is ready to share that reason with you, me, or anyone else, she will stay here as long as she wants. Her work so far is impeccable and I find her company most enjoyable. I would be gravely disappointed if she were to leave."

Lily looked at him and was surprised when nothing but fondness and maybe even a small amount of admiration was reflected in his impossibly blue gaze. The usual mocking was lacking, as was the superiority. She returned his smile. "Thank you, sir."

"You're welcome. Right and now..." He clapped his hands together. "I would like Jane sent up to my room to pack my cases as I will be going to Lord Winchester's for a week or so. That will leave you ample space to arrange this blessed ball."

"You are leaving today?" Nicholas asked.

He nodded. "Yes. I need..." He paused, glanced swiftly at Lily before turning back to Nicholas. "I need to catch up on a few things. Mrs. Harris, yourself and Lily will oversee things without me here, will you not?"

Nicholas bowed. "As you wish, sir."

"Good. Well, I bid you both a good afternoon."

He turned and walked from the kitchen. As soon as the door clicked shut behind him, Nicholas dropped into a chair. "I never thought I would see the day."

Lily frowned. "I'm sorry, Nicholas. I meant what I said; I really will behave from now on."

He waved a dismissive hand. "Not you. Him. The master."

"Yes, I know. That show of kindness was incredibly out of character."

"Lily." But when he looked up, she winked to show her jest. He laughed. "Very droll. No, I was referring to him coming to the kitchen. I have worked here close on ten years and never, ever seen him take as much as a step inside this room. Mrs. Harris won't believe her ears when I tell her." He looked up. "You are certainly having the most absurd effect on things around here. I can't help wondering what will happen next."

Chapter Four

September 1890 — The Day of the Ball

Lily pushed herself to her feet and smoothed her hands over the front of her apron. The ballroom looked spectacular as did the dining room which was laden with drinks and hors de oeuvres. The last two weeks had been a frenzied whirlwind of dusting and cleaning, polishing and scrubbing; as well as unpacking long-forgotten candlesticks and finery from the many boxes in a room on the very top floor of the house. When Nicholas had said the master hadn't entertained the idea of a ball for a very long time, Lily didn't think that meant the ballroom doors had not been opened in nearly half a decade.

It soon became clear Lord Westrop's father, the Earl of Marshfield, had been the one for dancing and merriment prior to falling ill, not the viscount. Although he had never before initiated a formal ball such as this at Cotswold Manor, Nicholas explained that the master was by no means adverse to the social season in Bath and London. It was just the master's home was his retreat and this ball should and would be the subject of much excitement and speculation. There could not be a clearer way of illustrating to Lady Tasmin and the rest of his inner circle that the viscount was opening his home to others—and her.

Ignoring the unwanted but incessant pang of nausea Lily felt every time Lady Tasmin and her lord's name were spoken in the same sentence, she drew in a deep breath. She turned her mind to her role as housemaid—rather than the idiocy of her inexplicable attraction to a man so above her station it was laughable.

Fisting her hands on her hips, she surveyed the combined efforts of the last two weeks. The entire staff had worked like Trojans and now the house was fit to receive Her Majesty herself let alone anyone else. The first time Nicholas had pushed open the double doors of the ballroom and gestured her inside, Lily felt as though she walked into a wonderland waiting to be discovered. Every piece of furniture was shrouded in white sheets or thick layers of dust. It had all been untouched and unloved for so long, but the moment Lily had closed her eyes, she heard the music. The distant play of a violin and the serenade of a flute had washed over her, making her feet want to dance and spin and rejoice in such a beautiful room.

And now after hours and hours of back-breaking work, every dusty surface had been polished, every black-spotted mirror shone and each crystal of the chandeliers had been carefully cleaned and buffed to a blinding brightness. Her fingernails were no more, every bit of the skin on her hands cut and sore, but it had all been worth it. Her smile widened. The viscount had taken her aside just before he left and told her to make the ballroom the living vision of her dreams no matter the cost. He asked her to try and imagine how a potential lady of Cotswold Manor would like it to be. And to her, at least, she had accomplished the task to perfection.

The walls butter cream, huge heavy drapes of pale green brocade hung at each of the many windows and either side of the gleaming French doors leading to the garden. Highly polished candlesticks and gilt-edged mirrors reflected the flickering candles and the crystals of the chandeliers. Lily clamped her hands together in

front of her as she rolled back and forth on the balls
of her feet like an excited child. Glorious! And just a
few short hours from now, the music would play and
the room would be a tempest of multi-colored glory
as the men hunted and the women preened. Maybe
there was something a little romantic about the
pursuit of a nobleman after a woman after all. A
small shudder tickled her spine.

She glanced at the huge circular, oak-framed
wall clock at the very far end of the room. Time was
bearing down. Each passing second meant less time
to convince Nicholas it would be a more efficient use
of her time and skills if she were to stay in the
kitchen this evening rather than the dining room.
His constant murmurings about designating her to
serving drinks in the ballroom were stretching her
nerves to breaking point. She fingered one of the
many silver candlesticks lining the mantelpieces as
she began to devise yet another plan. She could not
be in the ballroom tonight and risk being recognized
by the many people she socialized with during the
hectic Season in Bath.

If she was, her time at the manor would be over
and her disguise ripped bare for all to see. But it
wasn't the chance of ridicule and humiliation
making her stomach roll and her heart race. It was
the need to stay where no one knew Elizabeth,
where her old life already felt like a distant memory.
Lily had only just been born. Her slate was clean.
She had no regrets, only dreams and hopes and
desires. It was prevention of a confrontation rather
than the fear of one that had her longing to stay in
the background of the comings and goings of the
next twenty-four hours. Although her attitude had
somewhat softened since her last run-in with
Nicholas, Lily was not fool enough to think she
wasn't still teetering on a knife-edge. She'd lost
count of the times he'd reminded her she was still at

the manor on the Lord's say-so rather than his.

Ever since that afternoon in the kitchen, she had been on her best behavior and curbed her tongue in the most uncharacteristic way. Nicholas seemed to appreciate the change and for now at least, they were getting along famously. The arrangements for the ball were of equal credit between them.

At first, Lily had been suspicious of the lord's motives for disappearing without overseeing the arrangements of such a monumental event. But then Nicholas simply asked her if she had ever known a man, any man (Nicholas himself excluded, of course) of being the slightest bit interested in the ramifications of any social gathering. And as Lily thought of the master's masculine demeanor and noble stance, the idea of him fussing over the choice of linen versus cotton or the dilemma of whether to serve ham or tongue, she'd completely understood his decision to be far away from the manor.

The stout thud of footsteps against wood jerked her from her thoughts. She turned and the acoustics of the massive room enhanced her audible intake of breath. She immediately felt her face burn.

"My lord, you're back," she said, her heart turning over in her chest.

He looked magnificent. Slim black trousers skimmed over muscular thighs and down over his legs to brush the top of his highly polished shoes. His jacket was supremely cut revealing the ivory, subtly patterned waistcoat and snow-white shirt beneath. The high-collar of his shirt would have looked almost dandy on a less masculine man but on him, it was nothing short of regal. Big and strong, his wide shoulders accentuating his notably slim torso as he strode purposefully toward her, his eyes intently on hers. He seemed oblivious to the stunning transformation of the room around him.

"Lily." He held out a hand, his smile so wide, it made Lily's skin tingle to see him so happy.

She dipped her knees without thinking. "Did you enjoy your time at Lord Winchester's, sir?"

He reached for her hand and gently tugged at her fingers. "Come now, what have I told you about curtseying?" he asked as if he didn't hear her question. "No more."

She gave a tentative smile, while trying to remain impervious to the fact he had yet to release her hand. "I apologize, sir. I think it must be the way you are dressed. You are making me feel decidedly humble."

"You? Humble? Never in my life will I believe it." He grinned and broke his gaze to look down at his clothes. "Do I look like a fraud? A damn pansy dressed for the circus?"

A bubble of laugher tickled the back of Lily's throat to hear him laugh at himself in such a way. "I assume the clothes are not to your liking, sir?"

"Liking? My God, no. What I wouldn't give to be in my riding breeches and galloping at high speed across the country right now." He finally released her hand to push back his dark brown hair from his face. "This formal stuff is just not me. If my father..."

He stopped and his cheeks immediately darkened. His jovial mood evaporated. Lily watched as his eyes changed and whatever he'd been about to say waged a war behind two perfect circles of blue.

"Sir? You were going to say?"

He waved a dismissive hand and looked away from her. "It's nothing."

Disappointment plunged into her abdomen as the fragile moment broke. She suddenly wanted to learn something, anything about a father who, according to Nicholas, had managed to persuade the athletic Andrew Baxter, the unpredictable Viscount Westrop, to finally settle down. Also to open his beloved home to a future wife, instead of gallivanting around the county as he had before his father's illness struck. But the silence stretched between them like an invisible cloud, threatening to spread wider and wider until nothing but darkness shrouded them.

When he turned back to face her, Lily saw the wretchedness, recognized the suffocating feeling of helplessness in his gaze and her heart went out to him.

She might be wrong, but it seemed he was nowhere near as accepting of this situation as his staff wanted to believe.

Her strong sense of intuition had told her time and again the decision to hold the ball and everything that implied, was not in the master's best interests as Nicholas insisted. The man standing in front of her looked miserable and although the emotion confused her, everything inside her wanted his discomfort quashed and the brightness brought back. Forcing a smile she hoped as warm as a breaking sun, she threw out her arm to encompass the room.

"What is your opinion of the ballroom, my lord? Do you like it?" she asked. "Jane and I cut some roses from the garden and arranged them about the place. I also found some stunning candlesticks stored in the attic. I feel as though I have been polishing continuously for three days; but I think they look beautiful, don't you?"

He looked about the room, his gaze dazed. "Yes, yes, they're lovely."

"And over there I've put some silver platters on which we could arrange—"

"Lily?"

She turned. "Yes?"

"I hate to interrupt you but I am finding it incredibly hard to think about something as inconsequential as candlesticks when I am expected to find a wife under the most difficult pressure. I know this is something you could never understand. But please, just believe me when I say it will make this evening's entire debacle a lot more palatable if I didn't have to take into account the amount of work my staff has had to endure through preparation for a ball I no longer want to host."

The harshness of his tone dried her throat. A shift had invisibly taken place and now a new and hardened man stood in front of her. The candlelight turned his gaze midnight blue and indecipherable, his jaw appeared carved from stone. Lily heard the tell-tale beat of her pulse in her ears.

"Well? Have you nothing to say?" he demanded.

She swallowed. "I really do not think it is my place to—"

"No argument, no complaint at my rudeness after all your hard work? No rebuff how it is a small thing for a dying father to ask of his only son and heir?"

She took a breath, even though risking the sharp end of his tongue to pause and take the time to see what was really happening. There had to be a reason for the change in his personality. This constant battle within him was uncomfortable and confusing. It was as though he didn't know who he was—but he did, she just knew he did. And then she saw it. A heavy pressure pushed down on Lily's heart as an overwhelming sense of pain bore down on her. His words were tinged with anger but it was anguish that poured from the very core of him.

She tilted her chin. "You are right, sir. I would hardly notice the room myself under the same circumstances."

He shook his head, his eyes still boring into hers. "Come now, Lily. I know you can do better than that."

She would not get pulled into this game he so clearly liked to play with her. Little did he know that for the first time since she arrived at the manor, she could clearly see his sense of duty, his honor and depth of commitment to his family and what he was willing to sacrifice to uphold it.

"Well?" he pressed.

Lily's gaze did not waver despite the trembling in her legs. "I am positive your commitment will be recognized by a lengthy, happy marriage and a houseful of children, sir."

He stared at her, his pulse jumping in his jaw, his eyes wide with frustration. "Pardon?"

Lily fought for the words to appease him; but the weight of knowing she had run from the same problem, albeit on a lesser degree, prodded at her conscience. She wanted to tell him their lives would always be riddled with challenges and opportunities—it was up to them how they reacted. But she didn't. Instead she exhaled her words it in a rush. "All I mean is—"

He thrust a hand in the air. "Stop."

Lily started. "Sir?"

He squeezed his eyes shut and slowly shook his head. "Listen to me. My God, listen to me. Who am I to burden you? Why should I single out you as an outlet for my own misgivings?" His snapped his eyes open and exhaled a heavy breath. "I apologize, Lily. I'm sorry."

Shock at both his softened tone and the sincerity of his apology caused Lily to distrust any further comment. She dipped her head in silent acceptance of the apology instead. After a moment, he turned away and absently paced the floor.

"Can you imagine how it feels knowing you have made a promise of such magnitude, that if you were not to see it through, it would cause pain to everyone around you and even those who are not yet born?"

"I..."

He stopped and flicked his gaze over her hair and lips. Lily felt her body warm beneath his scrutiny. And then he blinked and the atmosphere shifted once more.

"What on God's earth is the matter with me?" he said, suddenly smiling. "If Nicholas heard me speaking to you so openly, he would partake in more than his usual horrified song and dance, don't you think?"

Lily opened her mouth and shut it again thinking her current state of silence was having a successful effect on him and it was best not to risk an about-turn.

"Well, anyway," he continued. "I know one day you will be lucky enough to marry a man you love and for that liberty, I envy you."

She nodded politely. "I hope so, sir."

He arched an eyebrow. "You hope so?"

Silently cursing her inability to further curb her blasted tongue, Lily met his eyes. "What I mean to say is, I hope I recognize the man I am meant to marry when I meet him and not miss such an opportunity."

For a long moment, he said nothing and then he cleared his throat. "And so I assume you have not met the man yet?"

The intensity of his stare made the blood rush to her face. "No, sir."

Another endless moment passed with each ticking of the clock and then he turned away and resumed pacing. Clasping his hands firmly behind him, he concentrated his gaze on the ceiling. "Do you know something, Lily?"

"Sir?"

"For all my resistance, it will be ironic if I actually enjoyed this evening, will it not?" He laughed. "Maybe I will dance a set or two. That will start the tongues wagging if nothing else."

Lily forced herself to talk over the anxiousness thundering through her veins. "Do you not usually dance then, sir?"

"Oh, I do. But when you dance under the beady-eyed scrutiny of a mother with marriage for her daughter at the forefront of her mind, it loses its romance somewhat."

And then it happened. The words tumbled from her mouth before she could stop them—and they were as reckless as if she'd suggested dancing naked in front of the queen. "If you really don't want any of this, sir, you shouldn't do it."

He halted, turning slowly to face her. "Sorry?"

She swallowed. "All I mean is..." Her voice dwindled to silence.

His Adam's apple shifted beneath the taut skin of his neck and then he took two quick strides towards her. Her breath caught when he came close enough for the musky scent of his cologne to hit her nostrils. She fought the irresistible urge to breathe him in like oxygen. She held her ground as his eyes narrowed.

"Why would you say that to me, Lily? Did I not just explain?"

"I..."

His gaze darted over her face. "You know, I thought of you often while I was away. You intrigue me. You interest me without any provocation on your part. I can't explain it, but...I just want you to know."

Her heart raced inside her chest as a new and tantalizing pull tugged at her center. Her voice cracked as his gaze lingered at her lips. "Sir, I...this..."

He smiled. "No more talking."

His voice was so soft it caressed her skin like feathers over silk. Her nipples tightened as his gaze

79

traveled lower over her now decently shrouded bosom. A profound longing flooded her senses as her traitorous body warmed beneath the intimacy of this forbidden situation. It felt so arousing, so dangerous. The room seemed to close in, cocooning them in a tiny space where no one else existed. Just for one delicious moment...

Lily snapped herself up straight. *This is madness. I should leave.* She should run out of the room before either of them said another word. "Well, I thank you, sir."

He raised his eyebrows. "You thank me?"

She shifted from one foot to the other. "Yes, thank you. Now if you'll excuse me I really have so much to do before your guests begin to arrive."

She turned to leave but he reached out and gripped her wrist. Lily dropped her gaze to his hand. He snatched it away as though she burnt him with her stare.

"I'm sorry," he said.

Swallowing hard, Lily forced herself to meet his eyes. "There's no need for you to apologize."

He wiped a hand over his face and looked to the ceiling. "There is. I should never have told you such a thing." He laughed wryly. "What on earth did I expect you to do with such a bizarre confession? I apologize, Lily. I must be losing my mind under the pressure of everything that is happening."

He dropped his gaze to hers. The rapid pounding of her heart echoed in her ears. Just when she considered running from the room to save the embarrassment of stretching up on her toes and kissing him, he turned and stepped away. The space opened between them like a lonely abyss. She released her held breath.

"Can you remember our discussion in the study?" he asked.

The sudden change of subject jolted Lily back to

the here and now. "Sir?"

He turned, a small smile playing at his lips. "You know, when you inferred that this evening was about me lassoing a virgin heifer?"

The crassness of his words were such a contrast to the shared intimacy of a few seconds ago, a nervous laugh bubbled from deep inside her. "A virgin heifer, sir? I am sure I never said any such thing."

He wiggled his eyebrows and smiled. "Maybe not. But do you still feel I am nothing more than a brutish buyer at a market? A man intent on seizing a woman and holding her vice-like in my arms until she surrenders to my prowess with a sigh of heavenly gratitude?"

Lily forced a laugh and tried to delete the image he had described from her mind before she found herself wanting to be the heroine in that particular play.

"You are making fun of me."

He held up a hand and grinned. "Guilty."

She fisted her hands on her hips and feigned insult. "Well, whether I still feel that way remains to be seen after this evening. I refuse to apologize for not liking the idea of young women parading around in front of potential suitors, truly believing that marriage is all they are worthy of."

"Oh? And women are worthy of so much more?"

Her smile dissolved as a heavy sense of disappointment whispered through her. Why had she thought him any different? Maybe he didn't want to marry, but he still believed women are nothing more than tools in a man's life.

"Lily?"

She glared at him. "Of course they are worth more. Much more."

He gave a slow nod. "I see. And are your parents still happily married?"

"Why would my parents' relationship be of interest to you?" Lily halted as a terrifying realization had her teetering back on her heels and her eyes widening.

Did he know? What if he hadn't been to Baron Winchester's house at all? What if he had been to Bath and discovered the truth of who she really was?

She looked into his eyes but they told her nothing. Her hands turned clammy.

He knew who she was and would take his time torturing her. She needed to leave. She needed to get out of here right now.

She turned her gaze to the blessed open door at the other side of the room. "Um...yes, sir...they will celebrate their twenty-fifth anniversary next year."

"Wonderful, just wonderful." His tone, the tormenting intensity of his eyes as he watched her, left Lily in no doubt her suspicion was correct.

"And they quite obviously idolize you having paid the money to see you educated. Your use of language is quite outstanding to one of a lower class."

She bowed her head. Not out of respect but out of the fear that her eyes would deceive the barrage of emotions raging a battle of survival inside her. "I taught myself to read and write, sir. I have an avid love of books and the written word."

"Well, then, I insist you feel free to use the library. I am not much of a reader myself and I am sure the books in there could do with an airing."

Keeping her gaze on the polished floor, Lily nodded. "Thank you, sir. May I go now?"

"Of course. Oh, there is just one more thing."

"Yes?"

"I would like you to serve the drinks in the ballroom this evening. You are as beautiful as you are intelligent. You will be a delight to my guests."

She forced herself to meet his gaze. "Thank you,

sir. It would be an honor."

And then she turned and exited the room with as much decorum as her frazzled state of mind would allow. Once in the corridor with the ballroom door firmly shut behind her, Lily picked up her skirts and ran to the kitchen. Panic threatened to engulf her. Nausea swirled and ebbed in her stomach.

What would she do? It was over. He had discovered she was an imposter and now he wanted to make a public display of her. She pressed a shaking hand to her stomach. She'd seen the guest list and there were at least twenty people from Bath attending. She didn't recall any of their names but that didn't mean they would not know who she was once they saw her.

****

The smell of cooking meat and roasting potatoes washed over her senses when Lily pushed open the kitchen door. But she only managed a single inhalation before Nicholas all but tackled her to the flagstone floor.

"Where have you been?" he demanded, roughly cupping her elbow. "I left the master in his chamber not half an hour ago, fully dressed and ready for his guests. I come downstairs to make sure everything is as it should be and what do I find? No Lily. Again."

"I was with him."

"What? Alone? Why?"

Mrs. Harris, Jane and Robert all stopped what they were doing. Lily met their eyes one by one. "He wants me to serve tonight."

Nicholas exhaled his breath and laughed. "Oh, thank goodness, is that all? Well, that's that then. What the master wants, the master gets." He paused and peered into her face. "But why are you looking as though you're about to be hung at the neck?"

"I can't do it."

"You can't do what?" Nicholas glanced over his shoulder at their audience before turning to face her. "Please, please, please, do not start your stubborn behavior again, Lily. I have warned you that if needs be I will stand up to the master and insist you leave."

To her horror, tears sprang unbidden into her eyes and Nicholas' face blurred. "But I can't."

His eyes widened and his face flushed dark red. He looked to Mrs. Harris, back to Lily, to Mrs. Harris again, his head thrusting back and forth like a deranged chicken. "Mrs. Harris," he sputtered. "She's...she's crying."

"Oh, for crying out loud, man." The cook stepped forward, elbowing him out of the way. "Come on now, Lily. Come and sit down. Whatever's brought this upset on?"

Lily slumped into a chair and looked at the four faces she had come to be so fond of in such a short amount of time. "It's hopeless."

"What is?" Mrs. Harris asked, her moon-like face crinkling. "It's nerves, that's all. Some of the guests may be rich, a few will even be rude, but on the whole, the master chooses his friends well, and they are more often than not polite and courteous. There is nothing to worry about, child."

Lily looked deep into her eyes, her features distorted through tears. "It's not that. Oh, God, what a mess."

"Then what is it?" Nicholas demanded, his need for manic organization clearly breaking through his momentary fear of a woman's distress.

She shook her head. "It's all so hopeless. Why did I think I would be any different than Isabella? Why did I think—?"

"What on earth are you talking about? Who's Isabella?"

Lily looked up, met his confused gaze. "My

sister. She's my sister."

Glancing about him, Nicholas hesitated before picking up a folded napkin from the freshly laundered pile on the table and pressed it into her hand. "Now look." He sighed, his gaze softening. "You need to tell us what this is about. Whatever it is that has you this upset can no doubt be sorted out. Come on, out with it."

"You don't understand."

"Then tell me."

She drew in a shuddering breath as she looked around at their faces once more. What was the use in pretending? Sooner or later, they would find out what she'd done and hate her all the more for keeping them in the dark for so long.

"I am not who you think I am," she said, her fingers rapidly picking at the hem of her apron. "My name is not Lily, it's Elizabeth. Elizabeth Caughley."

"What?" Nicholas' voice raised an octave or two. The sound almost female in its hysteria. "You're a charlatan? A fraud? Oh, how could you? What will the master say? What of his reputation?"

Tears burned painfully behind Lily's eyes. "I had no choice, Nicholas. I couldn't spend the rest of my life with a man older than my father as my parents wanted me to. The thought of having to lie with him..."

He threw his hands in the air, two spots of scarlet burning high on his cheek bones. "Spare me the detail, Lily, please!"

"But you have to understand—"

"Oh, I understand perfectly. You ran away. Am I right? Do your family even have any idea where you are?"

"Of course I didn't run away," Lily protested. "I would not do something so worrying to my parents. What do you take me for?"

"What do I take you for?" He huffed out a

breath. "I don't know. I don't have a clue who you are, do I?"

She squeezed her eyes shut. "My parents agreed to my leaving home under duress. I gave them no choice in the matter. They know how strong-minded I am. They never would have been able to keep me at home if I didn't want to be there."

"Then why the false name? Why the secrecy?"

"I'm a lady, Nicholas."

"A lady? But...but...you can't be. You work so hard, you bear no umbrage for scrubbing floors, washing dishes."

"I will do anything to reach the place I want to go."

He stared at her. "And where is that exactly?"

"Paris. I want to go to Paris."

"Paris? Paris!" he cried. "Isn't that where they sing in saloons and the ladies show their undergarments to all and sundry?"

Lily bowed her head. "Yes."

There was such a long silence that eventually she had no choice but to look up. Nicholas was biting down on his bottom lip. An expression Lily already knew to be the only way he could stop himself from screaming. She reached forward and clasped the hand he held to his heart.

"Nicholas, I'm sorry."

He shook her hand away. "Oh, the shame! You must be nothing more than a brazen hussy."

The disparaging tone of his voice scratched at Lily's resolve to fling herself at his mercy. Her leg began to rhythmically tap up and down beneath the table. "I am no such thing. Just because—"

He threw a hand in the air cutting her off. "And when do we find out the truth of who you are? Why, an hour before we have half the gentry of Wiltshire arriving!"

Lily's jaw tightened. "Despite what you may

think of me right now, I still believe that just because a woman doesn't wish to marry at the young age of three and twenty that does not make her a hussy. In fact, if she wants to kiss a man, maybe even let him touch her before marriage does not mean she is less worthy of a decent husband."

His eyes widened to manic proportions. "Lord, save us. You are serious." He turned to Mrs. Harris and the others, his finger jabbing at Lily over his shoulder. "She's serious. Can you believe what you are hearing?"

Lily looked from Nicholas, to Mrs. Harris, to Jane and finally to Robert. They all stared back at her, their expressions a mix of shock, animated interest and maybe even a hint of disbelief; but Lily saw no trace of disapproval or judgment. A small spark of hope ignited inside her. She turned back to Nicholas and was about to appeal to his better nature once more when Mrs. Harris' roar of laughter made each of them jump.

"Oh, good girl!" She cried, coming around the table and pulling Lily into a rough embrace. "Damn and blast to those toffs who think a woman can't be a woman. We have the same bloody desires as any man let me tell you. You're young and beautiful, lustful and gay. I say, fair play to you, Lily. Fair play indeed."

"Mrs. Harris," Nicholas snapped. "How can you say such a thing?"

"Oh, roll your neck in." She laughed. "Don't tell me you wouldn't have a bit of flesh-on-flesh action if you could."

Jane smothered her snigger into her apron and quickly turned away when Nicholas shot an icy-cold glare her way. "Indeed I would not. Sex before marriage is a sin, Mrs. Harris. You and I both know—"

"A sin, is it? Well, that's you for the virgin bin

87

then, ain't it? Can't see you ever getting married unless they legalize men with men and that ain't never gonna happen."

Lily bit down on her bottom lip. This was not what she expected at all. She disentangled herself from Mrs. Harris' embrace and reached for Nicholas' hands. Her hope leapt when he didn't pull away.

"Nicholas, listen to me. What Mrs. Harris is trying to say—"

He shot the cook a glare. "I know *exactly* what Mrs. Harris is trying to say."

"...is that sometimes our bodies need to be touched by someone who, if not loves us, at least cares about us. But it is not for that that I wish to disappear to Paris. I want to lead my own life, my own way. Why is that such a scandalous notion? Why should I not push the boundaries a little? My parents have, albeit reluctantly, let me at least try. Please, Nicholas. Try to understand. I promise you I have no more secrets, I have told you everything."

He stared back at her, his mouth drawn into a straight line. Lily's heart beat erratically behind her rib cage.

A long moment passed in silence and then Mrs. Harris cleared her throat with an exaggerated cough. "Come now, Nicholas. Can't you see the girl is in pieces? We all guessed there was more to her being here than just a job of work."

Lily stared at her. "You did?"

"Of course. What with the lovely way you speak and all."

The way she spoke? Hadn't the viscount inferred the exact same thing? For all her intentions, how did she not think to disguise the way she spoke?

"I think the master suspects something isn't right too. For the exact same reason," she murmured.

"Well, I wouldn't be surprised," Nicholas

88

exclaimed, pulling his hands from hers and standing up. "He is no fool. He would have seen beyond your charade from the very first day no doubt. Maybe that is why he has taken such a...What shall we say? Special interest in you."

Nausea swept a low loop-the-loop in her belly. Of course, why else would he pay her so much attention? Be so interested in what she had to say? He was undoubtedly biding his time to use her as an example to all his staff. He would physically eject her from the house with a public naming and shaming.

She looked around the table. There was nothing else she could do or say. The truth was out and her agenda revealed.

"So...now you know," she said, softly. "What is it you wish to happen next? Do I leave out the back door or will you let me stay?"

Chapter Five

When no one spoke, Lily felt encouraged to continue. She had their attention rather than their derision at least. "I was right to come here. I was right to change my name. I am my own person now and so far, I am enjoying every minute of what I hope will be my permanent independence."

Nicholas shook his head. "I don't know. You are still deceiving the master and so are we now that we know your true identity. You are Elizabeth, not Lily. A lady no less."

"Bah. Leave the girl alone," Mrs. Harris interrupted. "She don't want that life, can't you see that? It's written all over her face as plain as day. She should be applauded for having the nerve to leave a privileged home such as hers, not chided."

Lily's heart swelled in her chest and her courage right along with it as she smiled her thanks to Mrs. Harris. She drew in a breath. "I want to stay here more than anything in the world. Elizabeth is gone. Lily is who I am now. Who I want to be for the rest of my life."

Nicholas pushed his hands through his hair. "And now you expect us to keep this from the master? My God, we've barely known you three weeks, Lily…Elizabeth."

"It's Lily. And you're right. I haven't the entitlement to ask anything of you. I just hope you can feel how desperately I want to stay here, working side by side with each and every one of you."

Nicholas sniffed. "Well, until you have the

90

money to go to Paris and then you'll be gone."

Heat seared her cheeks and Lily found herself unable to meet his eyes as a strange sensation clutched her heart. She would be sad to go, but she would indeed go. "Yes."

Her palms turned clammy and her mouth dry. Mrs. Harris, Robert and Jane watched Nicholas and Nicholas watched her. The seconds felt like hours. Her gaze stayed locked with his. She could see the cogs of his mind working behind soft hazel irises as he weighed up the magnitude of what she asked them to do. Lily's heart implored him to understand, to give her this chance, but at the same time despising herself for asking him to forsake his own values.

She had never asked such a thing of another person her whole life. Is this what independence was doing to her? She pushed the negative emotions aside—this wasn't manipulation, there was no malice behind her pleading. This was survival. If she was forced to live a life other than her own her soul would surely die. But as she looked at the man who could easily become her friend, she felt neither virtuous nor brave.

"Whatever is decided, you have no choice but to serve tonight," he said.

She flinched. "But why?"

"Because, my dear, if this is what you want to do and where you want to live, you will carry out the master's orders. He has asked you to serve in the ballroom and that is exactly what you will do."

"But many of the guests are coming from Bath," she replied. "What if I am recognized? They could quite easily be part of my social circle."

He threw his hands in the air. "And what of it, Lily? What do you expect me to do in the ten minutes you've given me to come up with a solution?" His face turned bright red. "I have no other choice. I am giving you yet another chance to stay but I cannot, will not, allow your inopportune moment to confess your masquerade any chance of damaging the master's opportunity to seal his betrothal to Lady Tasmin. I have served him and the Earl of Marshfield for too long to put yours or anyone else's needs in front of theirs."

Lily swallowed. He was right. How could she expect anything else? "I am so sorry, Nicholas. For everything."

He batted his hand back and forth in the air, swatting her words away as though they hung there like a swarm of irritating gnats. "As well you should be. There is a huge risk of the viscount being made to look a fool in front of his peers. Do you realize that? What if he has no suspicion of you?" He chewed at his bottom lip. "Do you know what? I can't do this."

Panic surged through Lily's blood. "Nicholas, please. I want this so much—"

"No, no, no. This is absurd. You cannot ask us to shield you this way. How can we possibly keep you down here all night? The master specifically asked that you serve. How on earth—?"

"Please, Nicholas, I'm begging you." Lily sat forward on her seat, perspiration breaking out cold along the nape of her neck.

Mrs. Harris stepped forward and placed a hand on his forearm. "Come on, Nicholas. Everyone knows you are the real master of all that goes on in this house," she said, seductively lowering her voice. "With your brain and sharp wit, surely you can figure out a way to keep Lily's disguise intact?"

He met the cook's eyes and slowly, second by tense second, his frown softened until he lifted his eyebrows in boastful agreement. "I suppose I could make this happen if I so chose to."

Lily threw a grateful glance at Mrs. Harris

before turning to Nicholas. "Please, Nicholas," she said, weaving her fingers together in prayer. "I will be the best maid known to man. I will do everything you bid me. I will take on your duties as well as my own—"

He held up a hand and blew out a long breath. "If we do this for you, you must swear on the Holy Bible, that myself, Mrs. Harris, Jane and Robert will always be the focus of your discretion."

Lily nodded solemnly. "I swear."

"If the master finds out we have helped you and lied to him about who you really are, we will all be out of jobs. Do you understand? None of us come from wealthy families, Lily. None of us have anything else to rely on other than the viscount's generosity."

"I promise. I promise all of you will be at the forefront of my mind for every moment of every day. I will never, ever forget you all did this for me. Ever."

Another long moment passed before Nicholas gave a curt nod and looked at each of them in turn. "Right, well, gather round then. Here is what we are going to do..."

****

Andrew tossed the remnants of claret to the back of his throat and swallowed. *Where is she?* He had forced himself to dance two sets, talked to at least five young women and their awful chaperones as well as having to endure the object of Charles' latest desire at the pianoforte. The woman's fingers were as heavy as a giant's and twice as lethal; goodness knows what she'd do to Charles' manhood if he were to share a bed with her.

Andrew took another glass of wine from the tray Robert carried when he came close by.

"Ah, Robert. Where is young Lily? I specifically asked her to serve this evening."

"She's...ah...on her way I'm sure, sir. She was helping Jane prepare some desserts when I last saw her."

Andrew eyed him carefully. The young groom cum footman had distinctly reddened under his gaze. It was as plain as the nose on his face that the man was lying.

"I see," Andrew said slowly. "Well, can you send Nicholas to me in that case? I wish to speak to him straight away."

"Of course, sir."

Robert hurried away and Andrew took another swallow of his wine as he contemplated what was clearly a closing of ranks amongst his staff. They were up to something. Something that had enabled Lily to keep away from the ballroom for the last two hours. The girl had the gumption of a military man, for goodness sake! Did she not give a damn he requested her attendance? He bit his teeth together. He wanted her here. Did he not make himself clear earlier? He shifted from one foot to the other.

The weight of a man's hand landed on Andrew's shoulder, making him jump. He spun around. "Goddamn it, man. What's the matter with you?" he snapped.

Charles Winchester held up his hands in mock surrender, his handsome face splitting into two by his even more handsome smile. "I say, what's got you all riled up, my friend?" He laughed. "My young cousin giving the run around, is she?"

"Who?"

"Lady Tasmin." Charles frowned. "What's the matter with you this evening?"

"Nothing," Andrew growled, gulping at his drink once more. "Is it my fault that I am yet to come across a single girl in this room in possession of an aligned vertebrae let alone a spine?" He paused. "Including your cousin, I'm sorry to say."

Charles sucked in a breath. "My, my, we are in a good mood, aren't we? Despite what your staff seems to think, this ball was your idea not mine."

Andrew bit back a retort. Charles had poked this simple truth into every fiber of his being like the unforgiving end of a battering ram for the last one hundred and twenty minutes.

"You need a wife in order to secure an heir," Charles continued. "So whether you like it or not, my man, you're going to have to court my cousin very publicly before you can inject your essence into her— so to speak."

"Inject my...? My god, how do you ever get a woman to even kiss you?" Andrew snapped. "Do you ply them with opium first, is that it?"

Charles laughed, his emerald eyes glinting. "My sex life is more than ample. But what of yours? You would do well to follow my advice and then maybe that jaw of yours might loosen for at least a little while tonight."

Andrew opened his mouth to respond when there was a discreet cough at his side. He turned to find Nicholas beside him. He stood ram-rod straight with a tell-tale muscle in his jaw jumping around like an out of control leech.

"Robert gave me the message you wish to see me, sir?"

Andrew drained his glass while glaring at his manservant above its rim. If anyone would break, it would be Nicholas. "Indeed I did." Andrew pulled himself up to his full six feet three inches and glared down at his butler with all the ferocity he could muster. "I am going to ask you a question and I expect nothing but the truth in return."

Nicholas dipped his head. "Of course, sir."

"Why is Lily not serving this evening?"

Nicholas kept his eyes determinedly focused on a spot above Andrew's shoulder.

"She…um…she is just on her way. I will follow her up right this instant."

"Not good enough. Are you not in charge of this household? Have you not always ensured my wishes are carried out to the letter before Lily arrived?"

"As I do now, sir. Lily merely…"

"…seems to be running circles around both you and I."

The butler's cheeks darkened and his chin snapped up as though it was attached to an invisible string in the ceiling. "Not at all, sir."

"Nicholas?"

"Yes?"

"Is something going on that I need to know about?"

The butler threw his head back, his laughter so feminine and high-pitched, so obviously uneasy, Andrew grimaced. "Well?"

"No, no, of course not. Why would you think such a thing?" the butler said, walking backwards towards the nearest door. "I'll fetch her for you straight away."

The man was out of the door before Andrew had a lark's chance of reaching out and grabbing his lapel. "Damn it. What are they up to?" he muttered.

"Who?" Charles asked.

"My staff. They're up to something."

"For goodness sake, man, this has got to stop."

Andrew frowned, his gaze still concentrated on the door through which Nicholas had disappeared. "What do you mean?"

"You and that bloody maid. I know I said I would leave things be. But for the love of God, whatever it is that has you fascinated with her, it needs quashing before it erupts into flames and leaves you dying in its embers."

Andrew looked at him and although expecting his friend to be smiling at his droll summary of

Andrew's life, Charles' eyes were alight with dangerous flames. A ball of resentment curled in the pit of Andrew's stomach as he resisted the urge to clamp his friend's chin roughly in his fingers. What he did had nothing to do with Charles.

He lowered his voice and leaned close enough to ensure that Charles heeded his warning. "You read too many novels. Your descriptions of my life are growing far too elaborate. Maybe you should spend more time accessing your own life instead of other people's."

The atmosphere sang with the hum of their mutually suppressed anger. The female laughter and jovial music surrounding them felt a million miles away, as though he and Charles stood inside a transparent bubble. Their eyes locked and their chests rose and fell in unison.

Charles stepped back and waved a dismissive hand. "Maybe you're right," he said. "Why don't we forget your staff for the night and let them carry out their duties without a spectator. Come, there's dancing to be had and a certain lady to woo."

He turned and Andrew watched his retreating back until Charles was swallowed up by the sea of guests. Drawing in a long breath through flared nostrils, Andrew reluctantly stepped toward the center of the ballroom just as several guests were preparing to dance the waltz.

Cursing under his breath, he then did what was expected of him.

He sought out Lady Tasmin. Much to the delight of some and the chagrin of others, he graciously led her to the dance floor. The music began.

"I am sorry to have neglected you, my lady," he said, nodding a hello to a passing acquaintance.

"Not at all, sir. This is your home and your guests. They each deserve as much enjoyment of your attention as I."

He met her steady gaze. People often commented her eyes were the color of newly bloomed forget-me-nots. Andrew saw them only as blue. Her soft blonde hair was swept up into the latest fashion, a thick length left long and loose down her nape. It was intertwined at the crown with a dark amethyst ribbon to match her dress.

The color would look magnificent against Lily's blazing mass of curls. He blinked. Where the hell had that come from?

"Are you enjoying the evening, my lady?" he asked.

"Indeed I am. The food is delightful and the musicians wonderful. Can I ask where you found them?"

He lifted his shoulders. "Their discovery is all credit to your cousin. Charles no doubt accosted them to come here. He claims they were more than willing but I will not question that either way."

Her tinkle of laughter grated at his nerve endings. He glanced toward the open doors leading out to the balcony, suddenly wanting nothing more than to breathe in lungfuls of the fresh night air.

"You seem distracted, my lord."

"Sorry?"

She smiled, a soft blush appearing in her cheeks. She looked at him from beneath lowered lashes. "I have been watching you shamelessly for most of the evening, and I'm afraid you do not appear to be your usual vibrant self. It's..." She hesitated, looking at him directly. "It's as if you are waiting for a most favored guest to arrive."

He cleared his throat and took a few steps in time with the music. "Really? Well, to me, there is no one in the room except for you right now."

Her decidedly pleasant smile did not reach her eyes. Andrew forced his gaze to stay level with hers, despite feeling like a cad to be uttering such nonsense. He knew Lady Tasmin was as much aware of their being thrown together as anyone else. The silence stretched between them. Andrew longed for the dance to finish so he could make his escape. His gaze flitted around the room once more.

Still no Lily—and still no Nicholas.

"My father was beginning to think we would not see you again until Christmas, my lord," Lady Tasmin said, interrupting his meandering thoughts.

"Mmmm?"

"It has been a whole month since you invited me to ride with you. I wondered if maybe something...or someone was keeping you busy at home."

He met her eyes. "At home?"

She smiled. "Yes, Charles informs me you rarely leave the house nowadays."

Andrew felt a twisting sensation in his stomach. Damn Charles and his meddling. Andrew would most likely end up marrying this woman. Why couldn't everyone leave him alone in the interim? He returned her falsely serene smile.

"Then Charles is certainly misinformed. I have just come back from spending two weeks with my father in Bath. I managed to persuade him to take the waters there in the hope it will rejuvenate him somewhat."

A flash of color swept from her chest to her neck. "In Bath? So why would you tell your staff you were staying with Charles?"

Andrew stopped. "How would you know I have said such a thing? Have you been asking my staff of my whereabouts?"

Her face darkened to the color of ripened tomatoes. "Sir, I have angered you."

"Angered me? Angered me?" Andrew's hands shook with the effort it took to keep holding her hands instead of pushing her away. He snatched his gaze from hers and glanced around the room. People

were hesitant in their steps as they tried and
dismally failed to continue in their paces while
feigning disinterest in the host and his sweetheart.

He turned back to Lady Tasmin. "Never ever
inquire about my whereabouts again. Ever."

"My lord, I apologize if I have offended you. I
merely care so much…"

Andrew had been about to excuse himself and
lead her off the crowded dance floor but something
inside made him stop.

"You care so much about me?" he said. "Is that
what you were going to say?"

Andrew knew exactly what bothered her about
his absence and it had nothing to do with the density
of her feelings toward him. He couldn't help but
wonder if she would have the courage to challenge
him. Lily would have no such qualms whatsoever in
her position.

But slowly Lady Tasmin's smile returned and
her features drew flawlessly back in place. "Yes.
That and I hope your father is feeling so much better
now."

The music came to an end and with it a heavy
weight pressed onto Andrew's shoulders. "No. No, he
isn't. Not at all."

Throwing a harried glance left and right,
Andrew touched his lips briefly to her gloved hand
before hastening from the ballroom. His hands
tugged clumsily at the blasted cravat Nicholas had
insisted on tying so tightly around his throat. How
was a man to breathe?

He walked straight onto the balcony and drew
great mouthfuls of air. Curling his hands around the
polished wood of the balustrade, he looked out across
the great expanse of an estate that would very soon
be entirely his. But the beauty of the gardens
silhouetted beneath the moonlight did nothing to
cheer him. The pond, the huge stone statues, even

his favorite forest offered no joy as his thoughts locked onto the frail old man his father had become. A man once so majestic, so kind and full of authority had, over the last twelve months, become a shadow of his former self.

Andrew blinked as the view blurred. He would not let the great Earl of Marshfield die knowing his only son had done nothing to secure what his ancestors had held so beloved. Closing his eyes, Andrew lifted his face to the blanket of night sky above him. *I will marry and I will produce a son, I promise you, Father.* But tonight he could no longer lie, he needed to breathe.

When he opened his eyes again and looked around him, he was brutally aware of the whispers behind fans and hushed speculation at his preoccupation. But nobody could have guessed the thoughts running through his head as the desire to escape his responsibility encompassed him. The urge ran through his veins like blood.

He turned and re-entered the ballroom. For the next half an hour, he made sure his lips were cemented into a smile as he mingled and drank and laughed. He merged into the atmosphere, lulling everyone into a false sense of security that the dashing Viscount Westrop was just as he always was. And then, with perfect timing, Andrew disappeared without a single person noticing him leave the room.

Chapter Six

Lily ran from the servants' entry out into the brisk night air. Music filtered from the open terrace doors, above the incessant chatting and occasional chime of female laughter dancing along behind it. Throwing a hurried glance over her shoulder, she stumbled toward the edge of the woods standing not five hundred yards from the back of the house. She owed Nicholas a king's ransom for hurling her out the back door upon hearing the master's footsteps coming down the stairs. How were any of them to know he would come looking for her? They had thought his one visit below stairs three weeks ago was an unprecedented lapse in character, but now it seemed he had taken it upon himself to breeze in and out of the kitchen at will.

Sprinting unladylike across the dew-covered grass, Lily's blood pulsed hard through her veins and her heart burned hot in her chest. The others had been so good in covering for her. But if that meant landing one of them in trouble enough for the master to dock their wages—or worse, ask them to leave—she would never forgive herself.

Her refusal to attend to the master and his guests would clearly be the signing of her own dismissal. *But please, God, do not let any of the others suffer.*

Guilt clawed at her parched throat and seeped into her veins. She had not meant to put the others at risk this way. It was stupid and selfish. None of this was supposed to happen.

Deep down, it wasn't just the risk of Nicholas

and the others being punished that appalled her. She feared standing in that ballroom and being forced to watch countless beautiful women cooing and braying over her lord's every word. She scowled. Lily knew just how these balls were orchestrated. She did not want to witness potential fiancées to the viscount bestowing pitiful displays of hiding behind their fans and acting as though every flick was purely coincidental rather than a ritual of planned seduction.

Lily slapped at a branch blocking her path.

No doubt he had spent the entire evening mooning around under their admiring glances, enjoying every minute—pathetic! Why, he probably knew she'd have little chance of successfully biting her tongue having to endure him gauging each and every one of them. He'd eventually select his prey with a smile or a tip of his elegant head. In fact, it was more than likely the reason he wanted her in the ballroom in the first place—so he could purposely inflict her grievance to it in her face.

Lily swallowed and swiped a trembling hand at the tears on her cheeks.

The density of the trees had thickened and now all she heard above the roar of her own pulse was the crunching of bracken and leaves underfoot. She turned her head to check she was alone. Her foot hit a fallen branch and she fell, ripping her dress and bruising her ribs. Tears stung like hot needles in her eyes as her body gave up the fight. She rolled on to her back and the strength drained from her muscles.

The tension and strain since confessing her true identity to Nicholas and the others just a few short hours ago took its toll. Lily wondered why she bothered to flee from the house at all.

What did it matter if Viscount Westrop demanded she leave? She could work as a maid anywhere and still be free of the shackles of society.

It was her liberty, not this house that mattered. She drew in a shaky breath and released it. Yet the thought of leaving...

A sharp sob caught in her throat.

The unmistakable snap of branches beneath heavy feet caused Lily to freeze as though she'd been touched by Jack Frost himself. Icy cold perspiration erupted on her brow and upper lip. Squeezing her eyes shut, she lay very still and concentrated on the impossible task of slowing her rapid breathing.

Who would want to come out to the forest and away from such a grand ball? Maybe someone saw her from the terrace and now had every intention of dragging her back into the house to explain herself.

Then the unique smell of one particular man drifted to her nostrils on the whisper of breeze that slithered through the leaves. The delicious blend of musky cologne mixed with fresh air and pine leaves tickled her nose and warmed her body. She began to tremble as her blood burned but kept her eyes clamped shut.

Please God, make him turn around and go back. Please, please, don't let him find me.

His footsteps stopped barely a foot away from where she lay. Beneath the curtain of her closed lids, she sensed him studying her. She knew his intense gaze would be on her ripped dress and heaving bosom. She grew ashamed as her fear was replaced with a wicked yearning to keep his eyes on her forever. She suddenly wanted him to look at her. Not because he paid her wage but because she was a woman.

There was a shifting, a snap and crunch as he took the final step toward her. She heard the rustle of foliage and then felt a weight drop down beside her. Her pretence was shattered and her consciousness revealed by the sharp hitch of her breath when the length of his muscular body pressed against hers, side to side. Not an inch of space lay between them. Lily opened her eyes and stared at the star-spangled sky above her.

He sighed into the darkness, the sound of a contented man.

"Now then, this is a much better way to spend the evening, don't you think?"

Slowly, she turned her head. His eyes sparkled as he watched her. Lily's heart skipped and stuttered to see his cheek pressed so carelessly into the dirt like it was the most natural thing in the world.

"Sir, what are you doing?" Her voice held an uneasy rasp he was sure to detect.

"Why, the same as you. This is just wonderful."

He tipped her a wink and she felt that erotic pull at her center again. A sensation that felt so terribly wrong yet so wonderfully right whenever he looked at her that way. She couldn't fight the smile on her lips. His eyes danced with mischief as they glinted in the darkness with forbidden abandon. In his obvious state of inebriation, it was clear to imagine the boy he'd once been and Lily fought the sudden urge to clip his ear.

She inhaled a deep breath. "Are you here to chastise me, sir?"

He arched an eyebrow. "Chastise you?"

"Yes, sir. For finding me lying amongst the trees instead of attending to your guests—and you?"

Seconds ticked by as his gaze darted over her brow, her eyes, her lips. "Well, yes. Yes I am. I can hardly let my housemaid come out here on the night of a ball to take a leisurely nap amongst the wildlife without some kind of reprimand, can I?"

The tone of his voice set a flint to her skin. Its sultry connotation and illicit suggestion seared every inch of her body. She swallowed. "No, sir."

She waited. But he said nothing else, only

continued to look at her with those wonderful eyes. His mouth curved into a silly, childish grin that had her insides a mess of knots and tangles. She wanted to pull her own gaze away but she was trapped like an innocent rabbit under the watchful eye of a fox. Yet what she felt was far from fear.

After a long moment, he turned to the sky, his lips still drawn into a smile. Lily also turned. Each of her senses were on high alert as she watched the stars wink and shine above them.

Why didn't he speak? This silence was infinitely worse than having him come here and yell his indignation. She needed to know what he was thinking. If not for her, then for Nicholas and the others.

She drew her hands into tense fists at her sides.

"I can only presume by your silence, my lord, you are basking in the power you have to elevate or quash me."

"I am?"

"Yes."

"Ah, but will anyone ever have that power over you, Lily Curtis?" he murmured. "I'm starting to think nobody will ever be able to elevate or quash any decision you make."

She pursed her lips together, the sound of her false name on his lips making her stomach roll uneasily. She pushed down the urge to tell him the truth and stop this mocking. Surely he must know?

"I will take your lack of response as an affirmative, shall I?" he pressed.

Lily struggled not to look at him. His words weren't accusatory or even condemning; they were spoken as though stating a simple fact. One that didn't necessarily anger or disappoint him, but rather intrigued and inspired.

"Sir, why did you come out here?"

"Why not?"

"You should go back inside."

"Why?"

"Because someone will soon notice your absence, if they haven't already." She paused. "And also, if Nicholas finds you out here, lying in the leaves like this, he'll run screaming and shouting into Bath demanding the best physician in town to come straight here and examine you."

His laugh rose from deep inside him, rich and smooth. "I think you are right. In fact, I may even agree to such an examination."

She turned to look at him only to find him already looking at her. "You would?"

"Yes, because right at this moment I cannot think of anywhere or anything more appealing than lying here with you."

A thrill skipped across the surface of her skin making her to shiver. Nothing but sincerity shone from his eyes. "Sir, I really think you ought—"

"To enjoy the moment? Here, here." He grinned.

This was madness, he seemed drunk. It was her responsibility to stop this. "Why don't we both return to the house," Lily said. "If the other servants find us—"

"Please, Lily," he said.

Lily swallowed. He suddenly sounded so despondent, sad even. "Sir?"

"I mean you no disrespect. Just let me lie here with you a little while longer. Please."

The dejection in his voice brushed around her heart like the threads of the softest wool. A solitary tear escaped from beneath his dark lashes and disappeared into the ground.

Convinced he had no idea of its existence a lump rose in Lily's throat, cutting off her ability to speak. The sudden need to reach out and hold him bore down on her with a suffocating weight.

"What is it, sir? You sound so unhappy."

His eyes locked with hers. "I have to marry her, Lily."

An unexpected and guilty rush of disappointment, stupidity and regret swept through Lily's body in equal measure. Each emotion rolling and twisting together, delivering with painful clarity, the knowledge she had indeed lost both her mind and focus.

"Lady Tasmin, sir?"

He nodded. "Yes."

Whipping her gaze from his, she cleared her throat and pushed herself into a sitting position so her face was hidden from his view. She pressed a hand to her tender ribs, welcoming the pain it caused her. Physical pain was manageable—it inevitably healed.

"Well, that's good," she said. "It's good that you intend to adhere to the promise you made your father, sir. It makes you an honorable man. A compassionate man."

There was scuffle in the bracken as he came up to sit beside her. She clamped her eyes shut and stopped breathing.

"Do you really think that?" he asked.

She opened her eyes but did not turn to look at him. She didn't want to see his face and all the emotions it evoked in her. "Yes, sir, I do."

"But what of my integrity? My innermost feelings? Do they not count for anything?"

Why was he asking her this? Why would her opinion matter to him? She was a servant. He would wake in the morning with a banging head and an even more banging sense of regret. "I do not know, sir."

"You don't know? Lily, look at me."

Her heart picked up speed. "Please don't ask me to do that. I would do anything to make this easier for you, my lord; but there is precious little someone like me can do to help you."

"But you would if you could?"

"Of course. But there is nothing I can do, so we will speak no more of it."

She jumped to her feet but he deftly followed suit. Clasping his strong fingers to hers, he spun her around to face him.

"Do you really mean that?" he asked urgently.

He stood so close to her she had to tip her head back to meet his eyes. "Sir?"

"Would you do anything to help me?"

She looked deep into his eyes and what she saw roused a slow and steady warmth across her skin. She licked dry lips as she began to tremble. Her eyes were drawn to the shape of his mouth.

"Yes, sir. I believe I would."

For a long moment, their eyes locked. Lily could neither move nor speak. And then he blinked, dropped one of her hands and stepped back. Their breathing was ragged as they stared at each in the semi-darkness, still held together by one joined hand. And then the faint sound of applause drifted from the house before being followed by the opening bars of another piece of music.

Lily's eyes grew wide when he smiled and then dipped into a low bow. "Shall we?"

Confusion furrowed her brow. "Sir?"

The intensity of his gaze abruptly changed. His face became alive, buoyant with liberty. "Will you dance with me, Lily?"

"Dance? But we cannot." Relief, or maybe disappointment, slumped her shoulders and she threw a hesitant look in the direction of the house. "If someone were to come looking for us—"

He propelled her into his arms with one sharp yank of his wrist.

Her breath caught and laughter bubbled in her throat as he flashed a cheeky grin and pulled her

109

firmly against his chest. "Come now, Miss Curtis, at least do me the honor of dancing a waltz with me on this beautiful night."

"A waltz? But I couldn't possibly."

"What? Is it too scandalous? Too risqué for your faint heart?" he asked, wriggling his eyebrows suggestively.

She tipped her head back and laughed, suddenly caught up in his drunken rebuff of status and decorum. "For me, sir? Never!"

He grinned. "Then listen to the music, fair lady. Let its enchantment work its way into your soul until you have no choice but to move with me as though we are one."

Closing her eyes, Lily let her ears attune to the gentle muted melody coming from the house. Mozart's harmonious flute and violin duo swept and dipped along on the breeze, snaking its way into her limbs and heart. Opening her eyes, she gracefully inclined her head and yielded to his challenge. He took her in his arms and they mirrored each other's feet perfectly without word or instruction.

Pressed so close, with his hand placed protectively at the base of her spine, Lily molded into the heat of his body. The feel of her flattened breasts against the firmness of his chest aroused something so erotic, so primal inside of her she didn't know whether to be scared or delighted by it. Heat seared her cheeks as she forced herself to meet his eyes. His own gaze shone—carefree and devoid of the anger and frustration. Her heart leapt to see him so happy. He swept her around and around the limited space beneath the canopy of trees surrounding them. This was the antithesis of the man who so frequently seemed to want to escape Cotswold Hall, galloping away on his horse as though a raging fire chased him.

All too soon the music stopped and the faint

cries of "Bravo" and rapturous applause filled the night air once more. Their eyes locked as their chests rose and fell in unison—for the briefest moment, they were completely alone. And then he dropped her hands and took several strides backwards, opening the space between them like a gaping chasm. Lily quickly wrapped her shaking arms around her to stop from reaching for him. Standing face to face, with her heartbeat an erratic tattoo in her chest, Lily's mouth ran dry. His expression was unfathomable. She had no idea what would come next.

He turned and strolled in a wide circle before throwing his hands in the air. "I must go."

She nodded.

"Let's...um...let's keep what happened here tonight just between the two of us, yes?" he said.

A pain stabbed at the center of her chest. "I...yes...of course."

He stopped pacing and faced her. "You dance splendidly. Extraordinarily so."

The accusation caught her completely off guard and her stupidity crashed down on her like the weight of a thousand mistakes. She could think of nothing to say. Nothing to explain her dancing skills. But if he noticed her distress, he didn't comment.

"Promise me you'll stay here for the foreseeable future, Lily," he said as though nothing untoward had passed between them.

She blanched. "You...you want me to stay? But—"

"I want you to be happy here. I ask for nothing more. Whatever it is you bring to my home, it makes me and my staff happier than we were before you arrived. I know that sounds insane and overtly excessive when you take into account the time you have been here. But the simple truth is, you belong here."

Heat warmed her face and Lily felt pride rise inside her. "I am flattered, sir. Thank you."

He shook his head. "Don't thank me, Lily. Promise me you will stay here." His gaze pleaded. He stepped close and reached out his hand. It hovered barely an inch from her face. She drew in a breath, released it.

"I'm sorry, but I cannot promise that."

His blue eyes darkened and his hand dropped to his side in a fist. "Why not?"

"I...I just can't. I will stay here, but I cannot promise for how long."

A long moment passed before he dropped his chin to his chest. "I appreciate your honesty. You have no idea quite how much." He lifted his head. "If only you were..."

Deep inside her chest her heart hammered. "If only I were what, sir?"

The air crackled around them as time stood still. The seconds ticked by like the pendulum of a clock. And then he was moving. Not away from her, but toward her. Tick, tick, tick, the pendulum swung faster and faster.

"I know I shouldn't say this," he said softly. "But you are a beautiful woman, Lily." His breath skimmed her lashes as she brazenly held his gaze. His eyes turned from admiration to awareness, from adoration to unmistakable hunger. His hand stole to her cheek. "I have never met anyone who radiates such passion, such life, such..."

His mouth came down hard against her lips before she had chance to protest. His tongue searched hers with such ferocity she was unsure whether to cry out in pain or pleasure. Hot and certain, she kissed him back knowing that this would never happen again. Every ounce of her self-control dissolved, every thought, every yearning she had denied existed since first seeing him three weeks before burst forth into that kiss. A low groan escaped the back of his throat when she lifted her hand to touch the hair at the nape of his neck. Her fingers urged him closer and she almost cried out in wanton relief.

"Lily. Beautiful, beautiful, Lily."

His words pierced her suddenly desperate heart with their sadness. His warm lips traveled to the curve of her neck, lower to the hollow at the base of her throat. Lily clamped her lips together to prevent saying anything that would forfeit this intimate moment.

His hands burned like hot embers on her skin, branding his oblivious ownership of her with every stroke, every touch. She sighed when his fingers tugged gently at the neckline of her dress and scored across her bare shoulders.

"Open your eyes, Lily. Open them and look at me."

She did as he asked and what she saw set her heart racing. Pure, unadulterated need burned in the depths of two glistening pools of liquid sapphire. Lily knew she was trapped. Ensnared in his net for the taking.

He shook his head. "You...you are..."

And then he tipped his head back and drew in a shaky breath of palpable regret. She wanted to keep him with her, not let his attention drift away. But it was over. For a long while, neither of them spoke. The sound of their joined breathing, quick and relentless echoed around the trees. She forced herself to smile, releasing him from the chains of guilt he would soon harbor for kissing her, touching her.

"It's all right, sir. Go. Go back to your guests."

He dropped his head to look at her. "I am so sorry."

With a shaking hand, she gripped his elbow and

turned him away from her and the sight of her tears. "Go."

"But—"

"Sir, please."

But then he turned back around and pressed one final kiss to her lips before turning and sprinting back through the trees. He left only the scent of him lingering beneath her nostrils. She released her held breath in a rush and unconsciously touched her tender mouth. Her plan to stay here only until she had the money to pay for the passage to France had been well and truly quashed.

Chapter Seven

October 1890

Andrew strained to hear her dainty footsteps upon the stairs. He'd been listening so hard at the door, it was impossible he had missed them. He had to talk to her. Tonight. Two weeks had passed since their kiss and he had yet to explain to Lily the reason he asked her to stay. He was surprised—and relieved—she had even spoken to him after that night. He spun away from the door and marched back to his easel. But he didn't sit down and he didn't pick up his pencil.

The sketch he was working on stared back at him accusingly. He reached out a finger and circled the almond eyes, the small nose and full lips. The challenge to draw Lily from memory was not even worthy of being deemed a challenge. She was in his mind all the time and as much as he knew this attraction, this affiliation toward her made no sense, it was far too tangible to ignore. And it wasn't just her physicality—although he'd be a liar if he said her body did not continuously fill his nocturnal fantasies—it was the sense she understood him. He had the unshakeable belief she came to the manor to save him. Or maybe for him to save her.

He unpinned the sketch from the easel and rolled the paper into a tube and secured it with ribbon. The picture was almost finished and would soon be added to the two others of her he had drawn since she arrived. Never before had he felt compelled to draw anything other than landscapes and his

115

beloved horses, but now? Now it seemed the lead from his pencil knew only Lily.

He glanced at the clock on the mantel. It neared midnight. Surely she must have gone to bed by now? Making a snap decision, Andrew packed away his pencils and paper, carefully storing everything away in his art box and locking it securely. He pocketed the key and drew in a long shaky breath as he thought back to the night of the ball.

He had to apologize for his harassment, if nothing else. Why did he do that to her? What possessed him to put her in such a position? He touched her, kissed her and then asked her to promise she wouldn't leave. Why should she make such a promise? He must have been obsessed, possessed. He was surprised she hadn't bolted from the estate like a horse from a stable. Promises. *Why do I always insist on promises?*

But she hadn't promised. He truly had no idea who the real Lily Curtis was but he did know she was the most fascinating creature he'd ever met and with each passing day he wanted her more. He flinched against the sudden pain deep in his chest.

Maybe he was hiding behind these sudden feelings for Lily? Maybe he poured every ounce of himself into an impossible situation instead of facing reality? He walked to the window and looked down upon the garden below. He had stood in this very spot earlier in the day and watched her pass parcels to Robert as he filled the cart with things that needed delivering in town. Her hair had shone like polished bronze beneath the Autumnal sunlight and her smile was as wide and as infectious as its glorious warmth.

She was completely unaware of her beauty and that enamored Andrew even more. She was so different than anyone he had ever met before. He wasn't hiding. Why would he fall for a woman he could never be with? Surely that was the worst possible scenario of all.

He swung violently away from the window.

Ever since the ball he'd been careful to spend more and more time with Lady Tasmin so as not to raise suspicion about his growing fascination with Lily. But who was he fooling? Himself.

Although he had ensured they were never alone again since the night of the ball, tonight he had no choice. Time was running out and very soon he would have to make some grand gesture toward Lady Tasmin or risk becoming the subject of rumor and speculation. Andrew wanted to spare his father this at all costs. The Earl of Marshfield lay bedridden and dying. What would it do to him to catch even a whiff of smoke emanating from a rumor Andrew had changed his mind regarding his courtship of Lady Tasmin? And all because his son's days and nights were filled with the pursuit of a housemaid!

Andrew knew there was so much more to her than met the eye. Because what he'd seen thus far was enough to fascinate him, it only made his preoccupation all the more intense. He needed to know who she was and then praise be, his hunger would be sated and he could in turn focus on the important matter of securing his family legacy.

He looked to the closed door. His hunger grew. That is what he felt. He felt hunger whenever he was near her. She was beautiful and funny and kind and daring.

Maybe it was entirely physical? Maybe one night would satisfy this ludicrous craving. Could Charles be right? Did he just need to taste her? Experience one night of abandon with her and his thirst would be quenched?

He looked at the clock above the mantel. It was almost midnight.

What was keeping her? Surely she wasn't still in the kitchen at this time?

Putting his glass down with a decisive bang on the table, he marched toward the door and yanked it open before he changed his mind.

He'd go to the kitchen and find her. If Nicholas or anyone else was there, he'd... he'd...think of something.

The only sounds in the corridor were the hiss and crackle of the candles hung along the oak-paneled walls. Andrew drew in a deep breath. He felt like an intruder in his own home. Pulling back his shoulders, he headed straight downstairs to the kitchen. Oblivious to the way he pushed and fussed at his hair that so infuriatingly fell across his forehead no matter how many times he combed it, or the fact that he'd puffed out his chest just a little too far to be natural, he strode forward.

Until he reached the closed kitchen door.

Once there, he shamefully pressed his ear to the wood. No sound came from within but he knew somebody must be in there. The sliver of light spilling from beneath the door flickered every now and then as someone walked past the source. He touched the handle, sent up a silent prayer that the someone was Lily and only Lily, and pushed open the door.

His breath caught.

She looked up and the light from the candle sitting beside her at the table transformed her hair into a burst of red-gold flame. Her eyes were in shadow and appeared blacker than melted tar. But it was her smile that had Andrew clutching at the place his heart had been just a few moments before. She held a book in her hand and something on the page had amused her because even when she met his eyes, the innocent and delighted smile remained fixed as though she wanted to share what she'd read with him. Andrew struggled not to rush forward and press his lips hard to hers.

"Lily."

Slowly she put down the book and rose to her feet. The smile faltered and then dissolved. "Can I help you, sir?"

Andrew caught the way she looked at that moment and felt it pass his heart and into his soul before he could stop it. There was no turning back. He had to have her. He blinked.

"You're reading."

She frowned and then her smile burst open once more like a breaking sun. "Yes, yes I am. It is very funny." She paused. "But what are you doing in the kitchen again? Mrs. Harris will make me start polishing the floor if you're to become a regular visitor, I'm sure."

He forced himself to smile, afraid she'd think him insane if he continued to stare at her the way he was. "Well, there's no need for her to worry about that. It's you I came to see."

She smoothed her hands over her apron. "Is something wrong?"

"No, no, please. Won't you sit down?"

She lowered back into her chair, her wide and beautiful dark eyes on his the entire time. He wanted to rub his thumb over the line that had leapt between her brows and wipe it away. She suddenly looked afraid and absurdly vulnerable.

"Lily, I came down here to talk to you about—"

"It's about the night of the ball, isn't it?" She sucked in a breath and clasped a hand to her throat. "I knew it. I knew you'd have to let me go. It was inevitable. In fact I have been expecting you to come and see me before now. But you must understand, I will never ever tell a single soul what happened."

"Lily, please—"

"The truth is," she rushed on. "I shouldn't have

spoken so openly the way I did. I shouldn't have stepped into your arms... Mama always said I've got an impetuous nature that would land me in trouble so big one day—"

"Lily, for the love of God, will you stop talking?"

"Am I in trouble? I can't be. Not when you're smiling at me like that." She snapped her mouth shut with an audible clap and stared at him wide-eyed.

Andrew's stomach drew into a tight knot. She was adorable. A rare heat seared his cheeks and he quickly cleared his throat. "No, Lily. You're not in trouble."

"Honestly?"

"But I may be." He lowered himself into the wooden chair opposite her. "I don't know that I can marry Lady Tasmin, Lily."

Her hands gripped her apron until the skin across her knuckles stretched tight. "Oh?" she said.

He shook his head. "It is all so wrong. I am marrying her because of a promise to my father, no more. I have no feelings for her and if my father were not dying, I would not marry her. And that is neither fair to her, nor me. Don't you agree?"

For a long moment she stared back at him. The thoughts in her head remained indecipherable from both her expression and her still posture. She opened her mouth, closed it. Opened it again and swung around toward the open fireplace. She stood and snatched the kettle from its iron hook.

"Tea. I'll make tea."

She turned and filled the kettle. The sound of rushing water was not too different from the rushing of Andrew's blood through his ears. What was she thinking? Did she suspect his desire of her? Of course she did—he was a fool! He'd practically crushed her in two when he held her at the ball. Hardly the actions of a man in control. She probably feared for her person just by him being in the room alone with her. *Leave her alone—Now.*

Clearing his throat, Andrew stood up. "No, no tea. I'll go. I'm sorry, Lily. I shouldn't..."

She turned and their eyes locked. "Stay. Please. I'll help you." Her voice was barely above a whisper.

He swallowed. "Help me?"

She nodded and gestured toward the table, the kettle seemingly forgotten. Andrew returned to his seat and she sat down opposite him. She drew a circle round and round on the surface of the table with her finger, a nervous gesture that Andrew found he couldn't take his eyes from. The mesmerizing repetition provided an alternative focus to his fear.

The finger abruptly stopped and he was forced to look up. She carefully watched him.

"I once served a family with two daughters of a marrying age, sir," she said. "They were different in many ways but the most obvious difference was their ideas of their futures. One of them knew she would always accept her destiny of an arranged marriage; whereas the other always said she would find her own husband and knew in her heart of hearts no one would ever stop her from doing just that."

"Lily, why are you telling me this?"

"I think their story will help you realize that your courtship of Lady Tasmin is different to those of less noble stature, sir. I for one will not judge you for having to do what you have to do in order to keep Cotswold Manor and everything it entails in your family."

She blinked and tears shone like diamonds in the candlelight. Andrew's heart hitched painfully in his chest. He reached across the table and covered her hand with his own. She didn't pull away.

"If you believe it is so right that I marry her, why do you cry?" he whispered.

She quickly swiped at her tears, her eyes wide. "Oh, please do not think my tears have anything to do with your predicament, sir."

Her statement was so succinct and so assured, Andrew's heart hitched again. "Oh. No. Of course not, I wasn't thinking that."

"I am crying for the eldest daughter. She changed beyond recognition and now that she is with child she has no escape.

"Escape? You sound as though she has been ensnared in marriage like a hunted rabbit."

"You're right, I do. But as far as she is concerned, she doesn't feel trapped in the slightest. She thinks she is doing her duty, what is expected of her. In fact, she is oblivious to the change in her personality. It is only her sister who sees it so clearly and so passionately resists the same thing happening to her."

"And what of the younger sister's responsibility to secure the family's future?"

She swallowed causing the pale column of her perfect throat to shudder ever so slightly. "Her parents have released her on the understanding if her plans fail she will return home and marry whomever they choose."

Andrew frowned. "I see. So everything may yet go wrong for this girl."

"She won't fail in her endeavor, sir."

Andrew watched her. "How can you be so sure?"

"I just know."

"You seem very sure of this girl, Lily. Fervently so."

A whisper of a smile played at her lips. "She is a woman of great strength and virtue, sir. A real force to be reckoned with."

"I see. Well, explain to me how you can be so admiring of such a girl when you suggest my courtship of Lady Tasmin is a good thing when I too, do not love the person it appears I am destined to marry?"

For a long moment she said nothing. Her gaze locked on his with the confidence of a woman older and wiser than her three and twenty years. "Because, sir, I worry your intentions and sense of duty have been altered by a totally irrelevant situation."

He didn't look away, his fingers grasping hers just a little tighter. "What situation? What do you think has caused this change in me?"

She shook her head gently and dropped her gaze to their joined hands. "I know nothing except the fact you have infinitely more to consider than the younger sister I speak of."

"Who are you, Lily?"

Her eyes widened with surprise at his question and her hand slowly slipped from his. "Who am I?"

"Yes. Who are you really? You are intelligent and articulate. You take books from my library and devour them as though tomorrow may never come." He picked up the book she had been reading and put it back down. "I want to know you, the real you."

She stood and walked to the fireplace. When she picked up a towel to wrap around the handle of the kettle, it trembled in her hand. She put the kettle on a ceramic mat beside the hearth. "I am just me. I like to read, I like to talk."

He stood up and walked toward her turned back. "You like to laugh, you like to listen, you like to dance."

He placed his hands on her shoulders and she stiffened. "I like you, Lily. I just want you to stay at the manor forever."

"Sir, please."

"Just stay with me."

Her shoulders slumped beneath his hands and she turned. She tipped her head back to look at him.

"I can't. I need to go to France." She hesitated. "And you were wrong about one thing you said to me that night in the garden."

"I was?"

"I won't marry a man one day who I love and he loves me."

"Why?"

The defiant tilt that Andrew began to know so well came into her chin. "Because I am no longer convinced such a notion even exists," she said. "I look at you and at...the youngest sister I once served and you are both of considerable stature and yet you have little freedom to choose your own life partner."

"But surely you—?"

"I think I prefer to be alone anyway. If I live my life alone, no one will have a claim over me or what I do."

He smiled. "I think I finally know who you are, Lily. Or rather what you are."

She looked deep into his eyes, confusion swirling in their inky black depths. "Sir?"

He touched a finger to her jaw. "You're a bird. A bird who needs to fly and soar and sing."

She met his smile. "You may be right."

He stared at her. "But do you really have to go to France to do that?"

She closed her eyes as though she couldn't bear to look at him anymore. Andrew left her and walked back to the table. He curled his hands around the back of a chair until he felt the sharpness of his nails digging into his palms. "I am being selfish asking you to stay."

Her eyes opened and she looked directly at him, her gaze unwavering. "Yes, sir. You are."

Andrew bowed his head and felt the pulse throb at his temple. "Then you must stay only as long as you want to."

"Thank you."

"And I will marry Lady Tasmin and see my promise through to my father." He looked at her. "I made a promise to my mother that resulted in her death; I will never break another promise. Not ever. You are right, Lily. Thank you for keeping me grounded and so eloquently reminding me of the reason I was born."

"Sir?" She came forward and stopped just to his side as though remembering her station. "You could not possibly be responsible for your mother's death. What is it you talk of?"

Andrew looked into eyes he longed to fall into and knew to resist telling her anything she asked of him was now impossible. He wanted to share his feelings with her; he wanted her to know what had haunted him so cruelly for the last twenty years. He wanted to tell her how one day had changed his entire life, personality and belief system. He snatched his gaze away and pushed his trembling hand through his hair.

"Do you really want to know?"

She nodded.

"Then I will tell you." He drew in a shaky breath. "My mother asked me four times if I had been playing with her riding tackle and I said no each and every time." He stepped away from Lily and toward the open fireplace. Concentrating his gaze on the gray-white ashes, Andrew rhythmically kicked the hearth with the tip of his shoe. The motion matched his heartbeat. "She mounted her horse and rode like the wind across the estate. Just as she did every day. She died because I had crept away from her groom and thought I would double check the girth beneath the horse. I couldn't get the buckle fastened properly but, being the bull-headed fool I am, I didn't tell anyone. I thought it wouldn't matter."

He didn't look up when her shoes brushed over

the flagstones towards him. And he didn't meet her eyes even when her hand gripped his bicep. "You were a child. A child. Nobody could have blamed you."

He shook his head vehemently, swallowed the bile as it rose bitter in his throat. "I was prohibited from going near the horses unattended. I just wanted to show her how grown up I was, and in doing so I killed her."

"Sir, please listen to me. You were a boy. A boy who loved his mother very much."

He turned and her eyes reflected such sympathy, such undeserved compassion that it took every bit of his strength not to lean down and kiss her eyelids closed so he wouldn't have to see it.

"I promised her I didn't touch it. I *promised* her. And that is why I have never *ever* broken a promise since and never will again. I have promised my father I will marry Lady Tasmin and that is exactly what I will do."

Her eyes changed, a momentary glimpse of something he couldn't decipher, and then she blinked and it was gone. She nodded. "Good. That is good, sir."

The agreement on her lips struck his heart like a knife but he would not say another word to undo the inevitable. He had to marry and he had to marry quickly. But now, for this one moment, he would do something entirely for Mr. Andrew Baxter and not Viscount Westrop, future Earl of Marshfield.

He took her hand. "Lily?"

"Yes?"

"Can I hold you? Just for awhile?"

"Hold me?" She looked to the door, then back to his face. "I'd like that."

He swallowed her words with a kiss as he pulled her into his embrace. And slowly, second by second, her body melted against his and she cautiously, tenderly met his emotion. And after a time far too brief, Andrew withdrew and dropped his cheek to the top of her head and held her as tightly as he dared without hurting her. Finally, a blessed sense of peace enveloped him and Andrew Baxter closed his eyes.

****

The weak dawn light peeked into Lily's room through the sliver of space parting her drawn drapes. By the time the master left the kitchen, it had been nearing one o'clock in the morning. The last five hours had been the slowest Lily had ever known and now her eyes felt itchy and sore from lack of respite. She knew her growing feelings for the viscount would be relieved of their danger once she boarded the ship for France—which she must do now more than ever. Because although she knew herself to be both impulsive and fanciful, there was absolutely nothing imaginary about the way he'd looked at her last night. There was a genuine possibility that he felt something for her too.

But for better or worse, when Lily pushed the complexities of what that might mean if either of them acknowledged it, she also knew with shocking clarity that she was a woman first and foremost. Her thoughts throughout the passing of the early morning hours with regard to the master had been decidedly unladylike. She was left with little doubt of what would happen between them if they had met in gay Paris where no one knew of their stature or class.

Lily bit down on her bottom lip in an attempt to trap her lewd smile as she felt the urgent tingle of desire between her legs. Images of his face, his body, even the way he walked across a room added to an internal metamorphosis as frightening as it was thrilling. Turning over, she buried her face in the pillow. She had to banish him from her mind.

She would leave England for her own sanity as well as for those around her. She didn't belong within the bondage of England's society. She was a free spirit. A trailblazer. And yet another predicament had been presented with the lord's confession of his flawed belief that he was somehow responsible for the death of the countess.

How could she abandon him to the torture of continuing to believe it so? She had to make him realize the folly of this belief. If she didn't, then what would become of him but a future of tortured choices and eternal grief?

Muffling her frustration in the pillow, Lily shook her head from side to side as a torrent of emotions ricocheted around inside of her. She knew it foolish to care so much about a man who could never mean anymore to her than he did then...yet she could not bear the thought of walking away and ignoring the knowledge he'd clearly trusted her enough to share.

Lily froze. But what of Lady Tasmin? Had his lordship told her also?

Despite being initially suspicious of Nicholas' histrionic outbursts with regard to her ladyship, the others had convinced Lily that she was a wonderfully kind and beautiful woman. Lily flipped over and stared up at the whitewashed ceiling. Touching her fingers to lips still burning from their kiss, her conscience screamed that she needed to make the viscount accept what Lady Tasmin could offer such a man as himself. Her breeding was of the highest caliber. She'd been groomed to sit side by side with the master at the head of a massive estate such as Cotswold Manor. She would have the ingrained capability to oversee the arrangement of balls, and lunches, country weekends and hunts as though she were merely orchestrating tea for two on the terrace.

The match would help him, not harm him

surely? It can hardly be compared to that of Candleford and herself! Not at least with regard to Lady Tasmin's physical beauty—she made Lily feel positively elephant-like when she watched her float from one room to another. Good God, to share a bed with Candleford would be like lying next to a hippopotamus dressed in old-fashioned breeches and smoking a pipe!

No, she must help Andrew...his lord...to open his eyes to Lady Tasmin's beauty and benevolent nature. He will then realize the carrying out of a promise that means so much to him and his father does not necessarily mean a life of unfulfilled desire.

And if she failed? Lily drew in a deep breath and blinked back the tears stinging behind her eyes. Well, then she hoped if he decided he does not wish to marry her, it wouldn't make him less of a human being and the lady's initial hurt would heal in time. But he would see, wouldn't he? She pressed a hand to the quivering in her abdomen. Of course he would and then he'd be free to make his own decision.

Lily threw back the wool blanket and pushed herself out of bed with finality. Her mind was clear. She would carry out her plan to the letter and then the absurd and nonsensical fantasies she had about her relationship with the viscount would be quashed. Lily would be further fortified she was on her way to having something that Lady Tasmin could only dream of—an independent life. A life full of integrity and freedom—oh, and something else quite special in the interim. The precious gift of spending time with the real Andrew Baxter, not the viscount on duty, but the man who was as complex and as alluring as any man could be to Lily's capricious nature.

Chapter Eight

"Jane, if you take those through to his lord and his guests," Lily said. "I'll follow on behind with the dessert wine in just a few minutes."

"Yes, Lily."

The young girl walked through the kitchen door with a wooden tray laden with four strawberry tartlets and cream. Lily pressed a hand to her stomach as it rolled uneasily. Viscount Westrop, Lady Tasmin, her sister and Lord Winchester were all seated upstairs having spent the day shopping and socializing in Bath. Lily knew she couldn't postpone going into the dining room for much longer. The master had sent three messages down with Jane already asking for Lily's attendance.

She picked up the wine and added it to a silver tray holding four tiny crystal cut glasses.

"The tray is not going to make its way into the dining room itself, you know."

Lily snapped her head up.

Nicholas smiled. "What's wrong, Lily? You've been out of sorts all week."

She forced a smile. "I'm fine."

"Has something happened between you and the master?"

"No, of course not. Why would you ask?"

He narrowed his gaze. "I hope you haven't started answering him back at every turn again? You have both been getting on like a house on fire for the last few weeks. In fact, I swear the man would monopolize your attention at every opportunity if he could."

Her burst of laughter sounded far too loud to be natural. "What on earth do you mean? We do nothing but discuss this house, his next outing and the arrangements he wants made; occasionally he will mention his father's health."

"Really? You have gained enough familiarity that he would discuss the earl with you? Well, well." He gave an inelegant sniff as he adjusted one of the wineglasses.

Lily swallowed. Nicholas could be astoundingly intuitive with regard to the viscount and now was not the time to increase his obvious suspicions about the nature of her relationship with him.

"Sorry, I didn't mean to laugh. You and I both know how the master is. He loves company, any company. Whether that be me, you, Lord Winchester, or anyone else for that matter," she said quickly.

"I see. And which of his *outings* needed to be dealt with in one of the guest rooms, eh?"

Heat seared her cheeks. "Guest room?"

"Yes. I saw you coming out of the double guest room in the west wing just a few days ago." He paused for obvious dramatic effect. "Closely followed by the master."

"I have no idea what you are—"

He raised a hand, cutting her off. "I don't want to know. I just hope you know what you're doing, bearing in mind your real identity, Lily. If he were to ever find out..."

She snatched up the tray. "I have done nothing for you to worry about. And as I have said before, I will be leaving as soon as I have the money to get to Paris so you can stop pulling that disdainful expression at me."

"And yet you're still here."

Lily looked away as her heart picked up speed. "I didn't realize you were so desperate to be rid of me."

He stepped forward and took the tray from her shaking hands. Placing it carefully on the table beside them, he then took her hands and held them tightly.

"I'm not," he said, the look in his eyes softening to one of concern. "I care about you, Lily. We all do. Probably too much to be good for us but there you are. But none of us are blind to what is happening. It doesn't matter how much it scares you, or how hard you are trying to fight it, your feelings will never come into consideration as far as the master is concerned."

Lily sucked in a breath against the unexpected pang deep in her chest. "I do not have feelings—"

He shook his head. "You know, it is not unheard of for a lesser man to take advantage of a maid's infatuation of him while she is in his employment. But fortunately for you, the master is so far removed from such a character, it is laughable. He is a proud and responsible man who will endeavor to do his absolute best by his father and the future of this estate. Which means whatever you feel for him, will never *ever* be reciprocated. You must see that?"

Lily searched his eyes looking for some disapproval; but it wasn't judgment staring back at her but sorrow. Nicholas quite clearly had her heart at the forefront of his mind. She dipped her head.

"I will be leaving as soon I can."

He tightened his grip on her fingers. "I am not saying I want you to go, you know? All I am saying is you must cut off your growing affections and realize the futility of them. Then you can stay here with us and we'll all be the happier for it."

She gave a soft smile and looked up. "You are sweet, Nicholas; but I always intended for my stay to be a short one."

"I know, I know; but now you are here and such

a big part of us—"

"You know," she said. "There is a far more worrying factor concerning me than the extent of his lordship's non-existent affections for me or anyone else. Far more worrying."

His brow furrowed. "There is? Then you must tell me."

Lily drew in a shaky breath and released it. "He holds something so painful, so inherent inside of him, I fear it will destroy him from the inside out if it's not released." She gave his hand a decisive shake. "Before I leave, it is imperative I make him see just how good and noble a man he is. I need to make him understand he deserves as blameless a life as the rest of us."

Nicholas' frown deepened. "But what is it you speak of? What blame?"

Lily shook her head. "I can't tell you."

"But you must! I know the master so much better than you."

"This isn't a test or a competition of our care or loyalty to him, Nicholas," Lily chided softly. "I've seen it in his eyes and it is slowly smothering his soul. Please. Will you trust that I know what I am doing?"

His anxious gaze darted over her face. "I really don't think—"

"Please. Trust me."

For a long moment, they locked eyes. Lily's heart beat steadily in her chest as she pulled back her shoulders. She had no intention of looking away or relenting in her mission. Nicholas would either have to trust her or fight her. Her determination to help the master was unshakeable. She had felt her own wings clipped by the constraints of society, but the imprisonment of the viscount's existence was inconceivable to her now—now that she...

He would never be free to live his best life

unless he broke the chains of his own frame of mind. He was not in any way responsible for his mother's untimely death and Lily would ensure he saw that with clear and unreserved vision.

Nicholas cleared his throat and gently released her hands from his grip. "The one vice the master cannot abide is deceit, Lily," he said, taking a step back. "You cannot escape the fact you are a lady masquerading as a maid and if he were to ever find out…"

Lily shivered. "I know. And I hate to do this to you. To all of you."

"I cannot contemplate the extent of his anger if he were to find out we have been lying to him for these past two months. I do not doubt for one moment we will all be out of jobs." He looked to the ceiling, his bottom lip trembling. "And I am positive I am not alone in saying my position here is more than a mere job, Lily. It is my life. A life that I love and do not wish to have snatched away from me for the sake of a woman I have barely known more than a few weeks." He dropped his chin, his eyes shining with unshed tears. "Even if that woman happens to be you."

Lily swallowed the lump in her throat. "And I do not like putting any of you in this position. Sometimes I feel as though I should never have come here; yet another part of me, a bigger part, thinks this is the place I was destined to be all along. But clearly it is not true, otherwise I would not be exposing you, Mrs. Harris and the others to so much risk. I will do my utmost to ease the master's pain and then I will leave."

"But this is madness. Surely it is only a matter of time before your subterfuge is revealed?"

She sighed. "Maybe. And that's if he doesn't know already."

He started. "What?"

"I think the master may already suspect something is not quite right."

His eyes widened. "You mean…?"

"He has mentioned certain things."

"Such as?"

"Such as the way I speak, my love of books."

"So you think he knows?" He squeezed his eyes shut. "Oh, mercy me."

Lily reached out and clutched his forearm. "He has yet to say anything to any of us so let's just presume he is not unsatisfied, shall we? I will endeavor to leave as soon as I can." Dropping his arm, she turned and picked up the tray from the table. It trembled in her hands. "And best of all, your concerns regarding any relationship between myself and the viscount can be laid to rest. Very soon, I will be nothing more than a memory to you all."

She turned to the door but then his hand touched her elbow. She met his eyes.

"You'll be sorely missed, Lily."

She smiled through the sudden tears in her eyes. "And I'll miss all of you too."

****

Leaving Nicholas standing at the open kitchen door, Lily hurried upstairs and along the corridor to the dining room fighting the nausea rising bitter in her throat.

She'd left home to seek her independence and now despite her best efforts to deny it, she was falling for the one man she should avoid. It would be funny if it wasn't so pathetic. And he knew she was not who she claimed to be. She was convinced of it. Which meant it was only a matter of time before he let them all know what he intended to do about it.

She stared at the closed dining room door. The burst of female laughter and male hilarity scratched at her nerve endings making her squeeze her eyes shut. She drew in one, two, three steadying breaths before balancing the tray in one hand and pushing open the door. It was as though she'd announced her entrance with a trumpeted fanfare. Their conversation immediately fell to silence and all four diners turned and stared at her.

"Good evening," Lily said, politely nodding her head.

"Good evening." They replied in unison.

Holding her head high, Lily strode toward the viscount at the far end of the table. She placed a glass in front of him before walking around the table and positioning the others. Sending up a silent prayer the jumble of nerves coursing through her body was not visible to the four pairs of eyes watching her, she walked back to the master and filled his glass. The intensity of his stare felt like two red-hot fire pokers on the side of her face. At last she'd filled his glass and could make her way around the seemingly endless table filling the other glasses in turn.

Knowing her escape was nigh, she topped off Lord Winchester's glass with a flourish. "Do all enjoy your dessert. Jane will serve coffee shortly."

She moved to walk away but as she did, she briefly met Lord Winchester's steely cold gaze. The hairs at the nape of her neck stood to attention. His glare bore pure unadulterated loathing. The force of it pushed the breath from her lungs and into her throat where it caught, scraping the tissue like barbed wire against flesh. She couldn't move. She daren't move.

"Lily?" Lady Tasmin called from her left-hand side.

Forcing herself to breathe, Lily swallowed hard and managed to dislodge the hard knot of fear in her throat. She turned around and met Lady's Tasmin's stunning green eyes.

"Yes, Lady Tasmin?" She smiled, hoping the

quiver in her voice went unnoticed.

"I just want to thank you so very much for this evening. The entire meal has been absolutely faultless."

Please do not show me any more kindness. "You are welcome, my lady."

"I do hope we have not caused you and Jane and everyone else to be running backwards and forwards too much?"

"Not at all."

"Good, good." She gave a small laugh and threw a glance from beneath lowered lashes toward the top of the table. "Andrew, sorry, Lord Westrop was adamant we joined him for dinner this evening despite such an exhaustive day."

Lily briefly looked in her master's direction and their eyes met over the rim of his wine glass. Pure blue circles of sapphire. She snatched her gaze away.

"No problem at all. We enjoy your company as much as his lord does, my lady."

She grinned. "Good, because I in turn *adore* spending time at the manor. Every single one of you is always so welcoming." A playful twinkle sparkled in her stunning eyes. "Of course, I still haven't entirely broken through Mrs. Harris' tough exterior, but I still hold hope I will one day."

Lily smiled despite the dull ache in her chest. Lady Tasmin was lovely. Lord Westrop must see that she was perfect in every way. There must be more to his resistance in marrying her than he told her. How could any man not want to call her their own?

"Oh, she's not so tough once you get to know her, my lady." Lily tapped a finger to the side of her nose. "Of course, it would be far better for me if she never found out I said that."

Lady Tasmin's laughter was as warm as the first spring sun. "You are a true delight, Lily! No wonder Andrew is so fond of you all. This house is a welcome change to the usual stuffiness we have to endure elsewhere."

"I'm glad you feel relaxed here, Lady Tasmin."

"Oh, I do. I really do."

With a final dip of her head, Lily left the room. Once the door was closed, she released the breath she didn't even know she'd held. The atmosphere in the room had been palpable and it seemed Lady Tasmin was the only one oblivious to it. Having always been proud of her instinct, Lily's intuition and every fiber of her being had been on high alert when she'd been in the room.

And then, when she'd met Lord Winchester's gaze...she pressed a hand to her thundering heart and took a step toward the kitchen.

She'd barely walked more than a few feet when she heard the dining room door open behind her. She turned. Lord Winchester strolled toward her, his mouth stretched into a wide, predatory grin. Icy-cold perspiration broke out on Lily's forehead and upper lip. She gave a tentative curtsey, praying he'd stop coming toward her. Praying she had the strength of character not to turn and run like the commands screaming inside her head warned her.

"Sir? Is there something you need?"

He came closer. His perfectly aligned, gleaming white teeth glowed stark in the semi-darkness, his lips hardly visible they were drawn back so far.

"Sir?" Lily took a step back.

"I know what you're up to, Lily."

"I don't—"

He held up a finger. "Shut up."

She flinched. His voice broached no argument and Lily's mouth ran dry. She looked left and right but the corridor was deserted. The only sound was the rich silky laughter of the viscount drifting along the corridor from beneath the sealed dining room doors.

She took another step back.

He lunged his hand toward her and grasped her about the waist before she had time to draw breath. He pushed her into an alcove and down onto a cushioned seat that lined the back wall.

"You want him, don't you?" he whispered. "You want my friend's penis in your cunny."

Revulsion rolled through her stomach on a tidal wave of fear. His eyes glittered manically with drink or hatred, she didn't know which. Danger poured from deep inside him like leaking poison.

"Sir, please, let me go. You are drunk, you don't know—"

He pressed his hand across her mouth and the bitter scent of cigars filled her nostrils. He used his other hand to pinch her breasts painfully through her dress. "Do you like that? Do you want Andrew to touch you here? Or somewhere else? Maybe lower?"

Lily squeezed her eyes shut as he leaned so close. The faint whisper of his breath assailed her eyelids. She pushed his hands away. Fear clawed at her throat, threatening to close her airway. Her blood pulsed in her ears and her skin burned.

Please God, surely he wouldn't think he could force himself upon her here?

"Leave her be, Charles. Leave her be right this minute."

Lily's eyes snapped open at the sound of Lady Tasmin's voice. It was barely recognizable in its coldness. She stood beneath the arch of the alcove, her hands fisted at her hips, her regal face in shadow. He turned in slow motion, his hand slipping from Lily's mouth as he faced his cousin.

"What did you say?"

"I said leave her be."

He pushed to his feet and Lily put a shaking hand to her bruised mouth as she watched him

139

approach Lady Tasmin. If he laid one finger on her...what could Lily do?

"You're getting a little ahead of yourself, cousin," he sneered. "You are not the mistress of this house yet."

"That is neither here nor there, Charles. If I were to shout out now, Andrew would come running, and what do you think he will do to find you assaulting his favored servant? Do you think he will not eject you from this house and his life in one fell swoop?"

He tipped his head back and laughed softly for a moment before the laughter abruptly stopped. He reached out and gripped Lady Tasmin's arm in the exact same way he had Lily's. With the exact same amount of disregard for her wellbeing, he tossed her onto the seat beside Lily. Lily slipped her arm about Lady's Tasmin's shoulders and protectively drew her close.

"Ah, comrades in arms!" His laugh was frenzied. "Two ladies joined in battle. God, it is the most pathetic sight I have ever seen. Both of you need to understand something about the relationship I have with Andrew. Are you listening, mmm? Are those pretty, teasing little ears of yours wide open, eh? We grew up together, Andrew and I. We are closer than any husband and wife will ever be. I will take what I want in this house as Andrew has often told me to do. I will help myself to his staff the same as I do his food."

Lily swallowed down the revulsion in her throat as Lady Tasmin began to shake with anger or fear beside her. She bit down on her bottom lip to stem the flow of angry words building inside her.

"I want you to make your excuses and leave, cousin." He tilted his chin.

Lady Tasmin stiffened under Lily's embrace. "I will do no such thing. Andrew will think I am refusing his hospitality."

Lord Winchester strode toward her with such ferocity that both women pushed themselves hard against the seat. "You will leave. Now. And you will not come back here until I give my specific permission for you to do so. Do I make myself clear?"

"But, Charles..."

He smiled, tilted in his head to the side and softened his features in mock concern. "What is it, my dear? You love him, is that what you were about to say?"

"I—"

He snapped his head up straight. "Don't talk such rubbish! You do not love Andrew, and you never will."

"That is neither here nor there."

"Good. At last, something we agree on, so get out and leave me to enjoy a night with..." He leered at Lily until she had to look away. "...my best and most devoted of friends, the honorable Viscount Westrop. Take your sister and get the hell out of my sight. Go. Now."

Neither woman moved. He grabbed them both by an upper arm and flung them out from the alcove and into the corridor. They stumbled, but Lily managed to steady herself. She gripped Lady Tasmin's hand and saved her the embarrassment of lying face down on the tiled floor in front of a housemaid.

"What are you staring at," he spat at Lily. "Get her out of here, she is leaving. And as for you?" He swiped away the spittle that pebble-dashed his mouth and chin. "You, I will make sure are thrown out of Cotswold Manor with as much shame and disgust attached to your name and reputation as possible. Now get out of here. Both of you."

****

"What the bloody hell was all that about?"

141

Andrew demanded as Charles languidly pulled a cigar from the box on a side table. "Charles, I'm talking to you."

His friend took his time clipping the end and made a show of rolling the cigar back and forth over the tips of his fingers. His drunken state was clearly evident in the way he swayed a little back on his heels before lifting his eyes to Andrew's.

"What?"

Andrew shook his head. "Lady Tasmin and her sister. What happened? They left at such a speed I'm surprised their faces were not pulled back from the sheer force of it. What on earth happened between you and that cousin of yours? Did you have crossed words?"

"Nothing that won't be resolved once she's had time to sulk." His handsome face split into a smile. "God, was it really that obvious?"

"Short of grabbing her by the hair and hurling her down the graveled driveway, you could not have been more conspicuous."

"Oops, sorry." Charles grimaced and sucked in air through his teeth. "I just wanted rid of them."

"But why? Most of the time you adore her. My God man, you push the woman on me often enough."

Charles walked to the drinks cabinet and poured himself a hefty measure of brandy. He carried it to an armchair and sat down. He took a slow drink, meeting Andrew's gaze over its rim.

Andrew frowned. "Well? Am I right?"

Charles nonchalantly lifted his shoulders. "Yes, you're right. Maybe I shouldn't have been quite so heavy handed about it, but sometimes Tasmin can annoy the hell out of me." He took another drink. "Anyway, judging by your lack of interest in her over the past few weeks I would have thought you'd appreciate the gesture."

Following his friend's example, Andrew walked

to the cabinet to pour a drink. Or at least use the action as an excuse to break away from Charles' accusatory glare. "I have other things on my mind right now."

"Such as?"

"Things, Charles. Things that do not concern you."

"Is that so?"

Andrew turned and met his gaze. "Yes."

For a long moment, neither of them spoke, their fiery gazes locked in challenge. Charles put his glass on a table beside him. "Come on. I'm your friend, am I not? I might even be able to help."

"With what?" Andrew asked innocently. "I have nothing worrying me."

"Don't be an arse. You know damn well it's been five months since your courtship began with Tasmin. Society is speculating, the gossip magazines dribbling in the odd caricature, yet you do not even as much as hint at the notion of a near engagement."

"And why would I?" Andrew lifted his drink to his lips and winced against its potency as he swallowed the entire measure in one gulp.

"Are you serious? How can you say such a thing?" Charles' voice rose. "You have my father, her father, our entire family waiting with bated breath."

Andrew's fingers tightened around his mother's engagement ring sitting neglected and idle in his trouser pocket. He had thought himself strong enough to carry out his promise tonight. Especially after having shared a final sealing kiss of regret with Lily the week before, and witnessing the relief in her eyes at his decision to carry through with the betrothal.

And why wouldn't she feel relief? He had no right. No right to put Lily, wonderful beautiful Lily, under such pressure. What was she supposed to do with his advances? Was he really that man? The stereotypical aristocratic monster that employed his staff far and above the call of duty? *No, No, I am not! And I intend to put a permanent end to the pressure in the only way possible.*

He poured himself another measure.

"Andrew, damn it man. You owe me an explanation."

Andrew blinked at the sound of Charles' clear frustration as it cut through his musings. He tilted his chin. "I know you are all waiting for the day I get down on bended knee and no doubt it will happen soon. Just not tonight."

"But it will happen?"

Andrew strolled across the room and lowered himself into a chair. "A proposal will be forthcoming but I cannot promise when. That is the best you will get from me for now."

Charles slapped the arm of his chair. "Well, I'm glad to hear it, my friend. Tasmin is yours for the taking."

"Which is exactly what is holding me back." Andrew blew out a heavy breath.

"What on earth is that supposed to mean?"

"I just don't know if I can spend the rest of my life with a woman who does exactly as I ask without challenge or opinion."

Charles eyes widened and he shook his head. "I see. So the obstacles delaying this union is Tasmin's beauty, etiquette and utter devotion, is that it?" He drew a long puff on his cigar before slowly releasing the smoke in a stream of perfect circles above his head. "Well, that may be what you like, but to me, a woman who knows her place is a gift from the Gods quite frankly."

"Yes, well, you would think that," Andrew muttered, closing his eyes. "I, on the other hand, want more than a lapdog standing side by side with me at Cotswold Manor. I have dogs already. What I want is a woman with fire in her belly, someone who will test my intellect, arouse my body, fill my soul—"

"Whoa, steady on. You're in real danger of sounding like a man who wants an actual *wife* beside him."

"Very funny."

Charles laughed. "You would be insane to risk any woman knowing what you are thinking, what your plans are. Don't be fooled, these fillies can be very astute when they want to be. They push out their tits and bat their eyelashes to reel us in so they can pounce when we least suspect it."

Andrew opened his eyes and looked at him. "My God, you really are a piece of work. I swear you'll never fall in love with anyone other than yourself. You've no idea what you're talking about."

A flush of color stained Charles' cheeks. "What's love got to do with anything?" He paused. "Just get on with the job in hand and propose to her. There's no such thing as an equal and happy partnership between a man and a woman. If you want to expand your mind, read a book, if you want to arouse your sad excuse for a penis, pay for a high-class whore. But for crying out loud man, do not let this estate slip through your fingers because you were blinded by the notion of true love."

Andrew stared at him for a moment before snatching his gaze to the window. The earlier sun of the carefree day had set and the sky was now a sheet of untainted black. Not a single star broke the darkness. His heart picked up speed. Maybe Charles was right. Maybe what he felt for Lily wasn't love at all. Maybe if he tasted and experienced every inch of her, these thoughts of love would disappear and then this pressure around his heart would be released.

"Has something happened between you and the new housemaid?"

A heavy weight dropped low into Andrew's

145

stomach. The seat seemed to shift beneath him. He turned, determined to keep eye contact with Charles lest his friend guess the truth. "I'm sorry?"

"You heard."

"Between me and Lily?"

Charles grinned. "The one and only."

Andrew cursed the icy-cold sweat that broke out on his forehead. "In what way?"

Charles suggestively wiggled his eyebrows. "Well...you know."

"Don't be absurd."

"She's damn good-looking," Charles said, crudely adjusting the front of his trousers. "That bosom of hers is positively screaming to be fondled."

"Charles..."

"And those lips? God, a man could devour them given half a chance."

The fire in Andrew's chest rose fast and hot. "Don't talk about her that way."

"Or what?" He smiled, his bright white teeth glinting in the candlelight. He drew in a long breath through flared nostrils. "Mmm, indeed. And I bet her pubic hair is the same shiny copper as the hair on her head."

"Enough!" Andrew's anger burst forth like a breaking dam. But the moment he yelled, he regretted it. Pursing his lips tightly together, he waited to see what happened next.

The cigar halted at Charles' lips. It shook as it hovered in mid-air. Andrew tensed, prepared for battle when he recognized the crazy glint in Charles' eyes. Possessiveness that would become out and out rivalry if Charles wore to see into Andrew's mind and the graphic detail of the way he began to feel about Lily. But Charles' possession wouldn't be for Lily, it would be for anything that Andrew wanted. In the many years the two men had been friends, Charles could never abide not being the focus of

Andrew's undivided attention.

He knew. He knew how he felt towards her. And Charles being Charles would not let it be until Andrew admitted every last nuance of his ridiculous infatuation. Well, Charles would be waiting a bloody long time. His friend would not come after Andrew but Lily, if he became angered enough.

Charles drew in a deep and lengthy lungful of smoke. "Well, well, well."

"I won't have you talking about her that way, Charles. I am a bloody good employer and because of that you should have enough respect for me to not even jest about such things as the chastity of my staff."

Silence.

Andrew took a throat-burning gulp of his drink and sent up a silent plea for the strength to hold his temper. "Well? Say something. Are you going to stop this outrageous line of insinuation or not?"

Charles' lip curled back from his teeth and his eyes positively shone with satisfaction. "I bloody well knew it."

"Oh, for God's sake."

Charles leaned forward in his seat and peered into Andrew's face, his eyes narrowed to slits as he studied him. It took every ounce of Andrew's self-control not to look away.

"I mean it, Charles. You stop this. Right now."

Charles grinned. "You've got that look in your eye, my friend."

"What look?" Andrew snapped. "The look that's telling you to hold your tongue before I do something that will leave everyone in the country wanting to know who gave you the worst thrashing of your life?"

Charles laughed, sat back in his chair and held up his hands in mock surrender. "I'm only playing with you, old boy. I've seen the way you look at her and why not? She's very...I don't know...interesting, shall we say?"

Cursing the rapid thump of his heart, Andrew got to his feet and walked to the window purposely turning his back to the room. *Damn the man! Damn our friendship and the way Charles can see straight through me.*

"Andrew?"

"What?"

"Don't you agree?"

"With what?"

"That your maid is an interesting character. One you might want to learn more about?"

The mocking of Charles' tone poked and prodded at Andrew's curiosity. It left little doubt in his mind that Charles knew something Andrew wouldn't want to hear. He never said anything with such a triumphant tone unless he had the upper hand. Andrew pressed a hand against the cold glass of the window pane and bit his teeth together. He clenched and unclenched his jaw in rhythmic pattern as his gaze fixed on the woods. The place where the reason for his current unease had been ignited—she'd been like a flint to a dying ember.

He squeezed his eyes shut. Every time he thought of her his contemplation swung from erotic fantasy to petulant childish jealously. Whatever Charles said to him now was going to affect him—and to that he had little resistance. But fortunately, he did have the weapon of familiarity at his disposal. Andrew knew how to burst his friend's bubble, knew how to slap his legs out from underneath him with words rather than violence. He took another gulp of his drink before turning and meeting Charles' provocative leer.

"In what way is she interesting?" he asked, his tone dispassionate as he casually paced the room. "Is it the way she manages to look effortlessly striking despite that dreary uniform she has to wear day in day out? Or is it the way she uses that wonderfully dry and quick wit of hers to say something that has my staff laughing with such unadulterated aplomb, I sometimes fear their sides will split?"

Charles' forehead creased with confusion. "What?"

"Or maybe it's how for the past few days she has managed to be in a different room than me no matter the time of day or night, or the way—"

"The way she's been in a different room? What in God's name...? You're actually *aggrieved* that she hasn't been in the room with you?" Charles' laugh was as merciless as a punch in the gut. "Do I need to remind you that it is a servant's job to remain unnoticed unless their master demands differently?"

Andrew glared at him, his heart pulsing out the seconds like the beats of a drum before battle. "Exactly. And as far as Lily is concerned, I want it differently."

Their eyes locked, two life-long friends standing barely two feet apart, their chests rising and falling in unison.

"You have no idea who she is, Andrew." Charles' voice was a whisper. "No idea at all."

"And what of it? I don't know who any of my staff are outside of their work."

Turning on his heel, Charles walked to a side table and stubbed his cigar out with unnecessary force into a crystal ashtray. "She's dangerous."

"What?" Andrew laughed. "Don't be ridiculous."

"You are losing your mind and you can't even see it."

"I see plenty," Andrew said, his voice trembling with barely controlled anger. "I am not foolish enough to think she is all that she seems."

Charles eyes widened. "Are you telling me you already know?"

Unease prickled at the hair on the back of

Andrew's neck. "Know what? That there is more to her than meets the eye? Of course I do. Do you think I have not noticed the way she speaks, her use of language? Not to mention the way she dances—"

"Dances?" His friend's eyes grew to manic proportions. "You have danced with her?"

Silently cursing his penchant for verbal slips at the most inopportune moments, Andrew made himself stand still despite the weight of Charles' incredulous stare. He waved a dismissive hand. "No, of course not. I'm just saying you have no fear of me being blindsided by any woman, least of all Lily. So she has secrets. No doubt Lady Tasmin does too. None of us are perfect, Charles." He looked at him meaningfully. "Are we, my friend?"

"But—"

"Now, for God' sake, can we forget about Lily, Lady Tasmin and every other female on the planet and get plastered?"

But Charles didn't concur as he usually did at the mere mention of a drinking session; he continued to watch Andrew. His eyes shadowed with deeper and deeper darkness with each passing second. After a long moment, Andrew relaxed a little when at last Charles turned and strolled to the drinks tray. The charged moment wavered. Charles took his time filling a tumbler before he brushed past Andrew and dropped back into his seat.

"Something happened between us when I left the room earlier, you know," he said.

Andrew tensed, his heart picking up speed. "Between you and...?"

"The maid."

"What are you talking about? Did you follow her out into the corridor? You did, didn't you?" Unadulterated rage seeped into Andrew's blood like molten lava. "What did you do to her?"

His friend tipped his head back and laughed.

"What did I *do* to her? Oh, for crying out loud, man, will you stop looking at me like that. You'll be bloody glad I did what I did when I tell you what I found out about the girl."

Chapter Nine

Lily lifted the hem of her nightdress and sat back on her haunches. Nothing but maddening silence emanated through the closed drawing room door. Resting her cheek against one of the balusters lining the huge oak staircase, she strained to hear something, anything. The hallway was in semi-darkness, the only light coming from the candles lit sporadically along the wood paneled wall behind her. Even though the time was nearing midnight, Viscount Westrop had yet to retire.

Two hours had passed since Nicholas escorted Lady Tasmin and her sister through the front door. Lily had not seen them leave, instead busying herself in the kitchen waiting for her heart and hands to settle after the Baron's unprovoked attack. When Nicholas came back downstairs he'd announced Lady Tasmin had been taken ill. He said her high color and brusqueness were clear signs she was telling the truth as both were not of her usual manner.

Lily had been unable to look at him. After everything she'd asked Nicholas and the others to do for her, she refused to involve him in yet another censorship to be kept from their master. She would not and could not tell him about the baron's attack. She was perfectly well on the outside—the inside would not be seen. It scared Lily senseless that the other people who did know what happened tonight were the viscount's best friend and intended. What chance did she have of the master believing her version of events if it were ever revealed to him?

Squeezing her eyes shut, Lily pressed a hand to her stomach. She would not condemn Lady Tasmin for denying all knowledge in order to save herself and her family after seeing such evil in the baron's eyes. Who knew what a man like that was capable of?

Lily shivered and leaned forward. She strained to hear his footsteps or the faint rasp of a cough but there was nothing but silence.

He must still be in there. She'd watched the door with the staunchness of a devoted sentry for the past hour.

Lord Winchester had stayed for almost an hour after the ladies left. Nicholas had been sent away and told they were not to be disturbed. With the drawing room such a far distance from the kitchen, speculation quickly rose below stairs. Especially when Mrs. Harris added fat to the fire by planting a seed in Nicholas' head that the master was in cahoots with the baron in order to arrange a hasty wedding. Nicholas had been fanned into such a state of distress he'd had to sit down with a cold cloth pressed to his head.

But as much as she tried, Lily could not feign joviality and excused herself with claims of a migraine. And then not twenty minutes later, her heart had leapt into her throat when Lord Winchester slammed the front door behind him with such violence downstairs, she heard Nicholas calling for Robert to check the hinges were still in working order.

She gnawed at her bottom lip, willing the drawing room to open and release its occupant. Although how seeing the master would help her current state of unease, Lily had no idea, yet she needed to see his face. Needed to gauge what he thought, what his best friend had told him upon returning from the corridor after the altercation with her and Lady Tasmin.

Bony fingers of fear tip-tapped up Lily's spine as she heard the chink of glass against glass. He had refused supper. He may not be eating, but he was most definitely drinking. She swallowed.

If Winchester had told him she encouraged his advances, then the master would ask her to leave. In which case, her departure would be made all the easier. It was possible she might have just enough money saved for a one-way passage to France. Food and board would be a luxury she'd seek once she was there. She'd have to find employment immediately. She really had wanted to do this without her father's generosity, but she'd pay him back as soon as possible.

But what of his lordship?

Lily sucked in a breath.

Lady Tasmin as good as admitted she didn't love him. Lily couldn't bear the thought of allowing the other woman to take him and keep him from ever finding true love and happiness...but didn't he admit this was what he intended to do anyway? Wasn't this his answer to releasing the guilt of his mother's death by marrying and in turn honoring the promise to his father?

Lily swiped at a tear as it fell to her cheek.

A promise that masqueraded as nothing more than a cruel burden. He was not to blame for his mother's death and now her time at the manor was over and with it her chance to convince him otherwise thwarted. Lily pushed herself to her feet. And what of it? Who was she to meddle in other people's lives? Marrying for status might make her sick to her stomach but it had been the way of the world for centuries.

Picking up her candle, Lily cursed its trembling and hurried up the attic stairwell. She would involve herself no further in this. Her life, her independence—that's what she wanted, nothing more. What good would it do to stare at a closed door? The viscount was perfectly in his rights never to utter another word to her. If he wanted her gone, he didn't even have to tell her to leave himself. He could easily get Nicholas to do it. It would be best if she never faced him again.

With her heart beating like a lead weight in her chest and unshed tears burning behind her eyes, Lily strode to her room with her head held high. Once the door was firmly closed behind her, she set down the candle at her bedside and climbed into bed. Grasping the blankets, she pulled them under her chin. Too tense to lie down, she remained sitting bolt upright and stared blindly at the back of her bedroom door.

And then the harsh slamming of a door below made Lily jump so high she almost toppled from the bed. Her fingers tightened on the edge of the blankets until her nails dug into her palms through the wool. Hot beads of perspiration leapt to her forehead and upper lip. She strained to hear more. Then came the rapid thud of boot soles along the corridor below followed by the muted sounds of strained voices. She recognized Nicholas' higher pitch against the master's rich deep voice and grimaced. She was doomed. What else could Nicholas do but carry out his master's orders? She took this job as a means for blessed independence but Nicholas took this job to survive.

Heavy footsteps upon the stairs jolted Lily from her wretched contemplation. She listened carefully to their rhythm. It wasn't Nicholas. It was the Viscount. Of that she had no doubt. She dropped the blankets and ran trembling fingers over her hair. She glanced downward at her bosom and hastily tightened the knot there.

He must see her as nothing more than a maid.

She was good at her job, maybe that would be his main concern. His primary focus was marriage right now, maybe he'd not care about anything else but the right to an immaculately run household so that his energies could be pointed in a different direction. He knew of her wish to live abroad where women were granted a greater degree of freedom, maybe he admired her courage for such aspirations. Yes, of course. How could she possibly think he would fall into the vicious trap his friend had laid for both the viscount and her?

His footsteps came to a stop outside the door.

Lily's heart hitched and her mouth went dry.

The seconds passed but he did not come in or even knock.

With her eyes trained straight ahead, Lily's pulse beat hard in her neck. The wait was torturous but she would not call out and she would not crumble under the pressure.

Two loud knocks.

She jumped and blew out a breath. *Father, give me strength.* "Come in."

Then she remembered belatedly he should see her doing something other than staring wide-eyed at her bedroom door at this hour of the night. She leaned over and snatched the novel she was reading from her bedside table and opened it in her lap.

There was a brief moment before the door opened slowly. When Lily saw him, her heart skipped a beat. His physique was so big, so muscular that he completely filled the small area within the doorframe. He stood immobile. His soft dark hair brushed the wood above him and his wide shoulders left no space on either side. Lily longed to snuff out the candle beside her. Its light, cast across his features, made him look eerie and dangerous. It veiled his upper face in darkness, obscuring her ability to read his thoughts through those beautiful blue eyes.

What are you thinking, Andrew?

The whisper of his Christian name in her mind furthered her anxiety.

When had her feelings for him tipped so far in the wrong direction? When she first saw him? The night in the garden? Sharing a pot of tea in the kitchen when the rest of the house was asleep? What did it matter? The man was either here to sack her, or thrash her, and all she could think about were irrelevancies?

She mentally shook her head. "Sir? Is everything all right? It's past midnight."

A modicum of courage flared inside. Her voice sounded positively unruffled!

The silence stretched and tightened— lengthened and tormented.

Finally, he stepped forward. A zigzag of light shone across his face. The milky-white streak illuminated his mouth but only served to further conceal his eyes. She needed to see his eyes. His eyes would tell her everything.

"Sir?" she repeated. "Are you all right?"

His laugh was dry, making her want to reach for the glass of water beside her to wet her already arid throat.

"Am I all right?" he repeated.

She only managed to nod.

He stepped closer and at last she fully saw his face. Lily was unsure whether it was the candle or the anger inside him that flashed and burned in his eyes. She struggled not to reach out and close his eyelids with her fingers. She didn't want to see him look at her that way. Not after he'd looked at her with such tenderness as they laid side by side in the garden; or such yearning when they broke from their two stolen kisses.

"No, Lily. I'm not all right."

She swallowed. "Has something happened, sir? Lady Tasmin left in such a hurry but Nicholas swore I wasn't needed."

"Lady Tasmin has nothing, nothing whatsoever to do with what I want to say to you."

He spat out the words on a breath of such resentment, Lily flinched as though he'd struck her. "Sir, I—"

He held up a hand, cutting her off. "Not another word until I have at least managed to repeat what has been going over and over in my mind for the past hour."

Lily suspected her eyes were as wide as a doe's as she clutched at the blanket on either side of her legs like a lifeline. But she couldn't refrain from either. His smile so often vivid enough to brighten even the dullest day—the smile Nicholas said had only surfaced in the weeks she'd been here—was now replaced with thin-lipped anger. The hurt in his eyes unprecedented, and the fear she'd put it there was more than she could bear.

He took the final steps towards her. He stared at her for a long moment, hesitated and then her breath caught when the bed dipped beneath his weight. She smelled the faint scent of his cologne beneath the much stronger aroma of aged brandy. A single breath shook from deep inside her and whispered out from between her lips.

Lifting one finger at a time, he unlocked her hand from the blanket. He didn't speak straight away and the only sounds filling the room were his gruff inhalations merged with her quickened breaths.

"I really can't believe I am this angry about such a thing," he murmured at last. "What right do I have?"

"Sir?" she whispered.

But he appeared not to hear her. He stared at

the opposite wall as though the words he wanted to say were written on the stone. Tension had bunched his shoulders at his neck, his jaw rhythmically clenched and released. Lily watched him through lowered lashes, uncertain what to do or say.

"Do you know something?" His voice was lower now as he turned from the wall to stare at their joined hands. "I don't know why I am even here in this room with you. What I have come to say is not my task but Nicholas'."

Nausea swirled in Lily's stomach as her ponderings of just minutes before revealed themselves before her eyes. "What is it that is Nicholas' task, sir?"

He met her eyes. "To ask you to leave."

She snatched her gaze away to a spot above his shoulders. "Oh."

"Do you know the reason I may demand such a thing?"

"No, sir."

"No?"

"No."

He lifted his finger to her chin and it burned the skin there like an iron brand. He applied only the slightest pressure but Lily could not refrain from meeting his eyes. "Did you not offer yourself to my friend, Lord Winchester?"

The world seemed to stop turning. "I'm sorry?"

His jaw tightened. "I *said,* did you not offer yourself to Lord Winchester?"

"Is that what he told you?"

"Answer the question, Lily."

"And you believe him?"

"I have not yet made a decision."

The burst of indignation that shot through her blood came as a shock that she could not have predicted. When she'd been waiting for his condemnation, Lily had only anticipated fear. But with the two of them alone and so intimately shrouded in their own private world, she felt an overwhelming sense of disappointment. Profound and painful disappointment.

She jerked her chin from his hand. "Well, if you think so little of me, sir, I will save you the task of asking me to leave. I will gladly do so of my own accord first thing in the morning."

"Are you saying he lied to me? Misinformed me of your conduct and risked our friendship by implying improper behavior when he clearly knows how much I value each and every one of my staff?"

Her gaze didn't waver from his. Lily was entirely convinced that the passion, the rage swirling in the sapphire depths of his eyes was equally as tumultuous in her own eyes. "Yes, sir. That's exactly what I am saying."

Lily's bosom rose and fell with each ragged breath. She had guessed Lord Winchester would do this—would callously reverse the events outside the dining room—but it did nothing to soothe the pain of having Andrew accuse her of such a thing. He thought so little of her and disregarded so quickly what he had learned of her.

"Then I'm disappointed in you, Lily."

She swallowed hard against the stab in her chest. "That be as it may, sir, but if there is one thing I have, it is my candor. I assure you Lord Winchester's claims of my conduct are a blatant insult to my character. Yet they neither upset nor anger me. I expected nothing less of him."

He arched an eyebrow. "Is that so?"

"Indeed."

A small twitch moved at the corner of his mouth. "The trouble is, Lily, you misunderstand my disappointment. It is not disappointment with your alleged unladylike conduct—"

"There *was* no unladylike conduct," she said. "I

did nothing, nothing to invite such—"

"I am frustrated you would think for one tiny moment there was any possibility of me believing such claims about you. Whether they be from my best friend or a stranger on the street." His eyes softened, even twinkled with amusement.

A surge of relief and then incredulity surged through her veins. The man was incorrigible! One minute he wore the face of an executioner, the next the twinkling mischief of a schoolboy. She opened her mouth to protest.

"You have done everything I have expected of you, Lily. Everything I have paid you to do and more. You must never doubt that I will think of you with anything other than complete and utter respect." His gaze flicked from her eyes to her hair to her lips and back again.

Her cheeks burned as she dipped her head. "Thank you, sir."

"Lily?"

She looked up. "Yes?"

"My anger is not directed at you or even Charles. I am angry with myself. Why I ever thought I could behave as I have with no consequences to myself, my lineage or my reputation, I do not know."

The word reputation immediately resulted in Lily's perpetual itch starting to scratch. She huffed out a breath. "I often think the issue of reputation is given far too much contemplation."

He smiled softly. "And why do you say that?"

She hesitated as she realized what her words might infer. She looked down at the bedspread. "Sometimes I feel we are all guilty of wasting too much time fretting over what others deem as the right or wrong thing to do as far as maintaining a good reputation is concerned. The answer will forever change and so you will never truly attain what is supposedly right. A good reputation holds no bearing on personal happiness."

She stopped. A strange, indecipherable expression now clouded his face. She sunk further back into the pillow in a bid to break the invisible intimacy that had built between them. It hung like a hazy heat shimmering in the candlelight. If she were to reach her hand out, would she feel it like a tangible force? Would its intensity burn her fingers and shame her soul?

"You are a wonderful woman, Lily. A woman who has filled this house in a way you will never know."

Her heart raced, her hands moistened. "And you are a good man, sir," she said quietly. "And I believe your reputation should be considered one of highest bearing and if people feel otherwise, then they are not worth even a moment of your thoughts."

His gaze remained fixed on hers, making the tiny hairs at the back of her neck tingle and her heart beat faster.

"In an ideal world that may be so. But my father lies on his deathbed waiting for news that his only son has found a wife and impregnated her with an heir. The whole idea that I can do anything else other than seal my family inheritance is beyond any modern ideals."

His words were becoming slower, even slurred, and Lily was forced to see just how inebriated he was. Would he even remember being here in the morning, let alone what he was saying? It was her duty to persuade him to leave. Now. Before he said more than he should.

"Your father might have asked for those things, my lord, but I am sure deep down your happiness is at the forefront of his mind. If you marry Lady Tasmin, you will lead a happy life, I am sure. She is kind and beautiful..." He leaned forward and cupped a hand to her jaw. Lily stiffened. "Sir?"

"You are right. Lady Tasmin is kind and pretty, witty and gay. Maybe she will even make a perfect mother, who is to know? But she is not the woman I should be marrying, is she?"

Lily's heart kicked painfully in her chest.

What was he saying? Why was he doing this to her? Did he not know the way his words could be interpreted?

His hand slipped from her face and plopped onto the bed. "Yet I need an heir and I will have one. Even if that heir is created not with love but with necessity." He looked deep into her eyes and choked out a wry laugh. "Isn't that romantic? Isn't that how every child should be conceived?"

Nausea swept a low loop-the-loop in her belly. The pain in his eyes was horrible to see, too acute to bear. She longed to reach out and pull him to her. Tell him not to marry Lady Tasmin, to come away with her and forget the burden he carried with such intense duty and honor. Everything in society was wrong and sad and hopeless.

"No. No, it's not, and you should not do it." The words tumbled from her tongue before she could stop them. Her heart picked up speed and her mouth drained dry.

He stared at her. "Pardon?"

Lily swallowed. "I mean...what I meant to say is you are not like me. My heart breaks for the duty you carry. You have the weight of a family name to continue less everything your ancestors achieved will fall into another family's arms."

"But if I do not marry her, what then? I will be no closer to securing the family line and I will have broken my promise to my father." He snatched his gaze away and looked to the ceiling. "There must be an alternative. I cannot live my life in a lie. I just can't."

Lily watched his profile in the half-light. The

drink he had consumed seemed to fade right before her eyes, leaving him looking tortured and alone. Lily stole a hand across the bed and covered his hand with hers. His jaw tightened but he didn't pull away and he didn't meet her eyes.

"Sir, it is right that you want to ensure the future of this beautiful house, this wonderful estate. But the pressure that people expect it is a heavy burden for anyone to carry. Do you really believe your father will hold you to such a promise?"

He drew in a long breath and exhale. "I...yes, yes he will."

"Does he know you do not love her? Cannot abide the thought of marrying her? I am confident if you were to speak to him—"

"I promised."

The crack in his voice clawed at Lily's heart. She had to make him see, make him understand. "You were not responsible, sir."

He turned sharply and met her gaze. "Yes, Lily, I was."

She shook her head. "You were a boy. A son who loved his mother. Do you really think she looks down upon you now with blame and condemnation? Do you?" Lily drew in a shaky breath, forced a small smile. "She wants you to be happy, sir. Open your heart. If it is beyond your comprehension to consider Lady Tasmin as your wife, I am certain there are many others who would fall at your feet to take such a role."

His eyes darkened, their intensity shining like the flames of a fire. "But you have already said you have no wish to marry. Have you not told me that countless times?"

She swallowed and snatched her hand from his. "Sir, I did not mean it that way."

He pursed his lips together. His gaze darted from her eyes to her lips and back again. Lily began to tremble. What had she done? The alcohol still ran through his veins like blood. His brain was intoxicated and unaware. His frown deepened as his eyes bored into hers. Lily drew in a sharp breath against the pain in her chest as her vision blurred. If only he knew how much his drunken ramblings hurt.

"What are you thinking? Talk to me," he whispered.

She blew out a breath and purposefully pulled her mouth into a gentle smile. She hoped to encourage a modicum of humor back into his eyes rather than the heated intensity that resided there.

"It is not that I will never marry, sir. I won't marry until I meet a man who wants me for who I am, and I him." She laughed, the false gaiety sounding contrived to her ears but hopefully genuine to his. "What is it you suggest? If I was otherwise inclined, you would like to marry me?"

But he didn't join her laughter as she'd expected. Instead, he stroked his fingers along her jaw line, touching them briefly to her lips. She fought the sudden temptation to trap those fingers between her teeth. The physical need to touch him was unbearable. Why, oh why, did she want him so? And why now did she want to alter the sadness in his gaze to something infinitely more dangerous?

The intimate place between her legs twitched and heated. He looked so vulnerable yet so incredibility strong, sad yet completely in control. It made no sense, but the combination had her senses reeling and her skin more sensitized with each passing moment.

And then it happened without her having to do a single thing to initiate it. His lips tasted different than they had the last time they'd kissed. The difference was better, sweeter than ever. His ardent command excited her and she knew neither of them wanted to think why this was happening nor indeed how they would stop it.

But stop it she would. In a just a second... No, a minute... His strong arms provoked the most pleasurable, delicious sensation deep in her heart as he pulled her close. The novel slipped from the bed and landed on the floor with a thud, but neither of them inched apart. Instead he held her tighter against him. Lily felt his ownership, his possession, sweep over her.

She snapped her eyes open. *What am I doing?*

"Stop. We must stop!" She struggled from his embrace. When she looked at his reddened mouth, she knew the branding of their kiss would be just as evident upon her own lips.

"What is it? Why stop, Lily? We both want this. I can feel your yearning. Mine is no different."

Her breath came in erratic pants. "Sir, you are a viscount, I, a maid. This is...this is madness."

He shook his head, reached for her hand. "No, no it's not. It's powerful. I feel it, you feel it. Why not take what we both want?"

"What I want is independence," she cried. "To not have to rely on anyone or anything." Hot tears pricked her eyes. "I have dreams and goals. I came here as a means of earning money, nothing else. Entangling myself in anything other than work will only guide me off course. I can't let this happen, I can't!"

"And I would not dream of standing in your way." He gripped her hand. "Don't you see I have no wish to hinder you? I will not make any demands on you. I will surrender to what you want, how far you will allow this to go. Surely independence does not equate to loneliness? Do you not yearn to feel the heat of my skin as much as I do yours?"

She shook her head vigorously from side to side. "You don't understand."

"I will never hurt you. You make me smile, you make me laugh. If you do not want me to touch you and hold you, then I won't. But please, please do not think I am your master trying to take advantage. I want to offer you liberty, not bondage. I feel your need and it matches mine. Perfectly."

For a long moment their eyes locked and Lily saw the sincerity, the fear reflected in his gaze. Why was this happening? Her heart and her body ached for him. Her mind yearned to understand him. Yet, she desperately wished they had nothing to share, nothing to need from each other. How could there be feelings between them? This was *not* what she wanted.

He dropped her hand and lowered his head. "I'm sorry, Lily. If I have upset or God forbid frightened you."

She touched a hand to his muscular forearm. "You have not frightened me. I'm not sure you could ever frighten me."

He met her eyes, the corner of his mouth tipping upwards. "Isn't a master supposed to be just a little imposing?"

She smiled. "I'm afraid that isn't you, sir."

"Ah."

For a moment, neither of them said anything but stared into each other's eyes and that was when Lily knew she was in love. And yes, she was frightened beyond belief. She drew in a shaky breath and gently pulled her hand from his arm.

"No good can come from this."

His eyes widened. "No good? You know as well as I do that this...this feeling between us has to be dealt with. Is it really so bad?"

She swallowed. She couldn't acknowledge it— she wouldn't acknowledge it. But didn't she give in to her desire before and knew she would again? Perspiration broke out along her spine, its iciness tangible beneath her nightdress and upon her face.

"There is no *feeling* between us, sir." She pulled back her shoulders and forced herself to meet his eyes. "Feelings come from inside, feelings grow from time and shared experiences. What is happening here is purely physical, and the reason it is so strong is because anything physical in this world is frowned upon and denied..." She paused. "This is nothing more than a clear case of forbidden fruit. The apple and the serpent."

His Adam's apple shifted beneath the skin of his neck as his stare changed and shifted with each passing second. She watched in morbid fascination as the soft, almost desperate way he'd looked at her not two minutes before slowly evolved into something more feral. His eyes darkened from azure to gothic midnight blue.

He reached his hand slowly toward her and Lily's breath caught when he cupped her breast. His thumb felt as light as the brush of a feather as it whispered over her traitorously erect nipple.

"Then take a bite," he whispered.

Lily lifted her chin, fought to stay still and not push her breast further into his hand as her body urged her to. "I can't."

Heat flooded her body. She held her breath as the air crackled between them. He circled his thumb again and again. She shivered. He leaned close and touched his lips so gently to hers, Lily was unsure they touched at all.

"Please, Lily."

"Sir..." But the protestation died on her lips.

"You are so beautiful. Please, let me look at you."

He moved back. And then he was untying the ribbon above her breasts and she did nothing to stop him. She couldn't. She closed her eyes, hiding her secret emotional submission. He could not see. He could not know.

His hands slid inside her nightdress, opening the material wide, allowing the cold air of the room to bite erotically at her nipples.

"Lily, beautiful, beautiful, Lily."

"Andrew," she murmured. Instantly, her eyes snapped open. "Oh...I..."

But his eyes danced with pleasure, his skilful mouth stretched into a grin as he let out a soft laugh. "Sshh, it's all right. Say it again. Just here, just now, say it again. Please."

"Andrew."

The name curled around her tongue like the most delectable pleasure as it had so many times before when she'd whispered it in the silence of her room. But now, as she said it aloud with him looking at her with such tenderness, it became a connecting bond between them. She smiled softly.

"Andrew."

He groaned before taking her face in his hands and bringing his lips to hers. His tongue was hot and purposeful. Lily surrendered. Feverishly, she returned his kiss. She wanted his hands all over her but felt paralyzed by her hunger. She had no choice but to follow his lead. His hands burned like hot embers on her skin, branding their ownership with every stroke, every touch. She bit down on her bottom lip as he lifted the blankets.

Her nightdress bunched high upon her thighs and with his gaze on hers, he slid his fingers beneath the dress and along the sensitive skin of her inner thighs. Her heart pounded, her center throbbed. She threw her head back and clung to his shoulders. He scored his sinful fingers higher and higher until they were entangled in her pubic hair and a small cry escaped her lips.

He stroked the damp strands over and over. She whispered his name and he pushed his fingers deep inside, probing, discovering, and coaxing her body to a delicious frenzy. She'd heard of this, she'd even read of this. She wanted to laugh out loud…surely this was worth the risk of eternal banishment? Just for this one moment of utter insanity, she would risk losing everything….

"Please, Andrew. Please."

His fingers glided gently in and out. And then with what she could only presume was his thumb, he rubbed and pressed at her nub sending shockwaves of mounting sensations hurtling through her. Her body was damp, her eyes squeezed shut.

"Look at me, Lily."

She frantically shook her head. "I can't."

"You can. Please. I need to know you want this."

It was the soft and sincere concern in his voice that opened her eyes. He smiled. "Good. Now let go."

Pure lust burned in depths of two glistening pools of sapphire as he watched her. She felt so gloriously alive! Her breath shuddered and she became ensnared in his net. His for the taking, now and possibly for the rest of her life.

And then, with their eyes still locked, the most unbelievable sensations rocked her very core. The vibrations scared, yet delighted her. She dug her nails into his shoulders and opened her mouth to a wide O. She started to pant, to want, to chase whatever it was he was doing to her. She couldn't let him see her vulnerability, the naked helplessness reflected in her gaze. She squeezed her eyes shut once more.

"Open your eyes, Lily. Let me watch you go over," he whispered. "Let me have that blessed memory for the rest of my life."

And then her orgasm exploded through her, releasing her shackled heart and exposing her new love for him like an open book never to be closed again.

Chapter Ten

City of Bath—two weeks later

Andrew drew in a deep breath and pushed open the door to his father's bedroom. He nodded to the earl's devoted manservant who had leapt to his feet.

"You can leave us, Buckley."

The servant respectfully dipped his head. "Yes, sir."

The door clicked closed behind him and Andrew walked to his father's bedside. Nearing the age of sixty, the Earl of Marshfield still boasted a thick head of hair and barely wrinkled skin. Although these days the dark hair was peppered with streaks of silver and the faint lines gathered like sunbursts at the corners of his eyes, he was still an attractive man. Until recently. Until his pallor had turned almost grey and his body had shed over fifty pounds making the earl look beyond his years seemingly overnight.

His once muscular and masterful physique lay shrunken and useless under the blankets; his head lolled to the side upon a snow-white pillow. Andrew took a cloth from the bedside cabinet and wiped the drool shining in a thin rivulet down the side of his father's chin. The earl stirred and his eyelids fluttered open.

Andrew took his hand. "Father. It is Andrew."

His father's eyes slowly widened until recognition registered in their watery gaze. "Son. What are you doing here? Did Buckley send for you?"

Andrew smiled. "No, so there is no need to

171

reprimand the poor man. I came of my own accord."

"Why?"

"Why? Do I need a reason to visit my own father?"

The earl tried and failed to sit further up in the bed. His weak body floundered for its former strength but there was little left onto which to lever himself. Andrew waited, careful not to jump too soon to his father's aid lest he be struck down by the force of a proud man's tongue. After a failed second attempt, Andrew leaned over the bed and clasped his father's shoulders, their eyes making silent contact. After a tense two or three seconds, his father's gaze changed from steadfast determination to reluctant surrender. The nod of his head was barely perceptible.

Once he was settled comfortably, Andrew reached for a hard-backed chair sitting against the wall and placed it beside the bed. He sat down, his forearms on the bed, his hand gripping his father's. The earl coughed, the sound hollow in his chest.

"What is it, son? What is it you have to tell me? Have you good news?"

Andrew drew in a breath through flared nostrils and looked down at their joined hands. "It is not what you wish to hear, I'm afraid, Father."

"And how do you know what I wish to hear?"

"I am not yet engaged." Andrew ejected the words as though his tongue would be scalded if he let them linger in his mouth a moment longer. He lifted his head.

His father stared straight back at him. His once vibrant blue eyes were now quietly somber. Their luster was lacking but their intelligence ample nonetheless.

"I see."

The clatter of carriage wheels running over cobble stones filtered through the open window;

along with the shout of a flower girl selling her wares to the late evening walkers and passers-by. Andrew wondered if his father could hear the beat of his son's troubled heart over these familiar sounds— or the turbulent thoughts running through his head which seemed louder than everything else combined. It didn't matter whether the answer he'd come here for today was yes or no. Andrew's decided path was laid down in stone and there was little his father or anyone else could do to break it. The foundation in which they lay was too strong, too set with conviction to be destroyed.

"And that is all you came here to say?"

Andrew looked up. "No. There is more."

"I thought as much. You have the look of your mother when something…" He lifted an eyebrow. "….or someone has burrowed their way into your heart and soul, managing to consume every part of you. She had the same look each and every time she set eyes on you. Well? Am I right?"

"Yes, sir."

"And which is it? A something or a someone?"

"A someone."

His father's eyes widened. "A someone? Yet the first thing you say upon waking me is you are not engaged? What has happened to the young man I know so well? The man who takes what he wants and goes after his desires with both hands? You are confusing me."

"It is not as straightforward as that, Papa."

"No? Well, how can someone you love—"

Andrew snapped his head up. "Love?"

"Yes, son, love. How can someone you love be the cause of such strain on that handsome face of yours and you have not claimed her as yours? What is wrong with you? Surely you do not doubt Lady Tasmin's feelings for you? This is not the son I know and love." He started to cough, each hack catching in his chest and throwing angry color into his face.

Andrew leapt to his feet and filled the glass at his bedside with water. He cupped the back of his father's head and lifted the glass to his lips. Guilt scratched at the surface of his skin like the itchy boils of the smallpox as his father gulped at the water. What would it do to his father to hear Andrew confess his love—*his love*—was for a housemaid and not the woman the earl suggested? How would he confess that a marriage was not forthcoming in the time his father had left on earth?

The wretched coughing came to an abrupt halt and the earl waved Andrew back to his seat. "Tell me. Tell me what it is that has you looking so remorseful? Maybe this someone is not an unrequited love but a family or person in need? Do you wish to help someone? I am right, am I not? You do not only follow your mother in looks, Andrew."

Andrew shook his head. "It is not a case of need, Father. Well, at least not the need of which you refer."

"Stop talking in riddles and tell me what it is you have come here to say. My time is limited, is it not?"

"Papa, please..." Andrew stopped when he caught the weak smile playing at the earl's lips. He managed a smile of his own. "Very amusing."

"Well, come on then. Out with it."

Drawing in a shaky breath, Andrew clasped his father's hand. "Firstly I have to confess something that happened almost twenty years ago. I have never owned up to my error but this person...this person I talk of has somehow given me the strength to find the words I need to tell you. I need to tell you, Father, in the hope that it will release me from shackles that tighten each day."

"Twenty years ago? What is it you speak of? There is nothing I do not know about you that could possibly have been such a burden that you would carry it for such a time."

Andrew met his eyes. "I killed mother, Papa."

Silence descended like a curtain of incrimination. Dark and heavy and unbearably cruel. Andrew's shoulders shook with the effort it took not to crumble beneath its weight. His heart beat accelerated as his fingers curled tighter around his father's hand—the most solid anchor he had in the world. But slowly, that anchor slipped from his grip and settled itself cold and unforgiving in the Earl of Marshfield's lap.

"You talk nonsense," he said abruptly.

Andrew shook his head. "It was me. I was the reason she died that day."

Anger flashed like splinters of ice in his father's eyes. "Why are you doing this? Why are you doing this to me? To yourself?"

"I am not *doing* anything to you, Papa. I am freeing myself from the guilt I have carried for too long. It's time to be free of it."

"What guilt? What is it you think you have done?"

"I killed her through stupidity, admittedly childhood stupidity, but stupidity all the same. I have to accept my responsibility if I am ever to live a life free from the pain. I realize that now." He took a breath and wiped a hand over his perspiring face. "She has changed me, Papa."

"Who? This love?"

Andrew nodded. "Yes. This love. She makes me want to be a better person, a stronger person. And most of all, she makes me want to release the past and look only to the future. I love her and want to be with her. I want to stop adhering to promises I cannot keep and only agree to prospects that I know I can fully carry out."

His father looked at him, his eyes shrouded with

confusion. "I commend the woman who has brought this sense of pride so forcefully to the forefront of who you are. But was it not there all the time? Is it not the way I raised you to be? Have I really been blind to what you have been feeling for the last twenty years?" His voice cracked.

Andrew reached once more for his father's hand and squeezed. "No, no, you haven't. I have denied these feelings for a long time, Papa. None of this is your fault."

The earl stared at his son before reaching out a frail hand and cupping Andrew's jaw. "Then tell me what it is that has troubled you."

Andrew drew in a shaky breath and released it in a rush. "My only intention was to help Mother that day, to show her how grown up I was. I thought I tightened the girth on her horse but I couldn't have buckled it correctly. The reason her saddle slipped and she was thrown from her horse was because of me." His father's face blurred. "I killed your wife, Papa. I promised her before she got on the horse that I hadn't touched the girth. I promised her. And she tousled my hair and kissed my cheek…"

"Son…"

"Then she mounted the horse, turned and winked, looking at me as though I was her everything. Her pride and joy, the love of her life—"

"Son…"

"And then not twenty minutes later the saddle came loose, and she was flung into the air like nothing more than a rag doll." His gaze scanned his father's face in pleading. "Can you remember how they all spoke? Can you remember how everyone said she looked like a rag doll?"

"Enough!"

The earl expelled the command on another barrage of hoarse coughing that snapped Andrew's attention back from his anguish. He reached for the glass of water and lifted it once more to his father's mouth. Shame flooded Andrew's body, forcing him to realize his torrent of words had been nothing more than an exodus of his own ingrained guilt. Did his father need to hear such things on his deathbed?

"Father, I apologize for causing you such distress. But I had to explain the reason I cannot go on with the promise I made to you."

His father grimaced as he swallowed the water before dropping back against the cushion. "What promise?"

"The promise to marry Lady Tasmin and conceive an heir before you..." Andrew hesitated. "...before you die. The only way I have managed to seek penance for Mother's death was by never breaking a promise I have made to another person. Some way or another I have always managed to deliver...until now."

"But I never insisted on any such promise. Never." His father lifted a shaking hand to his brow.

"Well, no, not in so many words."

"Never! I would never insist on such a thing. What sort of man do you think I am? No, you are wrong, Andrew. Very, very wrong."

"But—"

His father lifted his hand in the air. "And you did not kill your mother. You are insane to think such things. What is the matter with you?"

Andrew shook his head. "I did. As much as you want to believe—"

"You had better listen to me, my boy. The loosened girth was re-buckled before she even mounted the horse."

Andrew's breath rushed out of him as though his father had punched him full pelt in the stomach. "What?"

"For God's sake, man. You never left the stables. You were always there playing or making a nuisance

177

of yourself. You insult me, your mother and the staff to think any horse would not be carefully checked and double-checked before leaving the stables carrying such precious cargo as my Lucille."

Andrew pushed himself to his feet and thrust his hands into his hair. "Then why? Why did I hear people talking about the girth? The way the saddle slipped from the horse as though its back was smeared with grease?"

The earl closed his eyes and for a moment Andrew could not move. His father lay gaunt and drained, his hairline dotted with perspiration and his hands lifeless at his sides. A burst of inappropriate laughter from a group of drunken revelers outside propelled Andrew into action. He rushed forward and gripped his father's shoulders.

"Father? God, no. Father!" He shook him.

Slowly, the earl's eyes opened. They were shiny with unshed tears. "She was a risk taker, Andrew. A woman so full of gumption I had no idea from one day to the next what she would do. Have you ever met a woman like that?"

"Have I...?" Andrew smiled. "Yes, yes I have."

He shook his head. "No you haven't. Else your mother's ring would already be on her finger. The morning of the accident was one of the happiest moments of her life. She was convinced a new baby would be arriving in the spring."

Horror sunk into Andrew's veins like glue, halting his heart and sealing his airway. "She was with child?"

"No. But she suspected it. She awoke and announced it was possible. All she wanted to do that day was ride into the country. She wanted to breathe the fresh air and rejoice with the world."

Andrew dropped his gaze to the floor unable to look at his father's reminiscent expression a moment longer. He had the most happy, faraway look in his eyes yet Andrew knew as he retold the day's events in chronological order, that look would turn to anguish and pain. Pain that he had put there.

"It was Lucille who took the decision to stand up in her stirrups," the earl continued. "And it was Lucille who threw her hands in the air in joyful abandon. And it was the cruelest, most horrible twist of fate that a gaggle of blasted, frenzied geese chose to burst into flight at the exact same moment and soared across the lake in front of her. The horse bolted, Andrew, and the girth somehow broke. Your mother was an expert rider but no one could have stopped that horse. No one."

Andrew dropped his face into his hands as the hot sting of tears burned behind his eyes. "Oh, my God. All these years. All these years I thought it was me."

The rustle of blankets and the stifled groan of his father's exertions made Andrew drop his hands. His father leaned forward and grasped Andrew's arm.

"It was not your fault. Do you understand me?"

Andrew looked at him. "But—"

"I said, do you understand me?"

Sincerity burned in his eyes. It had to be true. Never, not once had his father lied to him. He was not the type of man to shield his son from the despairs and disappointments of life through emotion and love. Andrew felt something lift ever so slightly from his shoulders. The burden didn't leave him altogether but a tiny part of it dissolved. The remainder would take longer; but for now, the tiny shift was enough to allow the air in his lungs to function a little easier.

He nodded. "Yes. I understand."

"Good." His father collapsed back against the pillows.

For several moments, neither father nor son

spoke. They both looked to the sounds coming from
the window, lost in their own thoughts.

"So who is she?" The earl's gruff and demanding
voice broke the silence.

Andrew started. "Sir?"

"The woman you claim has the same gumption
as Lucille. Who is she?"

Heat seared Andrew's cheeks and his heart
turned over in his chest as Lily's face filled his
mind's eye. A small smile tugged at his lips. "I'm not
sure your heart will take what I have to tell you."

"For God's sake man, get on with it. Nothing will
surprise me. Not anymore."

****

Lily woke and her thoughts automatically
turned to the only person who had filled her mind
for every hour of the day and night for the last
fourteen days. Ever since the night Andrew had
taught her the joys that lay deep within her body,
she'd thought of nothing else. Neither of them had
referred to it since. Yet the sexual tension hung
between them like an invisible curtain. The entire
scenario was one of novel, melodramatic proportions.
It was not real life—it was dangerous, selfish and
foolhardy.

Straying her hand beneath the covers, she
fingered the warmth of her newly awakened
womanhood. Her eyelids fluttered closed and
Andrew's face appeared behind them. Red-hot desire
in ocean-blue eyes. The blend confused and excited
her, thrilled and terrified her at the same time.
Danger lay like a burning stick of dynamite behind
the escalation of their relationship. If Lily did not
snuff it out immediately—today—it would explode,
maiming and possibly destroying everyone in its
path.

As much as her heart ached to be leaving him,
her yearnings were too strong to be ignored.

Yearnings that grew each day. She circled her hardened nub, a sigh escaping her lips. Contrary to what her mother and a hundred and one other women had led her to believe, Lily had felt neither shame nor guilt since their candlelit liaison. In a single night, Andrew had shown her what real physical attraction could entail. Did a relationship between a man and woman always have to revolve around propriety? Or future security?

Lily pulled her hand from its exploration. It dropped limply to the mattress as she opened her eyes.

Maybe, maybe not. But the love she had for him couldn't possibly survive. She'd lied to him from the outset; he would never trust her and she couldn't blame him. Would she ever trust or love someone who'd had ample opportunity to confess their true identity, the motivations behind their actions, yet chose to never utter a word? She could have risked his wrath, a sacking time and again by confessing the truth when they were alone but she didn't. Why? Because such a huge part of her still wanted to live her own life, her own way and that would not be possible without money—or as a viscount's lover.

Her mind turned to Lady Tasmin and the way she had risked her own banishment by intercepting Lord Winchester's advances on a mere servant. He was her cousin, her bond and association to Andrew. Lord Winchester could have quite easily struck her if he had so wished. Yet Lady Tasmin had taken Lily protectively in her arms and held fast.

She was a strong woman, a good woman. Who was Lily to come in here and destroy Lady Tasmin's dreams of a solid and affluent future? She had been good to Lily from the first day they met. The woman had a history here, a foot firmly in the door. Lily was a new presence, maybe even eventually an unwelcome one.

Lily squeezed her eyes shut. Neither Lord Winchester nor Lady Tasmin had returned to the manor since that fateful night. Nor had Andrew ventured to visit either of them at their residences. The estrangement between life-long friends and potential sweethearts came to rest at Lily's feet as much as it did Andrew's. But it would be Lily who would be solely blamed, of that she was certain.

She swallowed.

She'd tell Nicholas and the others she was leaving before they had the slightest inkling of the huge changes happening under the roof of Cotswold Manor. The simple truth was, Andrew had left her wanting more and she must leave before things became even worse.

With her mind made up, Lily flung back the blankets and jumped from the bed. Nothing had ever swayed her once she made a final decision and nothing—or nobody—would dissuade her from this either.

Half an hour later, she walked into the kitchen. Mrs. Harris was serving sausage and eggs, bread and butter to Nicholas and Robert. It was just the four of them today as Jane had left the manor the night before to spend the day with her family. Lily's stomach rumbled.

"Good morning, everyone." She sat down and smiled her thanks to Mrs. Harris as she slid sausage and eggs onto an empty plate in front of her.

"Lily, good morning," Nicholas said. "I trust you slept well?"

"Yes, thank you."

"Good, because we have a full day ahead of us today." He leaned back in his chair, pushing his empty plate to the side and picking up his mug of tea.

She chewed her mouthful of food and swallowed. "Indeed we do. I want to give the dining room, the drawing room and the conservatory a thorough going over this morning, and then this afternoon—"

"Lily, for goodness sake, it is not the cleaning alone that I talk of."

The disparaging tone of his voice alerted Lily to yet another unexpected obstacle appearing on her carefully planned timetable. She had designed to leave everything in the best possible state before announcing her resignation. Hopefully the shining silver and polished wood would act as a buffer against Nicholas' wrath.

She frowned. "Then what is it you speak of?"

He put down his mug and grinned. "I have come up with the most ingenious plot."

"Plot?"

"Indeed. I have every intention of gently persuading the master to call on Lord Winchester once he returns from Bath."

A heavy weight dropped low into her belly at the thought of seeing Lord Winchester again. As long as he visited the baron and not the other way round, all would be well. She forced her lips into a smile. "Is the master returning from Bath today then? I had no idea."

"Yes, with good news regarding the earl, I hope. If his father is feeling better, my lord may well be receptive to paying a visit to his best friend, don't you think?"

"Yes. Of course."

"So I can trust you will do your very best to get things in order here in case my lord opts to invite the baron to the manor instead?"

Lily forced a chunk of sausage down her suddenly dry throat. "Why would he do that?"

Nicholas frowned. "Why would who do what?"

"Why would Lord Winchester come here if you are encouraging the master to visit him at his own house?"

Nicholas laughed, shook his head. "What a strange thing to ask! You know as well as I do, it is entirely the lord's decision where they meet. I cannot possibly tell him where to meet. All I want is for the two of them to start talking again. I have tried and tried to understand how everything ended up in such a dismal mess but the master resolutely refuses to discuss it."

"You have no idea what the quarrel was about?"

"No idea at all. They have, of course, had misunderstandings before but this is different. Whatever caused this discord between them is serious."

"But surely they will make amends in time? They have been friends since childhood."

"Well, yes, but what happens in the meantime? What about Lady Tasmin?"

Lily put down her knife and fork and pressed a trembling hand to her stomach as a wave of guilt swept through her. "Has the master said he does not wish to see her?"

"No, no, but he has yet to visit her since she left in such a hurry. I could see she was very close to crying when she left that night and I told the master as much the next morning."

"And what did he say?"

"That I was mistaken; but I know what I saw. Something upset her dreadfully."

Lily turned her gaze back to her plate, feigning interest in the increasingly unappetizing meal sitting half-eaten in front of her. "But surely the master will not allow his quarrel with Lord Winchester to affect his relationship with Lady Tasmin? His feelings for her have nothing to do with his friendship with the baron."

"Feelings?" He gave a hoot of laughter. "Feelings have nothing to do with it. Don't you see? Lord Winchester introduced her to him. He is pivotal to

184

their courtship. Why, I fear the master will no doubt drop her like a stone if the baron is no longer involved." He leaned forward, his eyes bulging in their growing panic. "It has taken weeks...no, months for the master to show the slightest interest in her and now this! He needs to produce an heir, Lily. The earl is dying and my lord must continue the line else risk losing everything. He knows his duty is cast in stone yet he seems intent on allowing it all to slip through his fingers."

Mrs. Harris sat her bulk down heavily beside him. "Oh, stop fussing, Nicholas. You'll give yourself a hernia," she snapped. "The master's a man, isn't he? He doesn't need you, or Winchester, or anyone else for that matter telling him who he should or shouldn't marry. He'll choose the woman he wants to bear his children when he's good and ready. Give him time. And when he does, we'll all have to suffer her whoever she is."

Lily kept her gaze on her food and waited for her heartbeat to slow. The less she participated in this conversation the better. Her color might deceive her; her eyes might show their distress. Suddenly the thought of Andrew looking at another woman, let alone touching her made the little food Lily had consumed churn in her stomach. This brought forward the truth with such painful clarity. Lily could not possibly ignore it. She had to get out of there—and fast.

She leapt to her feet, plastering a smile on her face. "Right, well, I'm going to make a start on the grates in the drawing room and dining room. They need clearing out and rebuilding and as it's Jane's day off—"

"Sit down, child," Mrs. Harris said. "You are not going anywhere until you finish that breakfast. You're losing weight faster than a greyhound chasing a rabbit."

Lily forced a laugh and waved a dismissive hand before turning toward the door. "Nonsense. Now, I really must get on—"

"Don't you think we haven't noticed what's going on with you, young lady?" The cook sniffed.

Lily came to an abrupt stop. *Oh, lord, oh, lord.* They knew. They knew about Andrew and her. Feeling as though she was moving in slow motion, Lily turned. Her smile ever so slightly wobbled. "What do you mean?"

"You."

"What about me?"

"Well, you're working yourself to the bone for a start. Running here, there and everywhere. Staying up late, getting up early. The weight's dropping off you and it don't look good on a girl your age. The master is constantly asking after you. By God, if I hadn't insisted you were fine the night before last, I swear the man would've come up to your room to check on you. I'm just glad he slept at his father's last night, at least I could sleep easy that the two of you weren't up to no good." She emitted a booming laugh.

"Mrs. Harris!" Nicholas snapped. "Don't be so ridiculous. And you have the audacity to accuse me of being the melodramatic one."

She got up and took his plate. "I'm telling you. He cares about Lily. He cares a lot."

"As he does us all." Nicholas stood up and took Lily by the elbow. "Come on. Let's get to work before Mrs. Harris casts us both in the lead roles of her imaginary production of *Romeo and Juliet*."

Lily let Nicholas steer her towards the door.

"He cares for her, I tell you. I ain't blind, you know," Mrs. Harris said.

Lily stumbled out with the cook's words echoing in her ears.

Chapter Eleven

Lily stood at the storage cupboard door and watched Nicholas as he went on his way. Thankful to be alone once more, she quickly grabbed a dustpan and brush, polish and cloth before hurrying into the dining room. Closing the door firmly behind her, she embarked on her cleaning duties with abandon. She scrubbed the silver until it shone, polished the brass until it squeaked beneath her rag and wiped every surface smooth and clean from dust. But it still did nothing to appease the dread that Mrs. Harris sensed the attraction between her and Andrew.

But what would the woman do if she became convinced? Lily needed to leave today and save Andrew the humiliation of society knowing he cavorted with a servant.

She sat back on her haunches and wiped an arm across her perspiring brow.

Their solitary encounter would be seen as sordid and immoral. But it didn't feel that way, not for one single moment. And nobody would be privy to either of their protestations—if Andrew ever subjected himself to such a prospect, of course. The fact was Lily was known only as a maid and Andrew a soon-to-be earl. The scandal could ruin his reputation forever. She refused to allow that to happen to him.

Lily started as Nicholas entered the room. She quickly turned her concentration to brushing the remainder of the ash from the grate. Her hands shook and her heart raced. All she wanted was to be left alone to work out a strategy while ensuring the house was as clean and tidy as she could possibly make it. Her last offering to Andrew would be through the sweep of a brush rather than the touch of her hand. She blinked against the stinging in her eyes.

What a mess. A mess of her own doing. Her mother wanted to marry her off to the dreadful Candleford. They couldn't have forced her because she was of age. But by refusing, Lily had risked damaging her parents' reputation. Even though she'd promised to return if her bid for independence failed, the thought of going home made Lily sick to her stomach. She'd escaped and could not possibly return—but what had she run headlong into? A catastrophe of such manic proportions that she saw no way out without casualty.

The happy-go-lucky tune Nicholas whistled so merrily as he ticked off his duties on a notebook, scraped on Lily's nerves like a fork against china.

"Can't you stop that?" she snapped.

He turned to face her, his raised eyebrows hitched almost to his forehead. "Well, your good mood didn't last long, did it?"

Scowling, she turned back to the fireplace but still felt his gaze boring into the top of her head. The brush trembled in her hand as she slapped it back and forth, praying he sensed her foul mood was in little chance of improving and make his escape.

Instead, he held his hand out in front of her and Lily silently cursed her outburst.

"Come on, stand up," he said. "I knew something wasn't quite right at breakfast. You have a funny look about you. Now then. What is it? What's happened?"

"Nothing." She kept her gaze on the grate.

"Lily. Look at me." His voice softened as he eased the wire brush from her fingers and placed it on the hearth. "Mrs. Harris was only teasing before, you know."

She snapped her head up. "Pardon?"

His smile reached all the way to his eyes. "About you and the master. What a thing to say!"

She forced a smile and slipped her hand into his and let him pull her to her feet. "Oh, I know she was."

"Then what is it?"

For a moment she said nothing. Instead she studied his face in a bid to remember every detail; she'd create a lifelike painting she could hang on the inner recesses of her memory forever like a treasured piece of art. She had only known Nicholas three months, but didn't doubt he'd yield the uncanny ability to bury himself deep into her heart. And now she had no choice but trust him completely. What else could she do when she felt so incapable of carrying the burden of her feelings alone?

She blew out a heavy breath. "I don't know how to tell you."

He frowned. "But you must. You look so anxious."

"I...this is so hard."

"What is it?" He took her hand. "My goodness, you're crying."

She blinked and felt the warmth of her tears spill onto her cheeks. She lifted her fingers to swipe them away just as the drawing room door burst open.

They both turned and the sight of Andrew standing there had Nicholas leaping two feet away from her—as though Lily had prodded him with the fire poker.

She froze. Andrew strode into the room, smiling and smelling of fresh air. Lily's heart lurched. He looked so handsome, so utterly revived and refreshed. She longed to know how it felt to sleep so peacefully and wake looking the way he did at that moment.

He stared directly at her. Grinning, his brilliant blue eyes danced with schoolboy mischief. Lily struggle to not return the infectious smile that sent her stomach into a mass of knots and tangles. She wiped her fingers under her eyes and smoothed the crumpled folds of her skirt before clasping her hands in front of her.

"Sir, how lovely to see you," she said, pulling back her shoulders. "I trust you enjoyed your visit with your father?"

"I did, Lily. He seems a little better even."

The way he looked at her made Lily's skin grow sensitive. Her need for him was even more urgent than she'd dare acknowledge. She had to leave. Immediately. "Well, that is wonderful, sir. Really wonderful. Was it me or Nicholas you wanted?" she asked, her tone abrupt.

He arched an eyebrow. "You, Lily, it is you I want."

Her cheeks burned hot. The sexual connotation and hungry tone of his voice was so flagrant, he might as well have strode across the room and caressed her bosom. She cleared her throat.

"Is there something I can do for you?"

He blinked, and threw a quick glance at Nicholas as though remembering himself. He turned back and straightened his face to a more somber expression. "Yes, yes, there is. I...um...I will be making a trip into town today," he announced with exaggerated fanfare. "I thought it a good idea to purchase a little something with which to appease Lady Tasmin's disappointment after what happened when she was last here."

Nicholas gasped. "Oh, sir, you are to visit Lady Tasmin? That is good news."

Lily bit down on her lip as Andrew threw an impatient glare at his butler. "Do calm yourself,

190

Nicholas. Why did you think I wouldn't come to visit her in due course? I at least need to ask after her welfare after her hastened departure from our last dinner if nothing else."

"Yes, yes, of course." Nicholas bowed.

"Anyway, as I was saying," Andrew turned his gaze back to Lily, "I wish to buy her a present but have no idea about such things. So I would very much like you to accompany me into town if you will."

Lily stared at him. And then she stared at Nicholas...and then back to Andrew. "Me?"

"Yes, you."

"But, I couldn't possibly..." The sentence trailed off as words failed her. She looked to the carpet.

"And why not?"

Lily didn't need to look at him to know he was smiling. Again, she felt the urge to curse. It shocked her when words she didn't even know were in her vocabulary ran through her mind on an endless train of profanity. The silence lingered on. Birdsong drifted in through the open window and the grandfather clock standing in the corner gonged the ninth hour.

She tried to speak. She opened her mouth but nothing came out. Town? Had he meant Bath? Why, oh, why hadn't she just sneaked out of the house in the dead of night and been done with it. Now what would she do? This was the end of her pretence. Maybe he did not believe Lord Winchester's allegations about her, but when she was recognized in town while carrying his packages and thus exposed as a fraud, he would counteract his own embarrassment by publicly humiliating her. He would shout from the rooftops about her subterfuge and her family's name would be ruined.

"Lily?"

She jumped and looked up. His face was etched

with concern as he took a slow step toward her and then stopped, his outstretched hand dropping to his side.

"Are you feeling all right?" he asked. "Your face is dreadfully pale."

She tried to speak but her larynx had stopped functioning and only a mere squeak came from her open mouth. She threw a hurried glance at Nicholas, beseeched him for help but he stood stock still, staring wide-eyed at Andrew as though his master had dropped his breeches and danced the highland fling. In short, Nicholas appeared in a worse state of mind than she.

She had to think! A man like Andrew Baxter would never humiliate another person. He would ask questions, try to understand. She must tell him—now.

"Sir, I..."

"Yes?"

But what she should have said evaporated on her tongue. "Would not Nicholas be better able to assist you in such an important decision?" she said instead. "My experiences in such things as buying finery are limited to say the least."

Complete and utter coward, Elizabeth Caughley.

A flash of color appeared above the snow-white collar of his shirt as his smile dissolved. He cleared his throat and his jaw hardened.

"I would like you to accompany me. I feel a female point of view is imperative. Would a trip into town not make a welcome change from the monotony of cleaning and running around after me?"

Her cheeks burned. "Well, yes, I don't mean to be ungracious."

"Or is the thought of sharing my company for the day the cause of your uncharacteristic hesitation?"

She heard and felt the mock simultaneously.

She met his eyes. They told her nothing of what he thought but Lily knew that this request broached no argument. It did not matter what she said, he would find a plausible way to make this trip possible. This confirmed any doubt that he knew she was here on false pretenses and now he wanted her alone to demand an explanation.

Her stomach rolled. She dipped her head. "I apologize, my lord. I would be honored to accompany you. The change would be welcome."

His face immediately softened, his eyes brightening. "Good, good. That's settled then."

After a long moment, Lily looked to Nicholas as Andrew seemed reluctant to leave. Instead of making a retreat for the door, the viscount continued to grin at her while tipping back and forth on the balls of his feet. Ignoring the fact he looked completely adorable, Lily concentrated her gaze on Nicholas. But he didn't as much as glance at her. The man had not moved an inch from his open mouthed, wide-eyed stance.

Turning back to Andrew, Lily's heart swelled to see him looking so elated. Refraining from rushing forward and kissing the idiotic smile from his lips, she took a deep breath. "Thankfully," she said loudly, "I brought at least one dress with me that will be acceptable for a town visit."

Both men jumped from their trances.

Andrew cleared his throat and pulled back his shoulders. "Well, that is just excellent." He turned to Nicholas, once more all business, his face pulled into an expression of authority. "I have asked Robert to bring my personal gig to the front entrance shortly. Please let both Lily and I know when it is ready."

Nicholas blanched. "You're driving yourself, sir?"

Lily's stomach dropped. What was he thinking? They were to make the trip without a driver? But Andrew was without an ounce of reservation. His smile stretched to a grin and Lily silently cursed the tingle in her chest. The man was so infuriatingly desirable even when it seemed he'd completely lost his mind.

"And why not, good man?" he asked Nicholas. "I am one of the most able riders this side of Wiltshire. I'll ensure Lily's safety, don't you worry."

"Well, yes, I wasn't referring to your riding ability, sir. I—"

Andrew raised a hand and turned to Lily. "Splendid. I will see you shortly then." His eyes glinted with such buoyant anticipation that Lily's stomach gave an equally expectant tilt. She bit back the smile threatening to break out on her lips. He really did have the most maddening effect on her sensibilities.

"Um, sir, there is just one more thing." She stepped forward.

"Yes?"

She looked to Nicholas and back again. "Are we to go to Bath or Bristol?"

He raised his eyebrows. "Does it matter?"

Nicholas hurried forward and dug his fingers into her forearm. "Lily, the master is most generous to even consider taking you with him into town."

"Nicholas, please," Andrew said. "I am quite happy with either. Which would you prefer, Lily? Bath or Bristol?"

She swallowed, shifted from one foot to the other. "Bristol," she managed.

He clapped his hands together, making her flinch. Her nerves were stretched to breaking point.

"Bristol it is then!"

He turned and strode from the room leaving Lily to exhale a rush of breath she didn't even know she'd held. Nicholas collapsed onto a chaise longue with his hand clasped to his forehead like a swooning damsel.

****

Andrew paced back and forth along the same four feet area of gravel driveway for the umpteenth time in the last ten minutes. He did not know what he would say to her or how he would tell her what he knew. Once he'd told his father of his suspicions regarding Lily's background and the depth of his feelings for her, the earl had gained a pleasing and astounding lease on life. In fact, he had insisted Andrew, "Grow a pair of damn scrotum and find out for sure who this woman is before she walks out of your house without looking back."

A bubble of laughter welled up in Andrew's chest. His father was a man who took no prisoners and although Andrew had not even slightest intention of letting Lily go prior to visiting his father, his words had certainly propelled him into action. All he worried about now was her resenting him for investigating her life, and thinking of him as nothing more than a stuck up aristocrat who happened to live in a big house with an even larger ego.

Drawing in a shaky breath, Andrew reached into the inner pocket of his jacket and withdrew a cigar. His hand shook as his mind wandered back to the night they had shared in her room. The look in her eyes when he'd brought her to climax had been almost too much to bear. The need to take her, to feel her body surround his had been so overwhelming, he'd forced himself to leave before he ravished her right there and then.

He patted the pockets of his trousers for a book of matches, purposely dragging his thoughts from Lily's physicality and back to the reality of her masquerade. His father knew many people in Bath and Andrew had hung all his hopes on his father recognizing at least something about Lily from one or two of Andrew's numerous portraits he'd drawn of her. Portraits he had labored on under the fading candlelight in his room late into the night—every night for the last three months. There were some with her naked, some with her dressed, others of her smiling, and others with her face drawn into the avid concentration she always wore whenever she listened to what others had to say. Lily, Lily, Lily.

And his hopes had come to fruition. His father had studied the portraits closely and mentioned she looked very much like the lawyer, Gerald Caughley. Andrew had leapt on the possible lead like it was the anchor to a capsizing ship. First thing in the morning, he had called on a dear friend who enjoyed the social gossip like he was a frivolous woman instead of a man and quizzed him about the Caughley family. The friend in question had confirmed the earl's identification. The youngest Caughley daughter had taken off, not three or four months before on a tour of Europe with extended family and yes, she looked exactly like the girl in Andrew's portrait.

Not wanting to invite any more questions, Andrew had bid his friend good day and left. Now here he was waiting for Lily—or Elizabeth—and wondering just what he would say to her. He knew the truth but deep down Andrew wanted the confession to come from her. The last thing he wanted to do was beleaguer her into knowing what had led her to him. He wanted her to explain everything in her own time and words. He looked up to her bedroom window.

Even if he had to wait longer than his body could stand. He would not risk her bolting like a mare from a stable. He wanted her to stay here even if it meant her mask stayed in place for the foreseeable future. *I do not just want her to stay—I* need *her to stay.*

He struck a match on the heel of his boot and

held it to the cigar. He blew at the end, watched it burn brighter and fade, burn and fade. Just like Lily; alive and unpredictable, beautiful to watch yet...yet maybe with the potential to burn and scar. He flicked the match away from him in a perfect arc, distracted and deep in thought. A few seconds later, the crunch of stone turned his head to the servants' entranceway.

And his breath caught. "My God," he whispered.

Her dress was of the deepest emerald green. Its cream lace collar fell in elongated triangles to meet at a point in the center of her tiny waist. The hem swished over the surface of the stones as she glided towards him. He swallowed and dropped the cigar unwanted to the ground. Mesmerized, he quashed it beneath his boot and straightened to his full height.

If he'd any doubt of her being a lady before, now he was certain. She had exuded nothing but grace since her first day at the manor. Whether dressed in her uniform of black and white or a high-necked nightgown, her allure was impossible to hide. He felt heat rise in his face when a sudden feeling of inferiority rushed over him to be in the presence of such beauty. He turned abruptly to open the door of the gig.

Her footsteps came to a stop beside him. The fresh scent of soap mixed with something that was entirely Lily filled his nostrils. He inhaled deeply before turning to meet eyes blacker than tar.

"Lily." Her name came out on his exhalation and self-consciousness caused the heat on his face to burn deep. He coughed. "I mean...you look...you look just lovely. No one will ever think you a maid."

She smiled shyly and Andrew's chest burned. Lifting her skirt with one hand, she clasped his offered hand with the other.

"Thank you," she said. "This the only day dress I brought from home and the last thing I want is to embarrass you."

He smiled. "Well, rest assured, there is little chance of that. I...I will be proud to have you walk beside me."

Her eyes softened and her smile widened. His gaze strayed to her hair. Without the hindrance of her house cap, the true beauty of it shone in all its splendor. She had pinned and styled the glossy strands in two simple twists lying neatly at the crown. A few ringlets fell on either side of her exquisite face and framed it to perfection. The burnished bronze danced and gleamed beneath the November sun. Andrew longed to remove the pins one by one so he could bury his face in her crowning glory.

"Sir, you are staring." She flicked a hesitant glance toward the house. "If you have changed your mind, I can return to my duties."

He tightened his grip on her hand. "No. I haven't changed my mind. Please. Won't you...?"

Easing her forward, her hand so small in his, he helped her into the gig and then pulled himself up beside her. She arranged her skirts around her as he picked up the reins. A trip with Lily. An entire day alone. There would be plenty of time to find out who she was and why she was here. He need not say anything yet. All would be revealed in good time.

He turned to the house. Mrs. Harris and Nicholas stood at the entranceway watching them. Their hands were lifted to their eyes against the sun. But he did not need to see their gazes to know their curiosity would be piqued to its height at the sight of their master and his maid sitting side by side like lovers.

"Turn and wave goodbye, Lily," he said with a smile.

"Sorry?"

He tilted his head toward the house and she

followed the gesture. Her falter was brief but evident. Then she lifted her hand. Fearful that she would ask to return to the house again and he'd be powerless to refuse her, Andrew commanded Portland, his favored stallion, forward with a slap of the leather reins against hardened muscle.

They traveled in silence until they were on the main Bristol road. The sun shone high in the sky and clear blue skies promised its longevity. Andrew breathed deeply. The late autumn air filled each pore of his skin, every inch of his blood. He settled Portland into a trot.

"You're very quiet. Are you all right?"

She turned her head from the passing scenery to face him. The sunlight behind her set her skin to a golden hue and made her hair shine in shades of copper and gold. Her mouth bore the faintest of smiles and the pure sight of her was as tempting as a taste of the finest chocolate. She flicked out her tongue to wet her lips and Andrew was undone.

She sighed. "I'm happier than I expected, that's all."

Relief relaxed his shoulders. She wanted to be here. "I would hope I am not that much of a dreaded companion?"

"Not at all."

"Good. Because I want you to enjoy today. You work hard and I am not one for taking my staff for granted."

"Yet I get the feeling you would not have asked Mrs. Harris to take this trip with you."

Her tone was gently teasing and Andrew smiled. "Caught."

"So why am I really here?"

His heart picked up speed and he turned to the road ahead. He should've guessed she would not hold back with her own questions. She was naturally inquisitive and forthright. Why in the world did he think he could control the unfolding of the day's events as far as Lily was concerned? The woman led her life her own way. Hadn't she made that perfectly clear despite trying to dilute her outbursts?

"Sir?"

He kept his eyes focused on the road. Before he even brought up the subject of her past, a more pressing issue itched at the tip of his tongue.

"Do you regret what happened between us?"

Silence.

It continued for so long, Andrew was forced to look at her. She stared at him. A flush of pink stained her cheeks. But her eyes flickered with the unmistakable flame of desire, unconcealed and honest despite the curtain of thick dark lashes surrounding them. His own desire immediately ignited.

"No, sir. I don't regret it." At last she looked away. "Do you think less of me for admitting such a thing?"

His penis twitched and a flame of arousal warmed his body. "On the contrary. I'm relieved to hear you say so."

She inhaled a breath. "I...I enjoyed the discovery." She turned to face him and smiled gently. "Very much."

Andrew swallowed. The temptation to touch her again made his heart race and his skin itch. His entire body hummed with the effort it took not to act upon his instinct. He longed to hear her whisper his name in breathless excitement and cling to his shoulders as she did in that darkened room.

"Nothing is more important to me right now than making my own way in life." She once more looked out to the countryside around them. "And you have armed me with the invaluable experience of...of sexual awareness that I never knew before. It will no doubt stand me in good stead in the future."

She might as well as have slapped his face hard enough for it to ricochet back on a neck of rubber. A ball of jealousy furled in his abdomen. The future? If she thought for one minute he'd stand by and ever let another man touch her the way he touched her...

"As I have said before..." She sighed nonchalantly. "All I want is independence, sir. The right to live my life my own way and follow my own path. Which brings me to something I need to tell you."

Now? She was going to confess her deception now? If she thought he'd allow her to walk away from him just like that, she was mistaken.

Andrew held up a hand hoping to silence her. "And how will the night we shared aid you in the future?" he demanded. "In what way will our sexual liaison help you on this road to *independence* you seem so keen to repeatedly remind me of?"

She turned to look at him, her eyes wide with confusion.

"Well?"

"I...you..." She faced the road and clasped her hands in her lap. "It means the mystery is now vanquished and so I will not make mistakes with whom I share my body."

"With whom you share...? My God, woman!"

She snapped her head around. "I beg your pardon, sir, but you have no right—"

"I have every right."

"No, sir. You promised there would be no further demands."

Their eyes locked. Andrew's heart raced inside his chest. Their ragged breaths were audible above the clatter of Portland's hooves and the rumbling of the carriage wheels over stones and bracken. Her eyes were two burning pools of blackened fury. He'd promised her. Promised. His mind whirled with the words he needed to say to her. The accusations he needed to make swirled together like a myriad of dangerous mistakes waiting to happen.

If I say the wrong thing she will leave and never come back.

He turned away and concentrated on leveling his breathing. After a few moments, he felt under control enough not to scare her. "You're right. I apologize. I have no right to voice my opinion on anything you may or may not do in the future. I promised no demands and I meant it. Forgive me, Lily. I...I care about you, I meant no umbrage."

He heard her breath of relief.

"Apology accepted," she said quietly.

He swallowed hard as his mind grappled for a subject change. "So..." he said. "What are your goals? What is it that equates to independence for you?" When she didn't answer, he turned. She looked at him with a mixed expression of sadness and regret. "Lily?"

She blinked and the sadness was replaced with optimism. "That is what I wish to tell you. I will be leaving Cotswold Manor by the end of the week to pursue my dream of living in Paris."

"What? What are you talking about?" His gaze whipped to her face to the road and back again. Fear tripped along his nerve endings making an icy line of perspiration moisten the neck of his shirt. "You can't just leave."

She defiantly tilted her chin. "Yes, sir, I can. I have a little amount of money saved—"

"And what is it you expect to find in Paris that you cannot here?"

"Why...happiness, sir."

A weight dipped in his chest as his anger gave way to defeat. "You are unhappy at the manor?"

The sudden gleam in her eyes was the evidence of unshed tears. He drew in a breath as he watched her and bit his teeth together so as not to say something he would later regret. This would be the worst possible time to tell her what he knew and ask her not to go.

"I just want to live my own life and regrettably it seems in England that is not possible," she said.

"How can you think that?" His hands loosened on the reins. "Are you not your own woman already? You can live the life you want here. Your mother and father will not put demands on you to marry someone you do not love. They will be pleased to see you marry regardless of who the gentleman is."

Her eyes widened. "Are you saying they'd be pleased to see me marry anyone?"

Oh, Bravo, Andrew. Now she's angrier than ever.

"Well, no, I'm not saying—"

"And you presume to think that I am happy to marry *anyone?*"

"I..."

"Anyone is better than no one to someone of my class, is that it?"

God, she was good. She was a woman of class; she knew it and now he knew it. Yet her demeanor, her values, screamed of a strong sense of personal pride. She was fantastic. She was an inspiration and he wanted her for his own with every fiber of his being.

He straightened in his seat. "That's exactly what I am saying."

"How dare you."

"I beg your pardon?" The urge to laugh battled inside him.

"I don't just want *anyone,*" she snapped. "I want to be with a man I love. A man who excites both my mind...and my body."

He stared at her. "Your body, Lily?"

She didn't turn away. "Yes, Andrew." She narrowed her eyes. "My body."

"Andrew?"

203

Her cheeks flamed red but she didn't falter but merely nodded. "Yes. Andrew."

Locking his gaze on her, he knew the time to ask her was now. He couldn't carry on with this charade. "Tell me who you really are, Lily Curtis."

Her beautiful dark eyes turned black, her mouth opened, then closed. Opened again and closed.

He slowed Portland to a walk. "Well?"

She looked straight ahead. "You are a fool to think I don't know you already know exactly who I am."

She never ceased to amaze him. "I see."

"Why else would you risk taking a maid into town with you? What other reason on earth could you have of sitting side by side with her like two lovers taking a ride in the park? Nicholas wanted to call the doctor but I knew you needed to talk to me alone."

"Fine. Well, your instinct is right." He felt his heart soften or maybe his reluctance to know more increased. "But you don't have to tell me anything now if you don't want to, you know. I want you to tell me when you're ready. I won't ask again in the interim."

She gave an inelegant sniff. "And am I to presume that once again you will want nothing from me in return?"

He looked from her eyes to her hair, to her lips and inhaled through flared nostrils. "I didn't say that," he murmured suggestively,

Her jaw tightened and yet another scarlet flush rose from her chest to her neck. "I am not a whore, sir."

The use of such a coarse word slapped him soundly in the face. "Of course you're not!" he exclaimed. "I would never think such—"

"Then why do you look at me like that?"

He couldn't stop staring at her. "I am looking at

you with love, not lust," he cried. "I look at you this way because I want you as my own." He grasped one of her hands that lay fisted in her lap and held it to his heart. "But not as a whore or a mistress. As a wife."

Chapter Twelve

"As a *wife*?" Lily snatched her hand from his and clutched it to her thundering heart. "Have you lost your mind?"

His smile was wider than the River Avon and fifty times as dangerous. "What do you say?"

An avalanche of emotions ran through every inch of her body in a tumble of confusion. "What do I say?" Her eyes darted over his face. "Nicholas is right. You *do* need a doctor."

"I am perfectly well, my love." He laughed.

"No, Andrew, you are not." She threw her arm into the air. "Will you please stop smiling at me like that?"

"Do you want me to prove a doctor is the last thing I need? Do you wish me to prove how in control of myself I am?"

She slid an inch or two away from him. "What do you mean by that?"

He tipped her a wink. Turning, he gave a firm yank on the reins and steered Portland down a muddy path and off of the main track. Lily gripped the side of the carriage. She rocked from left to right as they bumped along the deserted track. He looked so happy as though an invisible weight had been lifted from his shoulders and tossed from the gig.

Lily stared straight ahead, the idea of flinging herself over the side along with Andrew's abandoned burden battled inside her. *This is madness. Complete and utter madness.* Why would he have said such a thing? She had to put a stop to this cruel pretence. Why had she thought him incapable of such torment? Was he not a gentleman after all?

"I demand to know where you are taking me!" She panted; the hoped for bravado in her voice failed dismally as she jerked like a puppet on a string.

He smile widened. "You'll see."

The rush of low slung branches scratching along the sides of the gig snatched her ability to respond, whereas the higher boughs barely spared her gruesome decapitation. Biting down on her bottom lip, Lily surrendered to her fate. She had no idea what he planned to do but sensed this detour had not been on the agenda before they left the house. She so wanted to believe he was a good and honest man despite the evidence stacking against it.

Please don't let him have brought her to this deserted place with preconceived ideas of depravity. She stole a frightened glance at him. No, he wouldn't. Of course he wouldn't. Even though his face was flushed with the excitement of a schoolboy, this couldn't be his plan. He'd lost his mind, that was all. *Oh, fantastic rationalization, Lily.* He'd merely lost his mind!

She gave her head a curt shake in a bid to rid her mind of her sudden skepticism.

No. All would be well. He had proven himself again and again to be a man of insurmountable integrity and generosity of spirit.

The trees above opened, allowing a triangle of light to fall upon them and with it a longed-for yet distorted and vulgarly romantic notion occurred to her.

Could she believe he knew her real identity but still wanted her regardless? Unless she was a complete fool, there was more between them than lust. He liked and respected her.

A knot tightened in her abdomen. There was not a hint of self-satisfaction or barely-controlled lust in his expression. He looked liberated. Her skin tingled.

If his desires were sincere...they echoed in each and every part of her.

He drew Portland to an abrupt halt and Lily looked about her. They were deep inside the woods. The road could neither be seen nor heard. No one could possibly know they were there. The gig lurched as he jumped down from his seat to tether Portland's reins to one of the trees. Lily's cheeks burned as she shamelessly stared at the perfect curve of his firm backside as the material of his trousers stretched taut. She swallowed back a nervous giggle at the inexplicable flutter between her legs. She clamped her thighs together in a futile attempt to stem the sensation.

So much for her lustfulness.

He straightened and held out his hand to help her down from the carriage. She slipped her hand against the soft leather of his glove and jumped onto the mossy ground. She tipped her head back to look at him and then he took her by surprise when he dipped his. The kiss was soft and as light as the breeze whispering around them. For just a few seconds, their lips caressed and re-acquainted, enjoyed and surrendered. He met her smile as they parted.

"I fear I shall never stop looking at you," he said quietly.

"What are we doing? We cannot possibly be together."

He twisted one of the curls at the side of her face around his index finger. His gaze fixed upon it so adoringly that her stomach tightened to feel this admired. After a moment, he met her eyes. "Yes, Lily, we can. I know you come from a good, well-bred family. There is absolutely no reason to continue denying what this is between us."

"And what is between us? You are courting another woman, Andrew. A good woman. Despite every other reason why this cannot happen, I could never do this to Lady Tasmin. She has been so good to all of your staff. Even more so to me."

She took a few steps away from him and turned her back. She could not stand beneath his respectful gaze any longer. Just being here, alone with him like this was a huge treachery to Lady Tasmin and everyone else at the manor. Even though Lady Tasmin as good as admitted to Lord Winchester that she did not love Andrew, she did not deserve to have Lily stab her in the back. The woman had almost certainly saved her from the Baron's assault.

Lily jumped when Andrew's hands eased around her waist. She squeezed her eyes shut as he gently turned her around.

"Lily?"

She shook her head. "She doesn't deserve to have me steal everything that is rightly hers."

"Steal what is hers? What am I? A possession?"

Her eyes snapped open and she cupped her hand to his cheek. "No, no, of course not. I didn't mean—"

"Why are you making this so hard? Why are you not as happy as I am? Are my instincts so completely off kilter? Do you not want me?"

His eyes burned with passion yet teetered on the edge of despair. Despair that Lily knew with painful clarity she caused him. She dropped her hand from his face. "This is not what was supposed to happen, Andrew. I was supposed to leave. Be on a ship bound for France."

He gripped his hands tighter at her waist and shook her gently. "Listen to me. I am not forcing you into making a decision right now. I just want you to know that the pretence can stop. You can go home and I'll court and woo you with everything I have and feel." He grinned. "I'll meet your parents and wait for you to arrive at social gatherings like a love-struck youth."

Despite the turmoil battling a war inside of her, Lily laughed. "You are mad!"

He lifted her off her feet and pressed a kiss to her lips. "I am in love. Nothing more, nothing less."

She stared at him. "In love?"

His smile dissolved. "In love."

The soft tender love that swirled in the dark blue of his eyes evolved into something more primal with each passing breath. Lily's heart picked up speed and her nipples tightened against the confines of her bodice. The way he looked at her was lustful, exciting and infinitely powerful.

"I…"

"You what, Lily? Tell me," he murmured as he lowered his mouth to her neck.

"Oh." She tipped her head back, silently begging for more. "I love you too."

And then she gasped as his mouth sucked hard against her delicate skin. The combination of pain and pleasure ignited her body. Suddenly she was desperate to rip open her clothes if he did not. Arousal thumped through her body at such a speed she suspected he felt her pulse against his lips. She sighed as his hand stroked the curve of her breast above the hem of her bodice.

"Lily, Lily, Lily." He murmured her name against her skin, his warm breath tickling the fine hairs and making her shiver.

She lifted her hands and scored her fingers through his thick head of hair, wantonly guiding him lower, urging him to take her breast in his mouth. She had no idea how or where these actions came from but delighted in the way her body reacted to him, wanting him.

He lifted his head just once and searched her eyes. And then Lily knew whatever he saw reflected there was the spark to ignite something wholly masculine in him. He ripped the gloves from his hands so he could unhook two or three fixings of her bodice before man-handling her breasts free of their inconvenient constraint. The roughness, the urgency, caused the very center of her to throb with the unexpected thrill of his domination. The cool air felt delicious against the scorching heat of her skin as he pulled back to gaze at her exposed breasts.

Lily tried stay still beneath his hungry gaze, but knew he would see she quivered. Her underwear was moist against her skin and he had yet to barely touch her. She swallowed as anxiety threatened to spoil this wonderful yet illicit moment. Would he think her shameless if he touched her there? Was it normal to be so wet?

"My God, you are perfect."

"Andrew…"

He met her eyes. "What is it, my love?"

"I'm afraid. I want to be everything you want me to be, but—"

"You are. My God, you are."

He covered her mouth with his. His tongue probed, searched and conquered. She smoothed a hand over the thick width of his bicep and up to the muscular shoulder above. Every doubt, every reservation she had was as feeble as her resolve to be away from him. She dug her nails into his skin and he leaned his weight into her. The magnificent sensation of his broad hard chest crushing her breasts pushed a needy breath from deep inside her.

"I love you so much."

He drew away, met her eyes for a brief moment before leaning down and flicking his tongue over one nipple and then the other. Lily watched him in erotic fascination. And when he took one of her hardened nubs into his mouth, she was lost. She dropped her hands from his shoulders and reached behind her to grip the tree. The mix of pleasure and the unknown coursed through her blood, making her alternately want to weep or demand more. She closed her eyes and reveled in the illicit pleasure, the stolen moment that was now.

He lowered his hand and she felt his hesitation as he ran it down the front of her dress, lingering at the place between her legs. *Don't stop—don't let me think.*

His lips left her breast and she knew he looked at her. She heard his ragged breathing, felt the warmth of each exhalation on her face. Reluctantly, she opened her eyes. Her heart hitched.

"What is it? Why do you stare at me with such doubt in your eyes?" she whispered.

"I need to be sure you want this. Because, as God is my witness, I will never take advantage of you. If you want me to stop..."

Her heart thundered inside her chest. Suddenly the whole notion of never feeling what she felt, to never have him look at her with such vulnerability as now was the most fearsome notion of all. More than ever, Lily knew they were trapped. Neither would ever be able to fight this overwhelming love swelling between them like the eye of a tornado.

She smiled and lifted a hand to his rigid jaw. "I want this, Andrew. I want you."

He gave her a long, heated look before reaching around and taking her wrist. He pulled her from the tree and together they tumbled to the ground. The earth was soft beneath them and when his weight came down upon her, Lily stretched languidly beneath him.

They kissed and the heat intensified.

The urgent pulsing between her legs frightened and delighted her in equal measure. And then he moved to the side and his eager hand traveled over the dip of her waist to the curve of her hips and then across her thigh.

Her heart seemed to stop.

He hesitated for just a second before pressing his fingers hard to her center. Lily shamelessly, instinctively lifted her hips, returning the pressure with lustful impatience.

"You want this, you really want this." He murmured the words as he watched her.

"Yes. I want all of it."

He turned away and the rustle of silk filled the air as he lifted her skirts. She shimmied and writhed against the ground and he helped her, until her undergarments were tossed to the side. The dampness of her cunny was shockingly cool beneath the open air. Lily felt no shame as his eyes drank in every part of her. She felt powerful, alive and utterly female.

She reached for him, gripping his tense bicep in her hand.

"Touch me, Andrew."

He traced his fingers across her stomach and down into her pubic hair. Lily clamped her teeth together and pushed the back of her head deeper into the ground as he slipped his fingers inside.

"You're wet," he growled.

A flash of heat rose in her face and she closed her eyes. "I can't help it."

His laugh was soft, pleased. "It's wonderful."

And then she began to tremble as he rubbed her erect nub while at the same time keeping his fingers nestled deep inside. She felt the delicious sensations building and building again like the night they had shared in her room. And as before she had yet to touch him.

"Andrew, you have to stop," she managed. "I'm...I'm..."

"Going to come?"

Her eyes snapped open. "Is that what they call it? Come?"

He grinned. "Yes, Lily. Come."

She returned his smile. The word was perfect. It encapsulated the feeling, the rush, the need. She wanted to come. Now. But she wanted him to come too.

"Come with me, Andrew."

He leaned down and kissed her with an urgency so potent, her entire body screamed its primal need. She closed her eyes as his fingers slid away from her. She heard the gentle pop of buttons, the whisper of material over muscle and spread her legs wider in hopeless anticipation. His naked thighs brushed hers as he lay back down beside her. She opened her eyes and turned her head.

He kissed her lips before covering her body with his own. She feasted her eyes on his manhood as he hovered above her. She waited for the fear, the regret, the need to stop, but it didn't appear and then he entered her.

He thrust a little deeper and a whimper escaped her as she broke.

He stopped. "Are you all right?"

"I'm happy. Don't stop. Don't you dare stop."

They exchanged smiles, their gazes locked in joy. He slowly began to move back and forth and Lily gripped the strong arms planted on either side of her. He felt so big, so virile and so hard. The sensations built but not with the same potency as when he touched her before. But then he lifted a hand and was sliding it down in between their bodies as he moved.

She swallowed. "What are you—?"

"Sshh, wait."

And then he rubbed her while picking up the strength and frequency of his thrusts. Lily's eyes widened as she looked at him, her mouth open and her breathing hard. How could women not claim this again and again? How could people be ashamed of their sexuality and withhold sharing this with people they cared for?

Her climax came without warning. Her body contracted around him, pulsing against his hardness as she exploded while crying out his name again and again. Barely a few seconds passed before he erupted inside of her, filling her entire body and soul completely—perfectly. For several moments, neither of them moved. He collapsed on top of her, spent and breathless with his head resting just above her breast. She raised her hand and pushed it into his hair, securing him there. His penis slowly slid from inside of her and she fought the urge to giggle at the new and wonderful sensation.

"Are you all right?"

She smiled. "How many more times do you intend to ask me that?"

He laughed. "I don't know. I'm just...I don't know."

****

Lily tried to refrain from stealing glances at him as they traveled along the road. But she found it just as impossible as it was to calm the butterflies in her stomach. She was no longer a virgin, and she could not have been happier.

"We'll stop here," Andrew said, squinting his eyes as he studied something behind her. "I've heard the food is excellent."

She turned to see what he looked at. The Rose & Crown Inn appeared as charming a place as she'd ever seen. Yet a heavy sense of foreboding strangled her short-lived romantic elation.

How were they to know who was inside? She had just lain in the bracken with a man out of wedlock like a...a cheap... Lily swallowed as her cheeks burned. Would her new and contented state be written on her face, in the rash of his stubble at her bosom?

She jumped when he placed a hand over hers.

215

"Lily? What is it?"

Her gaze darted over the surrounding garden littered with bright colored flowers and cheery ornaments. A huge willow tree stood in the center of the manicured lawn and the weather-worn bench sitting beneath it added just the right amount of charm. Lily felt oddly out of place, almost as though she didn't deserve to be here and risk tainting the peaceful atmosphere.

She looked back at Andrew.

"What are we doing here?" she asked quietly.

He smiled and touched a tender finger to her jaw. "To eat. Are you not hungry?"

"But I shouldn't go in there with you."

His handsome brow wrinkled in confusion. "What? Why?"

She looked down at their joined hands. "Andrew, you know why. I am just a housemaid. If people see you sharing a meal with me."

"You are not a housemaid." He lifted her face to meet his eyes. "And you have never been *just* a housemaid to me. Not since the first night I saw you. Not in any moment of not knowing who you really were. You have always been and always will be so much more to me than a maid, Elizabeth. Always."

She exhaled a shaky breath at the sound of the old and now seemingly foreign name on his lips.

Who was she? Elizabeth or Lily? Elizabeth was a girl whose wings were clipped. Her frivolous naiveté led her to play games in the ballroom in the hope her preordained future never came to pass.

She looked deep into his sapphire eyes as he gazed back at her expectantly. With her heart thundering inside her chest, her lips curved into a slow smile.

Elizabeth was gone. She was Lily now and Lily would walk into that inn and sit with her lover and eat a meal with her head held high.

"Elizabeth's gone, Andrew." She raised his hands to her lips and pressed a kiss to his knuckles. "I am Lily. I want to be Lily. And Lily will have a meal with you but when we return to the manor, I have no choice but to move on."

His eyes darkened almost imperceptibility; but the shift of his Adam's apple and the tightening of his jaw left her in no doubt her words had struck an unsatisfactory chord. For a long moment they sat in frozen silence and then he leapt from the gig and marched around to her side.

"We'll talk of that later. Right now, I am famished."

"Andrew."

He gave a wink and held out his hand. "Come, fair lady, come and dine with me."

His grin was infectious. How could she resist him? They would talk of her leaving later. She slipped her hand into his and met his smile. "Very well. On your head be it."

They ducked beneath the low beamed entranceway and into the semi-darkness of the pub. The landlord greeted them with aplomb. Lily could not help but be enchanted by both his cheery, red face, and the interior beauty of the age-old inn. Oak beams strewn with horse brass lined the ceiling and what looked like family portraits and amateur oil paintings littered the walls.

"A table for two if you will," Andrew said brightly.

"Of course, sir."

Andrew gestured for Lily to walk ahead of him and she almost believed she was a lady once more. The landlord led them to a small table, nestled in an alcove in the farthest corner of the pub. A log fire burned to the side, its embers a smoldering mass of yellow and orange in the grate. He held the back of her chair and Lily sat down.

217

"Is this table satisfactory to you, Mrs....?" The landlord's gaze dropped to her left hand. "Oh, I'm sorry. I assumed..."

"If I could have a minute with you, my good man." Andrew stepped forward and steered the landlord away from the table. Their voices faded into the background as the flames of the fire blurred in Lily's vision.

It didn't matter that she did not regret lying with him. Andrew was not her husband and never would be. The judgment she saw for the tiniest moment in the landlord's eyes was enough to knock any remnants of fantasy from both her mind and heart.

What else did she expect? Did she think she would sail to France happy and satisfied at having lain with the love of her life for one beautiful yet reckless moment? Her need for independence had clearly been imbedded in naivety. How could she claim to want independence when she had no idea what it really meant? She was no longer a virgin. Andrew gently and perfectly brought her to womanhood. But now she was nothing more than a broken and very soon to be, lonely woman.

"Lily?"

"Mmm?"

She turned. The landlord had disappeared. Andrew lowered himself into the seat opposite and as soon as he looked at her face, his smile faltered. "Are you crying?"

"Of course not." She shook her head; but as she did a lone tear dropped onto her hand which lay on the table. He leaned across and touched the tear with his finger and then brought it to his tongue.

"What is it that makes you cry and thus breaks my heart, my love?"

Her heart turned over painfully in her chest. "Oh, don't. Don't say that. I would never ever want to think I have hurt you."

"Then tell me. Tell me your story so you can be free of its burden if that is what brings you such grief to make you cry. Tell me everything and then you will feel free to be with me."

She dragged her gaze from his and looked about her. The room was empty except for some work weary men sitting at the bar nursing two mugs of ale, a plate of bread and cheese at their elbows. No listening ears strained for a scandal; no caricaturist stood on the sidelines waiting to draw her picture and herald it in next week's newspaper. She turned back to face him.

She drew in a shaky breath. "I left home because my parents were intent on marrying me off to a man that I not only did not love but cannot abide. But it was more than that. I was deeply hurt by their assumption I would ever be prepared to marry a man I did not love. If they knew me even a little, they'd know it would kill me to resign my life to another who I felt nothing for."

He looked at her for a moment before reaching across the table and taking her hand. "And yet you still think of my union with Lady Tasmin. You defend it. Ask me to honor it when I feel no love for her. My heart is entirely yours, do you know that?"

"Even if I allowed myself to bask in such a thought, she does not deserve to be cast aside like this, Andrew. No one does."

"I am not *casting* her aside," he protested. "We are not engaged. I have made no promise to her. It was a promise between my father and me only. Do you not see that?"

"But you know as well as I do that society will not see things that way. You have been seen together on numerous occasions. You have monopolized her company at balls and assemblies."

His laugh was wry. "Monopolized her? My God,

she was forced in front of me. If not by her parents, then by Charles."

"But—"

He tightened his grip on her fingers. "No, Lily. Enough. You will listen to me. I will not marry her. I have spoken to my father. He knows everything. He knows of you, he knows—"

She snatched her hand away from his. "He knows me? What are you saying?"

He smiled, his eyes twinkling in the candlelight. "He knows I love you. He helped me discover your true identity."

"But how? Your father has never seen me."

A faint color stained his cheeks and he looked away. "I...I..." He lifted a hand to his mouth to cover his cough. "I have drawn pictures."

She leaned forward to hear him more clearly. "Pictures?"

He faced her once more. "Yes, pictures. Pictures of you."

"Oh." A warm wave of delight swept a low loop-the-loop through her belly. She hesitated and then smiled shyly. "I think I would like to maybe see them one day."

His face softened. "Maybe you will."

Before she could say more, the landlord came back with a bottle of wine and two glasses. She waited while Andrew tasted the wine and after a subtle dip of his head, their glasses were filled and their food orders taken. Alone once more, Lily exhaled her words in a rush.

"If you truly do not intend to marry Lady Tasmin then you must tell her. But the reason should not be because of your feelings for me."

He leaned forward. "Why not? My feelings for you are too strong to deny. I love you."

She shook her head fervently. "Andrew, why can you not understand my motivation behind everything I have done?"

"I am listening to you, but your words do nothing but confuse me. I want to marry you, Lily. Why do you look at me as though I am an ogre who wishes you harm? I can give you anything you want."

"But don't you see? I don't want you to *give* me anything." She pressed a hand to her forehead and waited for the erratic beat of her heart to slow. Blowing out a breath, she said, "I left my home and everything I knew because I despised the fact my life had been mapped out for me. I will never be the woman you need standing side by side with you at balls and functions and—"

He waved a dismissive hand. "I don't give a flying fig about any of those things! It's you I want."

Lily glanced at the patrons sitting at the bar. But they were far more interested in their ale than the quarrelling lovers sitting by the fire. She snatched her gaze back to Andrew's.

"I want to live my own life," she said. "That has not changed despite my falling..." She swallowed hard. "...despite my falling in love with you."

He grasped her hand. "But you did."

She snatched her hand away again and curled her shaking fingers about the stem of her wineglass. "But I still despise the expected decorum; the false wooing and bowing and scraping. It isn't me. It will never be me and now I love my freedom. And if the only way I can maintain that is to leave Cotswold Manor and travel to Paris, so be it."

He watched her in silence. She waited. Each breath hitched her bosom; each passing second marked her sadness.

The landlord served their meal of bacon, potatoes and boiled turnips and left.

"Then I will come to Paris with you," Andrew said.

Her eyes widened until she feared they would pop right out of her head. "You are insane," she cried. "How can you say such a flippant, irresponsible—?"

"Because I mean every word." He smiled. "I will have you one way or another, Miss Lily, and if it means giving up everything I have, I will."

"But—"

"No, no buts. That's just the way it is."

"But—"

"Ah, ah, ah. Enough. Now eat before your food gets cold."

She narrowed her gaze as she snatched up her fork. "This conversation is far from over, *Lord Westrop*," she snapped. "Far from over."

She stabbed her fork into her meat.

His smile dissolved and he crossed his legs.

Despite her upset, she struggled to hide her traitorous grin.

Chapter Thirteen

By the time they arrived back at the manor, the sky had turned the dusky pink of twilight. Andrew looked up at the house as he steered the gig along the graveled driveway. He marveled at the way his home appeared more beautiful than ever in light of his current state of complete honeymoon-like love. He drew in a long breath through flared nostrils, filling his lungs. His gaze darted over the many windows as his heart swelled.

How many rooms there were to fill with noise and laughter—love and children. He had to persuade her to stay. But if he failed? Then he'd follow her wherever she wished to go.

He turned to face her. Her beautiful dark eyes were wide as she stared out across his land. He touched his hand gently to hers. "Thank you for today."

She turned. "You're welcome." A small smile curved her full lips. "Although it should be me thanking you. I've..." She paused. "I've...had a wonderful time. I enjoyed each and every second."

Her face flushed the same delicate pink as the sky. It took all of Andrew's self-control not to lean across and kiss her. To pour every fiber of his being into a kiss that would leave her in no doubt of his commitment. She turned back toward the house. Her gasp made him snap his head around to find out what it was that put such sudden fear in her eyes.

"Lily? What is it?"

"Is that Lord Winchester's horse Robert is taking to the stables?"

His gaze followed the direction of her outstretched hand and his jaw tightened. "Yes it is. What in God's name is he doing here? I made my feelings perfectly clear..." Any further word lodged in his throat as the hairs on the back of his neck rose, issuing a warning. He turned to look at her. "Why does his being here concern you so? Has he said something to you?"

She opened her mouth, but then closed it, her lips pressed so tightly together they showed white. Andrew's hands curled into fists. *If he has as much as taken the wrong tone with her.*

"Lily?" he pressed.

"He...he..." She met his eyes. "Can you not remember what he accused me of before?"

"Yes. Of course I do and that is why he's not welcome here." He moved to cup her jaw but remembered that there could be any number of eyes watching them from the house. He dropped his hand. "And when we announce our love to the world, he will have to accept it or never dare to as much as look at me again."

"But have I not told you our union is impossible? You must accept that." Her voice rose in panic.

Andrew's impatience grew. "Do you really expect me to ignore this? To bury the love I have for you deep inside me and never allow it to show itself again?"

"You have to," she said urgently. "We both do. It is not just the issue of whether Lord Winchester accepts me or not. There is Lady Tasmin to think of, Nicholas, Mrs. Harris...my goodness, Andrew, what will this do to all of them? It isn't fair to expect them—"

"Stop it. Stop it right now."

She flinched.

He shook his head. "This isn't about any of them, damn it. This is about you. You're afraid.

224

You're afraid of following your heart and giving up this notion of independence you insist on thinking you need."

For several moments she said nothing and Andrew wondered whether he'd been too cantankerous with his words. The last thing he wanted to do was upset her. But then her eyes narrowed to slits and her spine straightened. A knot tightened in his abdomen. This was Lily. This was who he loved.

She was by no means a subservient admirer willing to do anything in order to catch his eye. She would not be upset by his terseness, she would punish him for it.

She tilted her chin. "I am not *afraid,* Andrew. And my need for independence is not a notion, it is a fact."

"Lily."

"The reason I am hesitant in declaring my feelings for you to the entire world is because one, I do not know if I could be the type of wife you need by your side at Cotswold Manor, and two—"

"Of course you could!" he protested. "You are wonderful. And funny. The staff adore you."

She snapped her head around. "Yet I still wish to escape every form of formality, of servants and class divides and everything it entails. That has not changed and the sooner you understand that, the better."

A sharp pain assaulted Andrew's chest as the first crack splintered his heart. "Are you saying there is no hope of you *ever* becoming my wife? You still wish to leave despite everything that has happened between us?"

A lone and telling tear slipped from beneath her lashes. "It will never work."

"You love me, Lily," he said quietly. "Please don't do this."

She swiped at her cheek as the tear made its trail down her face. "And two, I owe Lady Tasmin my loyalty. She is a lady both by name and nature. I will not be the one to alter her chosen course."

Andrew's jaw tightened. "I have told you before that I do not, and will not, be anybody's *course,* Lily. Our love will not hurt Lady Tasmin; it will merely delay her family's wish to see her marry well. There are without doubt others on the agenda in preparation for my possible failure to offer for her. She does not love me."

Her head dipped and she drew in a shaky breath. "Maybe not. But if you won't consider her, will you not consider the feelings of your life-long friend?"

"Charles? Why should you care what he thinks after what he accused you of?"

She hesitated and then blew out a breath. "I do not want to be the one to change your entire life, Andrew. Everything will change beyond recognition if you and I were to marry."

"And what of it?" he snapped. "And as far as I'm concerned, it will be for the greater good." He swiveled around and snatched up the reins. "We will discuss this further once I eject my so-called *friend* from the house so quickly his breeches will catch fire."

"Andrew!"

He glanced at her. There had been a definite laugh in her protestation. He winked. "Trust me, all will be well."

"I do trust you, but you misunderstand me."

He shook his head, his smile dissolving. "No, Lily, I don't. Charles Winchester is the youngest brother of three. He has never known, and God willing never will know the pressure to marry and secure a family estate. He is merely playing at life. He will marry when he sees fit and have the added luxury of marrying someone he loves. If he ever grows up. At the moment, he is nothing more than a playboy intent on butting into my life as much as possible."

"But it feels so wrong that it is I who destroyed your long-term friendship. You should make things up, settle your differences. I will soon be gone from England altogether."

A spark of anger lit inside his chest. "Fine. Then leave. I have told you I love you and you have told me the same thing. If you are leaving England, then I am too."

"But—"

"That's my final word. There is no more to be said about it." He turned toward the house with his heart thundering. He gave the reins a sharp snap and Portland immediately stepped on. "You are right, I will speak to Charles and hear what he has to say. Then...and only then, will I decide whether or not I ever want to see him again. And that, my dear, is what you will have to be satisfied with."

They pulled to a stop at the front entrance and the oak door immediately swung open on its hinges. Nicholas rushed out to greet them. Upon sight of his obviously near-hysterical butler, Andrew's scowl weakened to such an extent he had to bite back a smile. He would not change any member of his staff for all the money in the world. Nicholas was worth his weight in gold just for his histrionics alone.

Andrew jumped down from the gig. "Nicholas, how good of you to be waiting for us."

But Nicholas' gaze was fixed on Lily. "It is always a relief to have you back at the manor safe and sound, sir," he said. "Did you have an enjoyable day? The weather was just wonderful, was it not?"

"It was indeed, and yes, we did have a good day." Andrew smiled. "Thank you for asking."

Finally dragging his gaze from Lily who ignored

him and instead made a fuss of gathering her skirts, Nicholas faced Andrew. "I assume the trip was successful, my lord?"

Andrew lifted an eyebrow. "Successful?"

Nicholas stepped up to the side of the gig. He stretched his neck forward and then stretched it left and right as he looked inside, reminding Andrew of an extreme nosy pigeon.

"Nicholas, what is it you are looking for?" Andrew asked, amused.

His butler gestured at the gig. "No packages, sir?"

"No. No packages."

Barely suppressing the urge to laugh, Andrew turned and held a hand out to Lily. She shot him a glare and jumped down unaided. He didn't know whether to spank her or kiss her.

She slapped at her skirts and met Nicholas' eyes rather than his. "I will rise extra early tomorrow, to make up for the time I have lost today. I am sorry we were absent so long. The master could not make up his mind what to buy Lady Tasmin despite my advice and so I'm afraid we came back empty handed."

The butler pulled back his shoulders, his eyes narrowing to slits. "I see."

Lily cleared her throat; her cheeks flushed pink. "Is there anything you would like me to do now?"

"Well, you can change out of your dress and into your uniform first of all and then I will see you in the kitchen."

"Yes, Nicholas."

Andrew failed to hide his smile any longer as she turned on her heel and marched toward the house without a second glance in his direction. He watched her until she dipped out of sight and then turned to find Nicholas scrutinizing him. Andrew straightened his face.

"So..." He nodded toward the house. "I see Lord Winchester is here."

Blinking, Nicholas clicked his heels together. "Ah, yes indeed, sir. Lord Winchester arrived just a short while ago. He is waiting for you in the drawing room."

"And did he say what he wanted?"

"No, sir. But I couldn't help noticing the bottle of brandy and box of cigars he was carrying. Maybe he comes with a peace offering."

"I see. Well, let's see what the man has to say for himself then, shall we?"

Leaving Nicholas standing outside, Andrew strode into the house and directly to the drawing room.

****

Charles immediately turned from the window upon Andrew's entrance and the two men stared at each other. A chaise-longue and low table stood between them like the dividing line across a battlefield.

"What are you doing here, Charles? What do you want?" Andrew asked stiffly.

Charles smiled and threw open his arms. "Come on, my man. Is that any way to greet a life-long friend?"

"Life-long friend?" Andrew sniffed. "The last time I saw you, you insinuated my mental well-being was not quite up to par. Does that sound like something a friend would say?"

Charles stepped forward, casually waving a dismissive hand. "Oh, forget all that. Water under the bridge. Now, see here. I come bearing gifts." He nodded toward the brandy and cigars on the table.

Andrew threw a cursory glance at the offerings. "So I see."

"Can I pour you a snifter?"

"I think I'll pass until I know why you are here.

If I remember correctly, I specifically told you not to show your face here again until you are ready to apologize for snooping around on my staff. You dug for dirt like you were nothing more than a Thames sewer rat."

"Hey, steady on, old boy."

"I mean it, Charles. You had no right to talk about Lily that way. I want an apology."

The room seemed to come to a standstill. One, two, three ticks of the grandfather clock sounded as their glares locked. Andrew's blood heated as he waited. The anger flashed and burned in Charles' eyes for a long, long moment, and then he blinked and it was gone.

He gave a respectful dip of his golden head. "I was wrong. I apologize."

"Wrong, Charles?" Andrew pressed.

"I was wrong to tell you what you should and should not do with your staff."

"And?"

"Andrew, for God's sake, man."

"And?"

Another flash of fire in his green-blue eyes. "And from now on, I will respect whatever decisions you make in your own home."

With his hands clasped behind his back, Andrew walked past him to the window. The view fell to the front of the house. "Let's see if you really mean that, shall we?"

"I'm sorry?"

"You saw Lily and I return from Bristol, did you not?"

Charles cleared his throat. "Yes. Yes, I did."

"And how does it make you feel to know I have spent the entire day with her? What did it do to you to see me sitting side by side with her like that?"

Silence.

A smile played at Andrew's lips. "Surely in your

atoned state of mind, it must have been a pleasing sight, was it not?"

Silence.

Andrew turned. "Charles?"

Their eyes locked once more. Charles visibly shook and Andrew straightened his spine. He had seen his friend like this before. And it was indeed a dangerous state of mind. Charles hunted with the same look upon his face. He could take a knife and slash a deer's throat without as much as a grimace when the blood boiled in his veins as it undoubtedly was then.

Caution curled around Andrew's small intestine, digging into flesh and waking his inner defenses. There was not a chance in hell of Charles coming within ten feet of Lily until that look on his face had changed and his anger cooled.

"What do you say, Charles?" he asked, his voice dangerously low.

"I say it is your choice how you conduct yourself with your staff." His voice was equally low. "I will endeavor to tolerate your actions. I will not interfere."

Andrew drew in a deep breath, exhaled it. "Well then, we have a starting point at least."

Charles leaned forward and opened the box of cigars. "Do you mind?"

Andrew gestured. "Be my guest."

Charles bit off the end, removed it from his teeth and flicked it into a crystal ashtray on the sideboard beside him. "I do need to say one more thing, though."

"Why am I not surprised?" Andrew sighed.

"Her name is Elizabeth. Not Lily."

"I know. Miss Elizabeth Caughley, in fact. The youngest daughter of lawyer Gerald Caughley."

Charles glared. "You know?"

"Yes, I know. So unfortunately you have no

further ammunition in which to insinuate betrayal on her part because she has told me her story, Charles."

His jaw clenched and unclenched. "Is that so?"

"Yes. She left her home of her own accord to seek an independent life abroad. She is here to work and save money before departing for France."

Charles burst of laughter was as cold as a winter wind. "And you are pleased about that? To have someone of such insolence working in your house? Changing the rules and thinking she can do as she pleases?" He curled his lip in distaste. "You are a fool."

Andrew flew toward him forcing Charles to step backwards. "Yes," Andrew hissed. "I do want her in my house. Why is wanting a life outside of what is expected so wrong? Have you ever met another woman with such self-sufficient sensibilities? Someone with goals? A plan for the future that doesn't automatically involve propriety and duty? Well, have you?"

Neither of them moved—both frozen in anger and resentment. At last, Charles spun away and stormed to the center of the room.

"You are right, I haven't met such a woman. But I'm sorry, Andrew, you are not seeing what is truly going on here."

"What?" Andrew's heart raced as he pulled his hands into fists and willed himself not to pummel his friend into submission.

"No woman seeks such a life as you describe unless she is running away from something." He paused. "Or else is blatantly wanton and devious."

"How dare you." Andrew's voice was barely above a whisper.

Charles pulled back his shoulders. "You've been blinded. Your maid is a harlot. She has drawn a veil over your eyes the only way a cunning seductress could."

"You'd be wise to stop talking, Charles."

"My God, man, will you not just listen to me? I am giving you advice here."

"And it is advice I do not want or need. You are pushing your luck with me."

Charles shook his head. "Fine. I will say no more. I am certainly not going to allow this woman to come between us."

Andrew threw his hands in the air. "At last. The man sees sense."

"I will say no more about it. If she is to stay working in this house, I will respect your decision. In fact, I will make an extra effort to get to know her as you do and who knows? Maybe I will be proven wrong about her and her agenda."

The tone of Charles' voice and his words lent zero comfort. Each breath Andrew inhaled scratched at his throat. "You will be proven wrong. Of that I am certain."

"I love you like a brother, Andrew." Charles moved slowly around the room toward the fireplace. "It's just..."

Andrew hands curled into fists once more. *Will the man never learn to quit while he is ahead?*

His friend turned and met his eyes directly. "I have never ever seen you like this."

"Like what?"

"So enamored with another person. Why, if it was Lady Tasmin who had your attention like this, then maybe I'd be a little happier; but it's not, is it? The object of your affections, while we now know is a lawyer's daughter, is a woman content to work as just a maid. It makes no sense but I concede that it is your own business."

Andrew cursed the angry heat that once more flared in his cheeks. How could anyone deride a woman such as Lily because she desired to work hard? She was perfection personified. A woman he needed as surely as the air he breathed.

He swallowed down his anger. "Then there is nothing more to say."

"Good. Well, then, I knew this wouldn't come between us. In fact..." He paused. "Where is Elizabeth...I mean Lily, now?"

Andrew narrowed his gaze. "Why?"

Charles threw the remnants of his brandy to the back of his throat and put the glass down on the mantel. "I'm just assuming she would have to return to her duties after her trip out today, that's all."

"And so would I."

"Good, well at least things haven't gone completely awry."

"Charles..."

Charles flashed a small smile before walking across the room and toward the door. "I am only jesting, Andrew. Right, well, I'd better be of my way. I am going to pay a visit to Lady Tasmin. I promised to find out how you are and let her know forthwith. She loves you, Andrew, and I hope in time you will come to love her."

A flash of guilt swept across Andrew's conscience. He drew in a breath knowing there was no time like the present to start things moving in the ultimate direction. "You can tell Lady Tasmin that I am well and will pay her a visit tomorrow afternoon. There is something I need to speak to her about in private."

Charles' face split into a huge grin, his eyes dancing with feverish delight. "Ah ha, now my confidence in you is completely restored! Have my suspicions been completely off the mark this entire time?"

Andrew frowned. "What do you mean?"

"Well, this surely means there will be an engagement, does it not? What perfection! What will it be, old boy? A New Year wedding?"

Andrew trembled with the effort it took not to grasp his friend by the lapels and yell into his face. How could anyone be so brainless? "Just tell her I will be there tomorrow at three," he said. "And if you respect me at all, you will not mention a wedding of any sort. Do you understand me?"

Charles tapped the side of his nose, his eyes still shining. "Of course, of course. I am just happy that you have not forgotten what it is you have to do, that's all."

The nonchalant observation was too much for Andrew to ignore. "Oh? And what is it I *have* to do?"

"Marry and sire an heir, of course. Your father can now pass in peace, knowing the Baxter fortune will not lapse but continue to flourish."

Nausea swirled deep in Andrew's stomach. "I know what a precarious and important role I have, Charles, and there is no fear of me ever forgetting or neglecting it. My father knows my intentions and fully supports them."

"Well, of course he does! You are to forge a union with a lady of considerable wealth. What more could he ask for? Everything is as it should be."

Andrew pursed his lips. Everything as it should be? Isn't that what Lily was fighting? Wasn't he now fighting it too? Only God knew if it would suffocate them both eventually.

"Exactly. Everything is as it should be." Andrew nodded. "Now if you don't mind..." He gestured to the door.

Charles turned and opened the door. "The stage will soon be set and I for one expect a front row seat."

"The stage? This is not a play, Charles. This is my life."

****

Lily ducked behind a pillar in the hallway as the

235

drawing room doors opened for a second time in the last half an hour and Andrew walked out. Lord Winchester had left just a little time before. He whistled a cheery tune that left Lily in no doubt her suspicions of what had happened between closed doors were completely justified. Men's friendships were notoriously strong; a woman rarely if ever came between a man and his friend. She pressed her back to the wall and closed her eyes against the harsh sting of tears.

She truly did not want Andrew to change his way of life or his future for her. She'd meant what she said. She did not want to conform to expectations any more now than she had three months ago when she'd first arrived at Cotswold Manor. Yet, she would not deny the reason for her tears and her galloping heart and clammy palms were because of the sadness of never seeing him again.

And knowing Lord Winchester was welcomed back in the house made her decision easier to execute. She could not possibly walk about this house in the constant fear he might attack or threaten her. What kind of life would that be? Not even for Andrew would she surrender herself to such a fate. She'd wait until the house was asleep and then leave.

She stopped gnawing at her bottom lip and stood up straight.

The thud of boots against wood made her breath catch in her throat and she pushed back farther into the wall.

"Lily? What on earth are you doing?"

"Nicholas! How are you?"

"How am I?" His eyes widened. "What on earth are you doing?" He threw a glance in the direction of the drawing room and when he looked back at her, disappointment clouded his eyes. "Are you spying on the master? My goodness, have you no boundaries? Is it not enough that he takes you out for the day?"

"You don't understand."

"I don't understand. Always your nonsense, Lily. Will you never stop?"

She gripped his forearm. "Please, Nicholas. It's important. There's something I have to tell you."

He hesitated, looked to the drawing room and back again. "My God, not another of your revelations. What is it now? I despair of you, I really do."

"Please. Will you please come with me?"

"What? Where?"

"Just come."

With her hand still on his arm, Lily rushed through the house and down the stairs leading to the kitchen. Relieved to find it empty, she gestured Nicholas inside and shut the door.

"I'm leaving, Nicholas."

He sighed heavily. "I know, I know. You keep saying."

A spark of indignation lit in Lily's chest at his irony, but quickly extinguished. Who could blame him for doubting every word she spoke? She blew out a breath. "Tonight. Regardless of what happens I will not be here come morning."

"Don't be silly. And what do you mean *regardless* of what happens?"

"Nothing. I just mean whatever else goes on in this house tonight, I will be leaving. I have to. I can't stay here a moment longer knowing what I do."

The crease in his brow deepened. "Knowing what you do? What are you talking about?"

She dropped into a chair and covered her face with her hands. "Everything is such a mess, Nicholas. Nothing is the way it's supposed to be."

"Lily, look at me." His voice softened and he dropped to his haunches beside her. Lily let him pull her hands from her face. "What on earth is going on?"

His features blurred and Lily swiped at her tears. "I love the master."

His smiled softly. "I know, my dear, we all do."

She gave a small laugh. "No, I'm *in* love with him. We've...I've..."

He looked deep into her eyes and then his own stretched to manic proportions as he shot to his feet. "You've...? You've...? You and the master?"

"Made love, yes."

"Oh, my Lord! My Lord!" He stepped away from her as though she had leeches about her face. Then he proceeded to pace circle after circle around the room, reminiscent of an out of control spinning top. Lily grimaced as his hands clawed at his face and expletives tripped from his tongue like stones into water.

After what felt like fifteen minutes, he stopped. Lily held her breath. He watched her for a few seconds before lunging forward and slapping both hands down on the table opposite her. Lily flinched. His entire body shook but his stare was unwavering.

"Now you listen to me. I will not let you take my lord's reputation and shred it into a thousand pieces by spreading such accusations. Why would you even do such a thing? All of us have done so much for you. So damn much, Lily!"

Hurt struck like a knife in her heart. "How could you think I would ever—?"

He held up a hand. "Moreover, why in God's name did you think I would ever believe it?"

"Because it's true. I would never lie to you. Ever. What reason do I have to say I have lain with him unless it were true? He went to Bath, Nicholas. He went to Bath to find out who I really am. He spoke to his father and told him he loves me and will not marry Lady Tasmin."

Nicholas blanched as the color drained from his face. "What?"

Lily swallowed against the harsh thump of her heart against her ribcage. "He even asked me to return home to my mother and father so he can court me as my beau. I've told him our being together is impossible. I do not want him to change his life for me. Everyone around us would judge and curse the union. The last thing I want is the man I love with all my heart to be cast aside by his peers."

He stared at her, his shoulders trembling. "He loves you?"

She nodded.

"He told his father as much?"

She nodded again.

"Then why on earth are you leaving, child?" He pushed away from the table and ran around it to pull her to her feet. "Viscount Westrop loves you. You are a lady from a good family. You can marry him, Lily. You will never have to leave. You love it here; tell me you don't love it here."

"But, Nicholas, it isn't just about what it would do to him. I don't want to be part of society; it is the thing I dread the most in the entire world."

"But he loovveess you!"

She laughed. "And I him, but what good—"

"No, no, no. No buts. Mrs. Harris felt this...this something between you almost as soon as you arrived. We argued until we were both blue in the face about it. But now, now it is true and you are both in love. All is wonderful in the world." He pulled his face into a stern frown. "Not that I approve of the premature physical aspect, of course."

Afraid his happiness may become contagious, Lily forced her hands from his and stepped away to inject a much needed distance between them. "You are not listening to me. I am leaving. Tonight."

"But why?" he cried. "This is good news."

239

She shook her head. "Our love is doomed. Don't you see? I am not the woman for him. He cannot forsake his family's legacy for me. He cannot forsake his life-long friends. It's too much to ask of anyone, let alone the person you love."

"I will not let you leave. If the master loves you, I will not allow you to disappear without his knowledge."

Lily's heart picked up speed. "But you don't understand."

"Then explain it to me!"

She looked into his kind eyes and her resolve weakened. Could she tell him? Could she really tell him about Lord Winchester? Would he believe her?

"Lily?"

She drew in a shaky breath and released it in a rush. "I haven't told anyone this, but Lord Winchester attempted to assault me."

For a moment he said nothing and then he slowly straightened until he stood ramrod straight. "Go on," he said quietly.

"It happened on the night Lady Tasmin and her sister last dined with the master. Can you remember how they left in such a hurry?"

He nodded.

"He ordered her to leave. Immediately."

"And where did this assault happen?"

"He followed me into the corridor from the dining room." Lily stopped as the night came back to her on a tidal wave of fear. She closed her eyes and concentrated on leveling her breathing. After a few moments, the panic abated and she opened her eyes. Nicholas had not moved an inch. She inhaled a breath. "He pressed his hand across my mouth to silence me and then clawed at my breast like an animal in heat."

"What?" Nicholas' impassive face collapsed and evolved into an unfamiliar mask of disgust and outrage. "In this house? He attacked you in this house and you thought it unacceptable to tell someone?"

"I had to! I love Andrew so much. I didn't want to see two friends fight when I have no intention of staying here. When Lord Winchester was banished, it did not matter; but now the two of them appear reunited, I cannot stay. I cannot stay and serve him and act as though..."

Nicholas came forward and wrapped her in his arms. Lily closed her eyes and savored the strength of his trust and support for what little time she had left.

"It is all right. Everything is all right. I understand," he said softly against her hair. "I will help you to leave undetected. When the master asks where you are in the morning, I will deny all knowledge of your disappearance." He stopped to press a kiss to her head. "And because the tears I will cry will be genuine, he'll have little choice but to accept you left of your own accord."

"Thank you."

"And with regards to his heart? Well, if that is broken, I will have to find a way to at least seal it, if I cannot mend it."

Lily shuddered, for her heart broke as well.

Chapter Fourteen

Lily walked into the final stall of the stables but that, as the others, was empty. It felt as though Robert, Mrs. Harris and even Jane were hiding from her. Preventing her from saying goodbye knowing she wouldn't leave without a final farewell. Lily gave a small smile as she ran her hand over the polished leather of a saddle hanging beside her. There wasn't one single object or person she wouldn't miss.

Why did she think it a good idea to speak to everyone before she left? Would it help them? Would it help her? Could they forgive her for everything she'd taken and the little she gave in return? They kept her identity a secret, helped her to cool her temper and learn to be the better, more mature person she was today. And yet what had she given them? Nothing but the burden of her secrets.

She stiffened as the smell announcing Baron Winchester's presence assaulted her nostrils. The pungent mix of too much cologne and male sweat, dripping with hints of brandy and cigar smoke curled itself around her like invisible bars of a cage. Lily squeezed her eyes shut and sent up a silent prayer for the Lord to show mercy. But the ominous clicking of the stable door closing and the harsh clang of the bolt thrown into place behind her raised the tiny hairs at the back of her neck. She was trapped.

Drawing on every ounce of strength she possessed, Lily turned. Although Lord Winchester was neither as big nor as wide as Andrew, his presence loomed large and threatening in the semi-darkness. She took a slow step back, then another and another until a hay trough pressed up against the back of her thighs. She had nowhere else to turn, and was in the very scenario her leaving meant to avoid.

Forcing her fear to the back of her mind, Lily tilted her chin. "Is there something you needed, my lord?"

His smile was wolverine, his green eyes dancing with lust and power. "Oh, I wouldn't say I necessarily *need* anything, Elizabeth. I just *want* it."

The sound of her birth name on his tongue hitched at her nerves, drying the saliva in her mouth and increasing her heart rate. She swallowed. "And what is it you want?"

He raised his eyebrows in mock surprise. "Why, don't you know? Surely a woman such as you..."

"Such as me, sir?"

"Yes, a woman of..." He looked to the beamed ceiling above them as though searching for the words. "...how did Andrew describe it? Oh, yes. A woman of self-sufficient sensibilities knows when a man looks to her to satisfy his sexual craving."

He lifted his shoulders and casually plucked a length of straw from one of the bales stacked beside him. Lily forced herself to keep her eyes locked with his even though every drop of her blood, every inch of her flesh longed to turn away from the evil residing there.

"Have you nothing to say?" He took a slow step toward her. "I think he meant it as a compliment, don't you? Whereas I on the other hand, think self-sufficiency in a woman equates to nothing more than a slut who wants her own way."

The word slapped at her face. "A...?"

"A slut, Elizabeth. Shall I define the title for you? A slut is someone like you. Someone who uses her body, her mind or anything else she has to hand to get what she wants."

She took two steps toward the door. "I am leaving."

But he lunged forward, gripping her chin roughly in his hand. "Isn't that what you are doing? Hasn't your entire time here been a well-constructed plan? A plan involving precious more skill than sticking your tits in a soon-to-be earl's face. And when that didn't work, lie down on your back and let him fuck you."

His face was barely inches from hers, his breath singeing the fine hairs of her face. His eyes were so close she saw bright sparks of emerald embedded in dark, dark green. Her neck screamed its protest against the exertion it took to keep looking into eyes colder than an English winter.

"Sir, please."

His smile widened as his gaze flitted over her face, her hair. "Please what? What are you begging me for, mmm?"

Fear skittered along her nerve endings as a lead weight dropped into her stomach. If he decided to force himself on her now, what defense did she have? Who would hear her?

"Why don't you walk with me back to the house?" She gripped the curved rim of the trough as her legs began to tremble. "It's getting cold. I could ask Mrs. Harris to make you some coffee. It will help in sobering you."

He tipped his head back and laughed. "Coffee, she says! Why in God's name would I want coffee?"

"You are drunk, sir. You need—"

"Shut your mouth, whore!"

She flinched as the threat of his words and his anger dashed her face with spittle. He moved his hand in a flash from her chin to her neck and shook it.

"How long, whore? How long have you been

fucking my best friend?" He sneered.

"Please...please let me go."

He shook her again, causing her head to snap back like her neck was made of rubber. "How long have you let him run his fingers over your body, dip his cock into your cunny like the cheap slut you are, mmm?"

She blinked as hot tears stung like needles behind her eyes. "I won't let you—"

"Won't let me what, Elizabeth?" He glanced down at her bosom and back to her eyes. "Won't let me visit the special place Andrew has already conquered, is that it?"

Lily's breath rasped painfully against her throat and her stomach recoiled in horror. He could overpower her with his height alone. "Sir, please. I only need scream and Robert will come running. He left to refill the food troughs, he will be back soon."

"Shut up, you stupid, stupid girl." He laughed. "Do you not think I know the routine of this house like it is my own? Once again you forget how close I am to Andrew, how involved I am in his life. We are alone for the rest of the night, my dear. Robert will not return to the stable until morning. Now...whatever will we do to fill the time?"

He ran his finger slowly along the length of her jaw line, his tongue flicking out sharply like a serpent's to wet his bottom lip. Lily stared as his lip glistened beneath the lanterns hanging in Portland's stable.

What was she doing? Why was she allowing him to get the better of her? If he was going to hurt her then he'd have to do it after enduring a damn good fight.

The ashes of anger smoldering deep in her belly lit like a torch to a flame. Ignoring the caution echoing around her brain, Lily knew if Andrew could see the baron standing so threateningly in front of her and knew what was about to unfold, he would kill him. And that knowledge, that certainty, gave her all the fortitude she needed.

Pulling back her shoulders, she stood firm despite the pinch of his fingers bruising the flesh at her neck.

"So we are alone," she said. "What of it? Are you to beat me? Have your way with me?"

"Mmm, now there's an idea," he murmured. "Why not dip my wick where the great Andrew Baxter has seen fit to bury his? What is good enough for my friend is surely good enough for me, is it not?"

Nausea rose bitter in her throat. "You will never get away with this. Andrew cares deeply for his staff. I wouldn't be surprised if he is asking after me right now. He—"

His mouth bore down on hers. His teeth ground viciously into her lips, his mouth bruising and his tongue choking. Lily dug her hands against his broad chest and shoved as hard as she could. Every ounce of her weight, every inch of her determination poured through her fingers and smashed into his chest.

She jerked her mouth from his. "Noooo! I will not let you do this!"

The force of her words and the hammering of her heart gave her the power she needed. She shoved again and he stumbled backwards, hitting first his hip and then slamming his head hard on the corner of the water trough. He tumbled soundlessly to the floor.

Lily's breast rose and fell in erratic rhythm as she watched him lie motionless at her feet. The straw to the side of his head turned red with blood. The only sound resonant in the enclosed space was her panicked breathing.

What have I done? Oh, no, no, no. Please God, don't let me have killed him.

Her hand hovered at her mouth as the seconds ticked by. Her mind whirled with terror and indecision. She should run for help, tell someone what had happened. Tell them it was an accident, self-defense. But what if Andrew saw no other obligation than to report her to the authorities? Would she be branded a murderess? Condemned without voice? Nicholas. She should tell Nicholas. No, the poor man couldn't take any more.

Her breath caught as a soft whimpering pierced the silence. She watched Lord Winchester curl into the fetal position and then realized the whimpering was in fact weeping. Slowly, she lowered to her knees and crawled toward him. She wanted to help him but her senses remained on high alert, knowing full well this could be complete pretence—a way to lure her into reach before he attacked and maimed.

But she couldn't let him just lie there in his own blood. What if her delay caused his death? That was a conclusion she could not live with.

Closing the final inches between them, Lily touched a hand to his shaking shoulder. After a second, he turned his head toward her but his eyes remained closed and only animal-like mews emanated from his slackened mouth.

Lily swallowed. "Sir?"

Silence.

"Sir, please. Can you hear me?"

He rolled her over and crushed her into the razor-sharp straw. It scratched and pierced the exposed skin of her neck and arms like a million thorns. Her scream was strangled by fear. He hovered above her. His hands pinned her arms to her sides as he gyrated his crotch against her. Terror thundered through her body, turning her limbs to liquid and her heart to a ball of fire inside her chest. She looked into his eyes and her fear exploded like a cannonball, rushing through her veins and

Rachel Brimble

obliterating any final nuances of courage. He was manic, crazed.

No reason shone in the terrifying emerald of his raging eyes. A hot, traitorous tear escaped her lashes and slid down her temple. She could do nothing to stop another...then another...and another.

He laughed. "Oh, now she cries! Now she cries like a lady about to be sexed instead of a wanton whore who craves it."

Lily tried to concentrate her breathing, tried to summon the strength she would need when he finally assailed her undergarments to gain access to his prize. She couldn't just lie down and let this happen. She had plans, she had dreams. The silent monologue screamed through her head as her bottom lip trembled and her body shook. He didn't know what he was doing. He'd stop. He'd wake up from whatever gripped him and realize this was not what he wanted; this was not the man he was.

"What are you thinking, Elizabeth? Your eyes are wide yet you do not seem to entirely see me. Are you thinking Andrew will save you? That he will still care for you when he discovers you'll lie just as easily with his best friend as you do with him?"

She struggled to draw breath as his weight bore down on her. Her tears came faster and faster. "Please don't do this. I am begging you to see sense."

"Shut your pretty little mouth," he hissed. "You are nothing but a dirty, filthy whore."

Gritting her teeth, Lily felt her internal explosion erupt. With an almighty roar, she fought to tear her arms from his grip. She writhed from side to side, pushed and pulled, yanked and strained.

But achieved nothing; he didn't move an inch.

His laughter bounced around the stable, chilling her bones but also fanning the fire scorching her veins. She pushed and struggled. Fought and cursed.

"Yes, yes, come on. Fight me, whore." Winchester laughed. "It will make the whole thing more arousing." He stooped down to run his wet tongue along the curve of her neck. Lily blinked against the burning sting of tears as his saliva slid over the surface of her skin, making her throat convulse with the urge to retch.

And then her breath burst from her lungs as he whipped her over in one swift and violent movement. His hand felt huge as it pressed down on the back of her head, crushing her cheek against the abrasive and unforgiving carpet of straw. He grabbed and snatched at her underclothes, pushed and shoved at her skirts. His breathing became more frantic, more excited as he struggled to slide her drawers over her hips one-handed. Lily screamed but the sound was muffled within the straw. She squirmed and writhed beneath him but his muscular horseman's thighs held her in a vice-like grip.

"Stay still, you fucking bitch," he said, spraying spittle over the side of her face. "Or I'll make sure your body is found on the banks of the River Avon."

"Andrew will kill you first," she spluttered, her voice high-pitched and hysterical. "He will kill you when he finds out what you have done to—"

The impact of his fist punching her in the ear eradicated any words. A warm trickle of blood snaked across her ear lobe as a loud ringing reverberated inside her head, a symphony of terror and surrender. Her body turned numb. The fight left her and her consciousness floated away. Closing her eyes, she looked down on herself from behind closed lids. This way she was removed from the sickening ordeal that was about to occur. It could not touch her and it would not break her.

Her skirts were at her waist, her underwear at her knees. The white skin of her buttocks shone in the candlelight, virginal and untouched.

The splintering of wood and screeching of metal woke Lily from her trance-like state. Winchester's weight lifted as he was snatched from her body. She snapped open her eyes and turned over as Andrew flung him against the wall like he was nothing more than a featherweight. A sob caught in her throat as she grabbed at her drawers, desperately trying to cover her intimate parts. Tears coursed down her cheeks and she mumbled nonsensically.

"What have you done?" Andrew roared into Winchester's bright-red face. "What have you done to her?"

Lily stopped breathing, a ball of hysteria catching painfully in the center of her chest.

Andrew's roar was terrifying. "I said what have you done to her?"

Lily watched in morbid fascination as a stain spread like an ink blot from the crotch of Winchester breeches.

"Answer me, damn you!"

"Andrew, please. I am your friend. She is nothing but a cheap—"

Andrew punched him hard in the face and the sharp crack of breaking bone resounded around them like a snapping twig. The other hand holding him to the wall didn't loosen even though Winchester now hung limp and undone. Andrew's arm shook as he kept him pinned there with his friend's nose bleeding profusely.

"Are you hurt?" he asked, without turning around.

It took a moment for Lily to realize he was addressing her.

"No. No I am fine." She touched a trembling finger to her ear. It came away red.

"Are you certain?"

She looked at the bloody mess of Lord Winchester's face and then at the clenched jaw of her one-time lover and in that moment Lily knew with painful clarity that her decision to leave was the right one. She licked her dry lips.

"Yes. I am unscathed, Andrew. I promise you."

He gave a curt nod and then focused his attention back on Winchester. "I should kill you for this."

"Andrew, I..."

"I don't want to hear it or I will surely break your neck. Not another damn word."

Lily gasped as he punched him again in the face before opening his hand and an unconscious Winchester slid to the floor. Moving in an almost frenzied blur, Andrew yanked a coil of rope hanging from a nail on the stable wall and tethered the baron to the sturdy metal legs of the trough in one fluid motion. The trough was filled to the brim with water and impossible to move.

At last he turned to Lily. She held her breath as he covered the space between them in two easy strides. He held out his hands and she tentatively slid her palms against his and he eased her to her feet. She should have been shaking all over, maybe even hysterically rocking her body back and forth with her arms clamped about her, but the moment he touched her, the trembling stopped and her heart slowed.

He touched a finger to her chin and turned her head. "You're bleeding."

"I'm fine."

He drew in a shaky breath through clenched teeth, his broad chest rising. "No, Lily, you're not."

"It will heal. Andrew, listen to me—"

But her words were cut off as he leaned down and lifted her into his arms like she weighed no more than a child. "What are you doing?" she protested.

"Carrying you back to the house where Mrs.

Harris can prepare some cloths and ointment. I am going to take care of you."

"But she will ask questions. They will all know and then the upset will be too much."

"I don't care," he snapped, his eyes blazing once more. "I love you and I am no longer willing to hide it."

He turned around and studied the limp mess of his once good friend. "And while I am tending to you, I will ensure Robert gets word to the authorities that we have a criminal in our midst. A criminal who will live to endure the results of his despicable, vile and unforgivable actions."

Turning away, Andrew marched from the stables and out into the darkness. Lily sensed now was a time to curb her objections and dropped her head against his shoulder as exhaustion overcame her. Just for tonight, she would let him care for her. Just for tonight...and then in the morning everything would change.

Chapter Fifteen

Lily glanced over Andrew's shoulder as he carried her up the stairs. Nicholas, Jane and Mrs. Harris looked on with their heads tilted upwards. Every bone in her body ached, every muscle screamed its exhaustion yet all Lily cared about was the thoughts of the three people whose faces drew away with each step Andrew took. Each of their expressions differed. Nicholas wore the look of a man on the verge of a mental breakdown, shaking his head while waving a hand in front of his face; Jane's expression was dreamy as she pressed a hand to her chest like she watched a scene from a romantic play; Mrs. Harris was puffed up with flustered motherly concern.

She closed her eyes. She wanted to walk to her room but Andrew had been impossible to talk to since they had left the stables. He had stormed straight into the kitchen and ordered Robert into town to alert the authorities. Once that had been done, he sat down, pulling Lily onto his lap as though it was the most natural thing in the world and looked expectantly at his remaining three staff.

Nicholas, Mrs. Harris and Jane had stood in stunned silence until Andrew's voice boomed out a barrage of orders and they all leapt into action. Jane had bathed and cleaned Lily's ear, Mrs. Harris had prepared a small supper of broth and freshly baked bread, which Andrew had then watched Lily eat with the keen eye of a cobra. And as for Nicholas? Well, he had stood to the side watching Andrew rub his hand up and down Lily's spine, his eyes misted

253

with tenderness.

Now at last, Andrew carried her to her room where she could rest. Or so she thought. But once he reached the top of the stairs, he didn't continue to the second flight of stairs to her room but turned left toward his own chamber. Perspiration broke out on Lily's forehead at the audible gasps of her friends at the foot of the stairwell.

"What are you doing?" she whispered urgently. "Andrew, the staff, they can see you."

"And I do not care one whit. I said I want to take care of you and that is exactly what I am going to do." The stern tone of his voice broached no argument.

He kicked the bedroom door open and carried her directly to the bed. He set her down as though she was made of glass and then walked back to close the door. Lily sat in bemused silence, too stunned to move, too bewildered to speak.

In the center of the room, his bath had been prepared and great plumes of steam rose and evaporated into the air. A neatly folded soft white towel, a stoppered bottle of bath scent and a new bar of soap sat on a table beside the metal tub. Lily began to tremble. Surely he didn't intend for her to bathe?

He turned the key in the lock. *Oh, my goodness…yes, he does.*

When he returned to her, the unmistakable look of possession in his eyes shone like a beacon to her soul. Her breath caught and her body heated. His eyes bore into hers. Her mind screamed with warning that Nicholas could easily have his ear pinned to the door yet she remained silent. He stood looking down at her as he unbuttoned his shirt, pulling it from his breeches and letting it slide down over muscular shoulders to the floor. Her body trembled as she feasted her eyes on the glistening tanned skin of his chest and torso.

He reached out and smoothed the fallen hair from her face. Head dipped, he pressed one soft kiss to her lips before slowly inching her dress from one shoulder and then the other. She shivered beneath his touch as their eyes locked in silent understanding and she stood up. With the slow, tentative hands of an adoring lover, he drew open the ties zigzagged at the back of her dress until the garment pooled at her feet.

She looked down and scorching hot shame seared her face. The evidence of Winchester's attack showed in the stray straw and debris trapped in the cotton of her petticoats. Humiliation thundered through her.

The baron called her a whore, a wonton slut yet she couldn't stop this. She couldn't stop from making love to Andrew for just one more precious time.

She bit down on her bottom lip and screwed her eyes shut, trapping the tears within. He turned her around with gentle persuasion, his hands barely touching her hips. He kissed her closed lids and took her hands, drawing her out from within the rumpled circle of clothes at her feet. She opened her eyes and his gaze widened briefly.

He hesitated for the briefest of seconds and his mouth opened as if to say something but instead he dipped his head and kissed her. Lily knew he'd seen her eyes were glassy with tears and silently thanked him for not coercing the feelings from inside of her. She didn't want him to know the ugly names his closest friend had flung at her like splashes of venom.

His mouth covered hers, his tongue searching and taking, loving and needing. When his fingers moved to the hooks of her corset, they came free without resistance. She stood before him naked. His eyes left hers and ran hungrily over her body. Her nipples tightened. But he didn't ravish her; instead he took her hand and led her to the bath.

She opened her mouth to oppose such cruelty but his grip tightened and his eyes pleaded her agreement. She nodded, managed a small smile. He grinned.

The hot scented water slid over her body like the fingers of a velvet glove. With a firm hand, he guided her neck into the curved head rest of the bath and every bruise Winchester gave her screamed its victorious triumph.

Their eyes met.

"Let me bathe you, Lily. Let me do what little I can to ease what that monster did to you."

She smiled and cupped a hand to his jaw. "I love you, Andrew."

He turned and pressed a long, lingering kiss to her palm. The warmth of his single tear branded her skin and scored her heart. Kneeling down, he drew the wash cloth into the water and squeezed the liquid over her breasts. She watched it snake down to her navel, some escaping into the dark mass of her pubic hair. He soaped her breasts and her body responded. Immediately, she longed for his fingers inside her, a desire she'd only thought about in her nocturnal fantasies before Andrew had awoken every sexual fiber inside of her. She closed her eyes and fought the sensations but they rose on a formidable wave of longing that she knew would not be silenced.

She opened her eyes to find his gaze hungry, and totally focused on her body. He ran the cloth from her breasts to her stomach, swirled it in soft circles as goose bumps of anticipation broke out on her skin. His eyes darkened, his touch deepened and then with blessed relief, Lily exhaled her held breath as the cloth was abandoned. His fingers trailed over her sensitized flesh as they made achingly slow progress toward her most private place.

Their eyes locked, his teeth bit together and then he was pushing his fingers deep inside her.

Lily gasped.

He continued to slide them in and out, his other hand delving into the water to rub at that secret nub at her slit that drew her climax from her toes to her hair. She felt it building, her breathing became ragged.

"Andrew, Andrew, I..."

"I love you so damn much, Lily Curtis. You will be mine forever."

And then her body shuddered to its surrender. "I will, I know I will."

For a long moment, she laid perfectly still waiting for her heart to return to normality. His forehead pressed to hers as his breathing slowed. She reached up and pushed her fingers into the thick abundance of his hair.

"Marry me, Lily."

He pulled away from her and she met his eyes. They were shining with love, excitement but most of all, determination.

Her heart beat harder and harder, it soared higher and higher. Yet... "Andrew, I can't. I can't be the woman you want me to be."

"And just who do you think I want you to be? I want you to be you."

The frustration, anger even, in his voice made Lily stand up and step from the bath. But the moment she did, she regretted it. Standing naked before him, water dripping from her body onto his carpet did nothing but leave her feeling exposed and vulnerable.

How was she supposed to add substance to her reasoning when she stood there with her breasts free and her....her womanhood wet?

Her panicked gaze fell to the towel on the other

side of the bath. His side. He followed her gaze and thankfully didn't torture her further and handed it to her.

"Thank you," she said, wrapping it hurriedly around herself.

The corner of his mouth twitched. "You're welcome. You were saying?"

"I have no desire to return to being a lady and if I say yes to you, I will have no choice. I will be more than the privileged daughter of a wealthy lawyer, I will be the wife of a future earl."

"And what of it?"

She threw her hand in the air. "Andrew, please, you know what the role entails. Isn't that why your first choice was the beautiful and gracious Lady Tasmin?"

His head ducked as though she hurled a sharpened knife at him. She had sounded accusatory, critical and extremely cavalier. He had not *chosen* Lady Tasmin; he had considered her the simplest choice in carrying out the promise to his father. She knew it to be so. And yet she had just thrown his confession back in his face.

She stepped toward him, lifted his face to hers and pressed a kiss to tightened lips. "I'm sorry. I didn't mean to criticize you. I love you but I cannot stay here."

He took her in his arms and kissed her back. For the longest moment, they shared a deep embrace that illustrated a million feelings in its intensity and silence. Finally they parted and Lily waited for him to agree to what she had said.

"So you love me?" he asked simply.

"Yes, but…"

"Then we will marry. What happens after that is entirely up to you. If you wish to stay here and we withdraw from society, so be it. If you wish us to move to Paris and never come back, so be it. None of this..." He stepped away from her and circled the room, his arms flung out wide. "None of it, not one single thing means as much as you do, Lily. Not one single thing. I will do whatever you want to have you. Anything at all."

Tears burned her eyes and her heart ached with the desire to rush to him and say yes, yes, yes, but he was lying to himself and her. She shook her head.

"You have told me over and over again what the Baxter name and heritage means to you. I cannot and will not let you do this."

"I have not said I will give it all up. Where would the sense be in that?" He smiled. "What I am saying is we can live as big or as little a life here in England or abroad as we see fit. I have discussed this with my father, Lily. He has agreed that once he dies, the legacy, the responsibility is mine entirely. He told me..." He drew in a breath. "He told me not to waste one single moment of time that could be spent with the woman I love."

The catch in her throat moved her toward him. "Oh, Andrew..."

He held up a hand to halt her. "My father said when he lost my mother, he lost everything that was good in his life—except for me. The estate, the money, the status meant nothing without her. I won't do it. I won't live a life without love, and you, Elizabeth Caughley, you are that love whether you like it or not."

Lily's mind raced and her heart thundered.

"Well?" he pressed.

Well, Elizabeth...Lily...what do you have to say to such a declaration?

She drew in a shaky breath and exhaled it on a grin. Running across the room, he caught her as her towel dropped and she wrapped her legs around him.

"I say yes."

His eyes widened. "Yes?"

"Yes!" She screamed. "I will marry you!"

His lips came down on hers. An almighty crash sounded outside the bedroom door, then a muffled curse and a mumbled, "Sorry, sir."

Lily stared at Andrew and Andrew stared at Lily in stunned disbelief as they listened to Nicholas thunder downstairs shouting at the top of his voice, "She said yes, she said yes!"

A word about the author...

Rachel lives just a few miles from the famous Georgian city of Bath in the UK with her husband and two young daughters.

The Arrival of Lily Curtis is her third novel with The Wild Rose Press but her first historical. She loved writing every word and heralds Lily and Andrew's journey as her favorite of all her heroes and heroines so far.

Her next project is a contemporary romance between a female nightclub owner and a male social worker—and yes, through it all, they will fight for their happy ending.

Lightning Source UK Ltd.
Milton Keynes UK
20 November 2010

163196UK00001B/3/P